SONG of the SUSQUEHANNA

BY

HERBERT E. STOVER

CATAMOUNT
PRESS

an imprint of Sunbury Press, Inc.
Mechanicsburg, PA USA

CATAMOUNT
PRESS

an imprint of Sunbury Press, Inc.
Mechanicsburg, PA USA

For information about special discounts for bulk purchases, please contact Sunbury Press Orders Dept. at (855) 338-8359 or orders@sunburypress.com.

To request one of our authors for speaking engagements or book signings, please contact Sunbury Press Publicity Dept. at publicity@sunburypress.com.

FIRST CATAMOUNT PRESS EDITION: September 2022

Set in Adobe Garamond | Interior design by Crystal Devine | Cover by Lawrence Knorr | Edited by Lawrence Knorr.

Publisher's Cataloging-in-Publication Data
Names: Stovert, Herbert E., author.
Title: Song of the Susquehanna / Herbert E. Stover.
Description: First trade paperback edition. | Mechanicsburg, PA : Catamount Press, 2022.
Summary: Peter Grove, in search of ginseng in upstate Pennsylvania, becomes embroiled in the events of the French and Indian War.
Identifiers: ISBN : 978-1-62006-970-7 (softcover) | 979-8-88819-032-6 (ePub).
Subjects: FICTION / Historical / Colonial America & Revolution | FICTION / Small Town & Rural.

Product of the United States of America
0 1 1 2 3 5 8 13 21 34 55

Continue the Enlightenment!

TO MY WIFE

PREFACE

PETER GROVE, a man no longer young nor yet old, is telling this story. There are times when his memory is a bit confused as to details, but, in the main, his references to historical events are sound. His trouble is that he was too close to great happenings to have acquired a perspective.

Outside of historic personages, the names of the characters are fictitious. Even Peter's family name is Anglicized from the Dutch.

Peter is not sure of Indian tribal markings or all the accouterments of English soldiery, but he is sure of the courage, the humor, and the steadfastness of his forest associates. He is also sure of the promise of the young Washington, of the ability of Governor Morris, of the warmth and kindness of John Bartram, and the vision of Conrad Weiser. All these feelings are fast in his memory like the spicy smell of sweet fern or the nostalgic fragrance of pennyroyal on a sunny hill.

FOREWORD

PETER GROVE, who writes this, am Dutch and therefore a little stubborn about having my own way. I find myself driven by a necessity almost as great as that which took me forth to battle in the days when the red men came through the mountain passes and laid waste the land like locusts. It is not easy for me to sit at my small walnut table and scratch away with a quill while Faith sits on the other side of the fireplace, her flying fingers busy with steel needles and bright-colored yarn. It is also hard because sometimes, when I am writing, I will hear the bell tones of a hound intent on his business in the hills or the high, lonely cries of wild geese going over. Yet, I hold to my task.

I must tell the true story of those years and prove to those who will read that I am not the bloody-handed killer of savages the scalp hunters were. I killed only in battle—to lay the enemy low before he cut my time on earth short. I must also show how these broad acres came to belong to Faith and me. I must explain about my father, that he had naught to do with the evil powder trade excepting to fight it.

It is not true that my Indian name of Powder Horn was given in connection with this trade or because of my temper, but, when little more than a lad, I had a new rifle, and Mart Reed and my father fashioned a most wondrous powder horn, carving designs on it. Because I wore it with so much pride, the Indians with whom we traded called me Powder Horn.

Nothing remains in my memory of early childhood. I remember only from the days when, as a small boy, I rode the packhorses of my father's train passing to and fro from the land of the tribes to our home in Lancaster town. He and I were always together except for the few years I spent in Philadelphia gaining a more formal education, although he had already taught me to love books as well as he did. But I was a more apt pupil of the lore of the woods and trails and keen about the mastery of weapons which he delighted to teach me. Whenever he picked up a new wrestling hold or something about the handling of guns, knives, or axes, he passed it on to me, drilling me until I was its master. It is little wonder that, as I grew to manhood, I became more and more like him, even in looks. We thought alike and had many of the same mannerisms and habits. Truly my life was shaped about my father.

Then, while I was still a young man, the cruel times gripped both him and me but found us trained for them. Those days of struggle shaped our living and his death. They were years of war, of long trails, of nights of danger and loneliness. But, in them, I met men of courage, men who would stand by in sharpest dangers, men of vision like Governor Morris and John Bartram.

Also, I must admit humbly that I was fortunate. If it were not so, I would have ended my days when Aurtah, the stupid, and his painted Senecas found me asleep in that abandoned cabin. Fortune was with me at Kittanning and at Bushy Run when better men than I died.

Our great stone house, built according to John Bartram's exacting suggestions, looks out over broad fields, but the back of it is within a pistol shot of the woods. Now, as I write these lines, I hear the high, arrogant barking of a fox back there on the hill. I must lay my quill down while I step out and listen. He is in the forest, lonely, alive, and free.

CHAPTER ONE

LYING THERE on the hillside among the rocks and bushes, I told myself there had been too much thinking and waiting. That was why the minutes dragged as if they would hold back the thing that must be done.

All about me was the light, monotonous tapping of the thin, cold rain on the leaves, but now I thought I caught another sound coming up to me. With fingers not too steady, I lifted the bush before my face and peered down.

Below me, the greasy slick of the slide pitched sharply toward the river, making a yellow scar on the face of the ridge. Far down, indistinct in this poor light, the narrow path crawled across the treacherous gravel, and beyond it was the sheer drop to where the river current gouged and worried the bank. Under the rain and overcast sky, the place was as evil and treacherous as the men we had come to thwart.

Nothing was moving; I dropped the screening bush and settled my body a little. Then I heard it again, this time quite clearly, the clink of a horse's shod hoof against a stone!

Thirty miles away in our little camp at the northern tip of what old people call the Shawnee Hunting Grounds, Mart Reed would be anxious at what we would do here at the Slide. He would want each detail. He had brought the word to us from the river where he had watched. I remembered how softly he had told his story.

"The canoe came at dusk . . . four pack loads of powder in little kegs."

Reed had done his part. What happened to those kegs was in our hands now. The click of hooves again—I put Reed out of my mind, and my father joined me so quietly that I would not have guessed his coming but for the movement of the brush that sheltered me. I turned, saw the flash of his white teeth in a quick smile. He held up four fingers and whispered: "Horses."

The sound of hooves was clearer and closer. His strong fingers clutched my arm. It may be that he sensed the tumult in me. "Steady, Peter."

Three figures appeared and stepped out on that narrow path below us. Two were Indians, for they wore their shirts dangling. They moved slowly; their heads bowed against the rain. But the third figure walked with the manner of one who scorns bad going. He was white, and even from this distance and in the tricky light, we could see the broad black hat and the white feather thrust through its band.

"Charteris," my father whispered, and I nodded.

The horses followed in single file, pack train fashion. Two bays were first, then a gray, and finally a fourth animal that looked black. They moved with hanging heads, and an Indian stalked with them and poked their sides with a stick in the savage, brutal way Indians have with animals.

"Now!"

The strong fingers came away from my arm. Even in this poor light, my father's eyes had a gleam of excitement or anger. We flung our strength against the huge boulder at the top of the slide. My fingers slipped a little on the wet rock. We shoved like giants. Then it moved like something half asleep. It turned over, then plunged forward so suddenly that I fell and would have followed if my father had not snatched me back.

It was too late now, too late for anything or for anyone. Too late for us and for the slow horses down there on the narrow path. The plunging rock pounded loose an avalanche of stones and mud.

Three of the horses plodded on, paying no attention to the thing coming down upon them. Only the gray, burdened with its heavy pack, stopped, then reared in a futile effort to save itself. Its screaming neigh of despair came up to us. Then the mass struck. One moment the train was there; the next, there was a fresh scar along the mountain and the surf-like roar of the debris plunging into the hungry river. A puff of air lifted up to us, touching our faces like wet fingers.

For long minutes we crouched in the thicket, waiting and looking up and down into the wooded Narrows that would widen to the valley of the Standing Stone. Mist and fog rested on the hills like a disordered coverlet, dulling the sharp crests and changing clumps of trees to indistinct dark blotches. Something moved down at the edge of the slide at the place where the far end of the path had been. I caught a glimpse of the white feather. Charteris was standing there, and with him were two Indians.

They stood while their eyes picked up the full story of what had happened. Then something else appeared; a figure that crawled slowly up from the direction of the river as if it had come out of the water and sought the hill. None of the three made any effort to help. We knew it must be the man who had been with the pack train. When the others turned away, he gained his feet slowly and followed, limping as he went.

With all below seemingly clear, we were up and away, both glad to be out of that evil place of rain and mud and sliding death. But our haste dulled caution and brought us very close to our undoing. There was something in my father that made him alert as any cat. We were passing a wide clump of sweet fern when he leaped to one side and dragged me down beside him until we were screened by the low, dense-growing shrubs.

For a little while, there was nothing. We lay without moving, waiting. Then, against the skyline, an Indian appeared. He was naked but for a breechclout, and in one hand, he held a bow with an arrow already notched on the string. Presently a second warrior, armed in the same manner, joined him. They were so close, less than a dozen feet away, that I could smell the sickish sweet Indian odor above the washed fragrance of the sweet fern in which we lay.

My hand went down along my father's arm until I touched the naked blade of his knife that already lay in his palm. He reached around me slowly and carefully until he drew my knife from its sheath. I knew that he would throw the one blade, fight with the other, so I loosed my war ax and felt with gratefulness its flat handle in my clutch. Mart Reed had wrapped this same handle with thin leather so it would not slip and fail me in a tight place. My father's elbow nudged my ribs. I did not need to look to know he was grinning, and it made me feel better.

I do not think these Shawnee watchers of the pass were too intent on their job of guarding the way while the pack trains came through. A Seneca or a Cayuga would have sensed our presence. Like their master, Charteris, they were outcasts who, through drinking and excesses, had lost much of their keenness. Barring accident, it would have been easy to account for these men, even though our rifles were with Mart Reed. But, two dead warriors on the hill would be a calamity. The tribes would take such a thing as an excuse to break their fury on the frontier.

Night was dropping like a curtain, and the first brave grunted, shrugged his bare shoulders, and turned. He gestured toward the valley below, then loosed his arrow and placed it in the quiver which was slung over his shoulder. The second man did the same. Presently they were gone as silently as they had appeared.

This time we waited until we were sure we were not watched, then followed the ridge top until we came opposite where the Narrows widened. There we dropped down to the level forest and traveled fast to the big rock where we had slept the night before. We burrowed deep into a huge pile of leaves that were dry a few inches below the surface and lay close together for warmth.

During the last half hour of traveling, I had thought how welcome sleep would be. Now, however, I dozed, then came awake shivering, though I tried to check it. I was not cold but was seeing that gallant old gray, rearing, doing what little it could in the face of death rushing down upon it. Then my father's hand seized mine. "Peter!"

When I did not reply, he went on. "I know it was the horses."

I do not remember what I said, but he continued speaking softly. "It was the powder and also the lives of men and women who would be killed with it, or the horses. Peter, once I saw the black post at Kittanning. The man who hung there had no eyes, no lips. He was slashed across the belly. Yet he screamed, and from the thicket, I sent the bullet that took him away from them."

I turned toward him. He had never told me this thing. He was speaking again, his voice tense but controlled. "Some devilish things are shaping in this backcountry, and Charteris has much to do with them. He is no man's fool, yet there are those who think they use him to find the lead mine for them. They trade him powder. There is naught I can prove, yet—"

He left his words dangle, but he released his grip on my hand and rolled on his back so he could look up toward the dimness of the sky.

This time I had been back from the schools in Philadelphia a scant six months, yet I had noted the uneasiness on the frontier. Even John Harris at the Ferry, who was always so gay, had seemed less so. My father mentioned lead; that story I knew: how men searched for the lead mine the savages were supposed to have and how some did not return. But then, no English scalp had been safe for years when, if it were laid down in a French post, it would bring the equivalent of eight Spanish dollars.

"Peter," he said after a little, "I taught you history. When this colony of Penn's was scarce six years old, England and France began fighting for the land, and they have been at it ever since. Oh yes, there have been times of peace, but they were short. Some day this trouble will have to be settled for all time."

He was quiet for a little, then continued. "There'll be another war, Peter. The French want the river valleys; they'll want the Forks of the Ohio, which you have seen." He nudged me with his elbow. "How would you like to see the lilies of France over Harris Ferry or our own Lancaster town?"

A French flag over our own places! Nevertheless, I said soberly, "I do not like English soldiers."

His chuckle was immediate. "Nor do I, for better cause than you have, Peter. But it is the French who will loose the savages on the frontier. Every pound of powder that reaches a Delaware or a Shawnee makes him hungrier for the scalp trail."

He sat up suddenly with a rustle of leaves. "Listen, the French make good powder, but they're afraid to send a shipload even when there's peace, lest an English ship gobble it. Peter, powder is gold. You and I do not love the English, but we rolled a rock straight into the face of a war-hungry French king this night."

We settled down to sleep again, but I studied a long time. It was hard to believe that this night on a muddy slide, we two traders had made a bit of history, that, for a little, we had thwarted the purposes of a king.

When sleep did come, it brought troubled dreams. There was a great hill of bright newly molded bullets. The pile broke, and the small lead balls rolled down upon me until I was suffocating and striking out my arms for release. But, awake, I found the pressure was my father's hand between my shoulders, shoving me down into the leaves to awaken me.

Mart Reed had a savory meat stew and his good cornbread ready for us when we came to our camp. The horses of the pack train looked good, though a bit pot-bellied from eating much of the lush grass in the small meadow. Bram, the small bay mare, welcomed me with her upper lip wrinkled in the way she had been taught by Reed.

We ate ravenously and finished before anything was said about our venture. Reed seemed content to serve well and appreciated our appetites, but he showed no curiosity until my father spoke. "Bitter business, Mart. The powder's in the river at the Slide."

"And the horses?" Reed's question came quickly. I saw my father glance at me, but I affected to be busy cleaning my tin plate so it could be placed in our kit.

"All went down, never knew what hit them."

Reed's eyes wandered to where our string grazed quietly. I do not think he heard the next thing father said. "Better them than people killed."

For all his kindliness, I am not sure Reed believed that. Sometimes I had the notion that if he had to choose between little Bram and me, it would be that small brown horse. Yet, truly she was a fine animal.

We were on the Raystown path on another day, a regular pack train bound in for the trade, either with the Indians directly or with other traders. At times the three of us rode; more often, we walked. I liked just as well as riding to stride along, listening, and looking about. Here would be a bird's nest, now empty; here, ruffed grouse would thunder from a thicket, or I would catch a glimpse of the white flag of a deer bounding away.

We came up quietly through the mountains. The trail was excellent; the horses' hooves made little noise in the damp leaves underfoot. The grades were not too bad over Sideling Hill, and we crossed the Raystown Branch so we could cut through the next ridge at Aliquippa's Gap. It had been so quiet in the hills that this Raystown place, when we reached it, was veritable confusion.

Just north of the stream, long yellow ditches showed where a force of men labored, digging, throwing out earth. Down by the two big taverns, Toby's and Prendergas', horses were tied to the hitching rails. There were more people in sight than one would see at Harris Ferry or even Carlisle town.

Just as we turned our train in at Toby's paddock, a man came running, waving his cap. "Peter," he yelled, "Peter Grove!"

There never was any question about this man's enthusiasm. It was too evident. Now he shook hands with my father, pounded Mart Reed on the back. Hartley Myers was only a few years older than I, but he had been a trader on his own for a number of years.

He grabbed my hand again and turned me around. "You young Dutch son-of-a-gun. Good buckskins, a fine linen shirt—Peter, this time we must step out. These young squaws would have you for free after what they see about here."

He winked gravely at my father, reached in his pocket, and donned his wig. Hartley had a good bit of fun with that thing. He was bald as an egg. With his beak of a nose, there were times when he looked like a huge predatory bird. He would go to an Indian village, palaver, for a time, then gravely remove his scalp. It always made an impression.

"Prendergas and I will want your goods, Michal. Or are you bound back?"

"No, I had hoped to unload here. It's getting late in the season."

Leaving everything in Reed's hands, we walked toward the tavern.

"You got here just in time for the news," Hartley announced.

Father looked at him gravely but asked no question.

"Word's down from Standing Stone that a mountain fell on Charteris' train, wiped it out, eight or ten loads."

We listened to Hartley politely. It was in my mind to wonder how much he knew. Hartley Myers always followed the talk of the frontier, knew the traders. He grinned.

"Charteris is put out, says somebody slid the damned mountain down. Now me, after a drink or two at Toby's and a couple more at Prendergas', I feel I could shoulder a horse, but I couldn't shift hills about. You, Peter, how many hills have you shifted?"

The men on the porch had heard our interchange. A lone Indian sat there, his back against a post. We went inside. Toby was just as lean as his fellow innkeeper, Prendergas, was stout.

"You will drink on the house. Friend Michal, you and your boy and Reed."

He looked at Hartley quizzically. "And Hartley this day as well, though he is a hard man at times."

It was pleasant there that evening. Both taverns were thronged. The ditches, it appeared, were for the new Fort Bedford being erected here. Fifty workers labored here under Captain Hance Hamilton, a quiet man but a heavy drinker. I saw him stand at the bar and drink deeply, but the liquor did not seem to affect him.

"These Scotch Irish," Hartley told me when I mentioned it to him, "are weaned on whiskey. Don't underrate the man Hamilton; drunk or sober, he is still a pretty able engineer."

Father leaned forward at the table where we were sitting. "That, Hartley, is what I would want Peter to be, an engineer."

I smiled back at him. He knew well enough I had small liking for any part of an engineer's work except that some of it was out of doors.

Next day we watched the men at work on the fort. Hamilton spoke gravely to my father. "I'd be glad to hire your horses, Grove. Need them to get out the timber."

Father agreed gravely. "I would help you, but these horses of mine are small for heavy work and untrained in harness." He glanced about and saw that, for the moment, we were alone.

"Captain Hamilton, what is this I hear of Charteris?" "Just what the men say, Michal. He got caught in a slide east of the Standing Stone in the Narrows. Says he lost his loads."

Hamilton looked into my father's eyes. "It is my notion that the loads that man loses may be gain to peaceful folks. Do you know the man?"

Father nodded. "I have traded many years and know the men of these hills. I do not love this Charteris as they say the Quakers do."

Hartley and Prendergas, who ran a store as well as an inn, were approaching. The talk of Charteris stopped. The two wanted to trade for our loads. We left the business to Reed, and father and I rode two horses northward along Sideling Hill. On Standing Stone Creek was a small Delaware village where we hoped to get some really good buckskin.

Most Indian villages are alike. This one was small, not more than a dozen and a half lodges, all made by setting up a circle of limber poles, bending the tips together, then covering the whole with bark. They had made a good job of it, using the bark of slippery elm, which is easily pressed flat. To the back of the village was a fair-sized corn field with pumpkins showing golden sides. The lodges formed a semi-circle open to a broad rectangle over which was sprinkled white sand. This would be the Chungke or ball ground. To me, this is a stupid game. The players each have a long smooth pole like a spear without a point. Also, they have rounded stones that they throw out on the field. Running, the players try to hit the stone with the hurled stick. He who comes closest wins two points. They play all day and bet on their skill. To me, the game of pitching horseshoes is far better, but the Delawares love this game. However, they are Indians.

This village seemed a little cleaner than the average, and the sand on the Chungke field was fresh. One communal fire smoldered before the center lodge, sending up a lazy smoke spiral. Three old men sat near it, smoking gravely. Women were busy dragging in parts of a dead pine tree and piling the faggots. One old crone sat by one of the lodges, her skinny fingers working a crude loom.

The smells were here. An Indian uses every part of an animal for food while a white man discards much of his game. Therefore, what an Indian eats sometimes reeks to high heaven, but it does not offend him. I always liked their venison, their green cornbread when made with maple sugar, and their stews which are savory enough if one is hungry and not too curious as to what went into the pot.

My father was welcomed, and one of the old men smiled at me and said: "Welcome, young Powder Horn."

He had remembered that when I had my first rifle. Father and Mart Reed had equipped me with a beautiful horn for my powder, carved with game pictures. My pride in carrying it had given me the name Powder Horn among the friendly Indians.

We produced gifts of tobacco for the men, big needles for the women, and our visit was formally begun, and from morning until well on in the afternoon, I watched the trading for deerskins. Then I recalled an errand John Harris had entrusted to me.

"Peter," he had said, "find me two or three of those doeskin shirts Indian women wear. I want good ones. Pay with this wampum."

I did not remember seeing anything of the sort down where father was trading with the older squaws; there were only raw skins. Nor had I seen any squaw wearing a garment that might please Harris. Nevertheless, I made a complete tour of the camp. One old squaw leered at me and spoke in English when I asked her about shirts. "White eyes, Indian hair, look that way."

She pointed up the small stream. I did not enjoy her reference to my hair or eyes, but I walked off in the direction she had indicated.

It was pleasant to be away from the camp smells. Leaves rustled lightly under my moccasins. The stream babbled its friendly nothingness. Certainly, I did not think anything important was up here or that I should find trouble.

A half mile from the village, I saw a small bark lodge built much like the houses of the Six Nations. It was set in a thicket of young hemlocks, and a skin curtain served as a door. I whistled; the edge of the curtain was turned back by a shapely arm loaded with copper bracelets. A girl stepped outside.

There was nothing remarkable about her, just a young squaw of about my age with a friendly and pleasing enough face. What I noticed was her deerskin shirt. It reached below her waist; it was softer than any cloth and was most cunningly ornamented with quills and beads. In color, it was the soft brown of an aspen leaf. I pointed to it.

She looked at me stupidly and raised one hand to her throat. The nails had been painted with red pocone root. I brought out some of Harris' wampum.

"Buy shirt," I said, and measured a string of wampum from my middle finger to my elbow. The more I saw of the garment, the better I liked it, so I doubled the string. "For the shirt, I will pay this."

She began to simper, then took the end of the wampum string. The sleeve of her shirt fell back as she measured. I helped her, my fingers clumsy on the warm copper-colored roundness of her arm. "Buy."

I tapped her shoulder with my forefinger, touching the soft skin of the garment. Her hand came up again to her throat and twitched the bright strings that fastened the shirt. She shrugged her shoulders and stood before me, naked to the waist, holding the garment in her hand. She was smiling.

Today I would see a squaw naked with no more disturbance than I would a cow or any other animal. But I was young then. The blood mounted to my face and neck.

"Put it on," I gestured to the shirt.

It is my notion she understood well enough what I wanted, but it was her business to misunderstand. Again a swift gesture to the waistband of the woolen skirt she wore. She was all-naked rounded Indian from the crown of her sleek black hair to the small beaded moccasins. She took my hand and turned toward the door of her lodge.

Then it came, the crunch of a quick step on a dry stick, and my father stood before us!

The girl stared at him for a moment. Suddenly he growled something at her in a gibberish she must have understood, for she snatched up her garments and scuttled into the lodge.

"Filthy slut," he muttered as we walked away. We had gone a hundred yards before he turned and faced me. "Peter, I have had it in my mind that you should be a gentleman. To that end, you've been sent to school. Also, to that end, I have worked with you since you were a child. Now you're a man, but back to school, you'll go again. So long as I live, my son will not be a chaser of any of these red sluts. I want none of mine loaded with the French disease. Once you chase squaws you're done as a white man. Look at Hartley Myers."

Never in my life had I seen him so angry. His voice choked. But my own rage matched his, only I could think of no word to say, choking on my stubbornness. I would not tell him I was not buying the girl. Within an hour, we were packed and off, and we spent the rest of the day without speech. Then we overtook Mart Reed and the pack train. The following morning came the show-down.

Of all in this world, I loved my father best. Since boyhood, my world had moved about him. Now that I was a man grown, I respected him still, the things he could do, the way he thought and acted. But he had hurt me. Never before had he failed to understand. Right after breakfast on this day, he signaled me to follow him.

There was a little glade here, and horses had eaten the grass until the place was like a small clipped lawn. He turned and faced me. I looked squarely back into a face just like my own, with long chin, deeply set gray eyes, rumpled black hair. We were about the same height; perhaps I was the taller. He may have been a half stone the heavier.

"'Peter, we are going to Lancaster. You'll go to Philadelphia, finish school and your surveying." His voice was gentle, but there was iron back of it. I stared at him. About us were the things I loved—the musty smell of trampled bracken, the spiciness of hemlocks, the clear air sharp as wine. He continued. "If I were to ask you to go, you would say 'no'?"

I nodded, and the ghost of a smile touched his lips.

"So I thought. Now I've taught you many things—riding, shooting, woodcraft, wrestling, and to be a sportsman." He stepped close to me, tapped my chest. "We are men, Peter. We'll wrestle for it; two falls of three. I win, back to Philadelphia and school. You win; we stay together in the trading business. But," now he angered me again, "either way, you'll keep away from squaws."

I said no word but tugged off my hunting shirt, tightened my belt. Rage pounded in my temples. He was ready.

"Don't hold back," he gritted as we came together.

Anger made me reckless, and I paid for it. His muscles were like iron bands. He caught me, and I went end over end on the grass with a thump that knocked the wind out of me.

"One," it was Mart Reed's voice. He was watching, his arm over Bram's neck. The little mare looked interested.

This time I was cooler and faster than I had been. It was a matter of rushing in, of tugging, ripping, no close meeting of bodies. And I brought him down. It did not matter that his shoulder touched but lightly. He nodded, conceding me the fall.

The third time we sparred for an opening carefully. Twice we locked close, body to body, straining. I saw the look in his eyes, the faintest sign of desperation. Suddenly all the anger was out of me. I thought of the time when I had had the fever, and he had carried me in his arms many hours until we came to a village. Back and forth, we strained until my chance came, the beginning of a hold I knew. My right arm locked back of his neck, my left, with elbow crooked, came upward toward his throat. He had taught me this hold. Pushed through, he would be helpless. But I hesitated, and the pause gave him time to drop his shoulders forward. His powerful arms went down. For the second time, I measured my full length on the grass.

"Two," Reed grunted, and my father seized my hand and drew me to my feet.

"Truly, you are a man, Peter. You nearly had me."

Hours later, Reed jogged quietly along beside my horse. He looked at me gravely, then gestured to my father up ahead. "Once you had him, Peter. Is it that you really want to go back to school?"

I gave him no answer but a surly scowl with which he seemed as pleased as though I had given him a whole package of our Mr. Demuth's best tobacco.

CHAPTER TWO

SO, WITH SCANTY loads, we came directly out of the land of the tribes over the foothill ridge we call Blacklog, thence through a narrow gap in Shade Mountain. From there, we followed the path that zigzags up the side of high and wind-swept Tuscarora, stopping often to let the horses blow until finally, we reached the summit.

Whenever I come this way, I like to stop and look since from here, it seems that, if vision were stronger, one could see far away Philadelphia. The ridge on which we stood runs south and west to the Maryland border. To the east and north, it is broken only by the river above Harris Ferry. With the Maryland border, this ridge forms the vast triangle of land we called in those days "Improved Pennsylvania." Here were the towns, the roads, the broad farms with stone buildings on them. Here was Lancaster, the largest inland town in all the English colonies.

But to our backs, there were only outposts. This tumbled, hill-broken land is the country of the tribes. Here were the displaced and unhappy Delawares, the tricky Shawnees, and their friends. Far to the north and along Penn's whole north boundary were the Iroquois. This was the land, too, of the trader, the elk, the bear, and the ginseng, which I was to value so highly later. Hidden in narrow valleys were bright streams large as English rivers. The forest covered the whole of the land, the great pines making natural cathedrals with their straight trunks and the shadows from their tops.

From the paths chosen, I knew we would cross the wide river at Harris Ferry rather than by Wright's, which is a score of miles farther south. To this place in the very early days, John Harris's father had come, and the crossing was increasing in importance daily. To the northward was the mountain barrier through which the river breaks; east and west roads converge here.

Truly this "improved Pennsylvania" is and was a great land from the mountains above the Ferry to the Maryland border.

While I stood on the ridge crest studying the land before me, my father sat on a rock and patiently whittled at a laurel twig. Mart Reed busied himself among the horses, losing a cinch here, tightening another there, and allowing little Bram to nuzzle a bit at his upstanding shock of white hair. When he thought the animals were ready, he gave the signal to march.

We dropped down through laurel thickets, through rhododendron, through pine and hemlock shade until our horses were treading level land once more.

In another hour or so, we were in settled country where stacks of hay and herds of fine cattle could be seen in the barnyards. Corn was nearly ripe on tall stalks; yellow pumpkins shone in the long aisles made by corn rows. There were almost as many farms here as down Lancaster way, though houses and barns were not so large. But the people here were Scotch-Irish, not German. Here were Ramsays, and Armstrongs, and MacDougalls, and MacDowells—a dour lot but good farmers and entirely indifferent to whatever danger threatened from behind the western ridges.

It had always been pleasant to come out of the woods with the train. After the timber, the rough mountains, the squalor and stink of Indian villages, it was fine to hear a cowbell, to see swept dooryards, to hear shepherd dogs bark, and to savor the opulence of rich lands well tended. This day I missed the charm. What lay beyond took the pleasure from me. I did not like to think about the crowded city filled with strange faces. There I have so often been homesick for mountains, for the sound of fast water among rocks, for the tangy taste of wood smoke in one's food. A matter of months before, I had thought myself finished with cities.

The most irritating thing was the attitude of my father. It was not that he said much, but satisfaction was around him like the smoke wreath from his pipe. For miles, he would ride with one knee across the pommel of his saddle. All the while, as he jogged along, he did another irritating thing—he whistled through his teeth in a manner that both Mart Reed and I disliked. Yet, neither of us hinted at our annoyance; we grudged him that satisfaction.

John Harris was absent when we crossed, being up river looking into his properties there. His place was really a village. There were many new cabins in which lived those who had work or fields about the ferry. In others were those who sought a home farther west or north and waited here at an outpost for the final step. Here were dogs, chickens, cows, and a half dozen Black men. Harris preferred them to the bound boys so common farther east.

Harris had kept his own home a little aloof. Set on a bluff, the ground around it was clear except for one huge walnut tree where the cardinal birds always whistled in early spring. Here he set the example for the others, having dug a well instead of using the water from the river. The sweep and the wooded bucket were monstrous things. At the edge of the bluff, a steep flight of steps led down to the river. All told, I always found this Harris Ferry a pleasant place and more homelike than our own edge of Lancaster. The Black man who set us and the horses over the wide stream said: "Marse John'll sure miss seeing you, Mister Grove."

For my part, I was not up to seeing him. It would be hard to explain about that wampum and the shirts I did not buy. I could not tell him that I, a man grown, was being packed off to school to keep me clear of Indian strumpets who had never been considered much of a danger before.

Beyond the ferry, the land is fairly well settled, at least the better part of it, though there are wide wooded tracts where it is too rough for clearing. Usually, our route home was that which goes down river away almost to Wright's Ferry, then eastward to Lancaster. This time we took the upper way because Reed insisted it was shorter.

Fifteen miles out, we came to an inn. It was new, except for the center section. Likely it had been a cabin with these new wings built on. The logs were squared, the chinking was an excellent job; everything in sight—buildings, barnyard—was as neat as such places can be. On a wide signboard hung from an iron bracket on a post was painted the picture of a huge blue goose and the legend "Blue Goose Inn."

Mart Reed thought in terms of horses and their comfort, so he led the train to the barn, but father and I entered the common room, which was as neat as the outside. A short bar stretched along one end; there was a wide chimney piece and plenty of benches plus some rush-bottomed chairs of massive design.

A few men who looked like farmers sat at the tables. They nodded civilly to us; then, an inner door opened, and a lady came forward. We pulled off our caps.

There was a smile of welcome on her face as she stopped and looked at us; evidently, she knew my father.

"Michal," she said and came up to him, one hand out thrust. "It is nice to see you. Welcome to the Blue Goose." There was warmth in her low-pitched voice. I knew little about a woman's age, but she was not much older than I in years. Her yellow hair was braided and twined about her head in the manner affected by Swedish women I have seen in Philadelphia. Not tall, she moved like a lady should, and there was dignity in the way she took my father's hand.

"Mistress Wright, I present my son, Peter. He is on his way back to the city to finish his studies."

She took my hand, smiled. "You are very like your father, Peter."

She studied my face a little and seemed to forget that her warm fingers rested in mine.

"Very like," she finished. "Cooney is at the barn. He'll help Reed with the stock and loads."

Nancy Wright, she was, and it seemed odd that an inn-keeper should be a woman. Mart Reed told me a little about her later. It was not known from where she had come, but she had two Germans and their wives with her, the stocky Cooney and the big dour John Stouffer. The Inn was a pleasant place; we found the food excellent, our beds fine and soft when we reached them.

There was little custom that evening, so Mistress Wright was kind enough to sit with us and talk. I liked her directness of speech and the way she understood the frontier and its work.

"You know, Michal, you should give this jenseng a trial. Have you seen it?"

Father nodded. "Yes, Peter and I have seen it on the Sinnamahoning where we hunted bears. It's an odd root having the shape of the human body. It is really called ginseng, not jenseng."

She tapped the toe of her bright buckled shoe against the leg of a chair, "There is real money in it. Chinamen will pay its weight in gold for it."

Father laughed. "No, Mistress Wright. I'll stick to furs, for I know them. I know the profit and risk. Also, I am not interested in medicine. It's hard to teach an old dog new tricks."

She laughed lightly, "Friend Michal, sometimes I do not think it is the age of the dog as much as what kind of a dog he is."

Father buried his nose in his tankard of brown ale. I wanted to laugh. Mart Reed blew a veritable cloud of tobacco smoke into the air.

Cooney served our breakfast the next morning, moving lightly on his feet despite his weight and look of clumsiness. Like our supper, this meal was excellent. Father paid the score and went out with Reed to the horses. I loitered at the table over the last corn cake drenched with maple syrup. The men had been gone a matter of minutes when Mistress Wright came in, her hair in long braids down her back. She wore a sort of quilted dressing gown, which she held together with her fingers at her throat, and she came directly to me. It was evident that she was very much in earnest.

"Peter, you are very like your father but perhaps more ready to listen."

I stared at her, then moved to rise, but she dropped into a chair, motioned to me to be seated. "Don't rise. There is little time for manners. Just this—try to keep your father from having aught to do with powder—either way."

"But," I stammered. "But—"

"The times are bad, Peter. Powder and lead mines! Honest traders should have naught to do with either. If evil men are doing wrong, it is not your father's duty to stop them."

With that, she rose and left the room, and she did not appear when our train filed out, the bells all a-jingle.

So there was plenty to think about on the way to Lancaster. A woman who ran an inn and warned a man she felt was too stubborn to listen; powder and lead—what did Mistress Wright know of them? There would be no way she could guess about a slide back in the hills, of a plunging avalanche, of an old gray horse that reared up in the face of death.

Also, I thought a little of an Indian girl with sloe-black eyes and with skin which had been wondrous smooth; then of the wrestling match. Sometimes I felt my father only wished to be rid of me, that he did not fear too much my adventures with Indian women.

Lancaster has changed so much it is hard to explain what the town was like then. I found little difference between it and Philadelphia except that the up-state town lacked the riverfront and the shipping. It was not then, as now, a Pennsylvania-German town—witness its name. The people were mostly English business folks who had come upstate after the rich trade that flooded in from the farm lands and the backcountry. It was not for many years that retired German farmers began to change the character of the place.

Streets were not named for plebeian things like trees but dukes, princes, kings, and royalty like Anne and James. Stone and brick houses crowded the sidewalks but left the room necessary for street travel. There were so many churches that one could see a spire from any part of the town. Business was excellent. Here was the first real hardware store in the colony and many tobacco warehouses, for tobacco was gold then and newly cultivated this far north. At the northern limits of the town were the trading posts. Here, men bound for the backcountry made up their packs; here, they brought skins and furs to sell outright or to barter. In this section, Conestoga wagons were built. Some Swiss and German gunsmiths had set up their shops to serve the traders and long hunters.

Socially, I knew little of the town. The people were cold, being intent on profits. Yet it was not so cold as the village of Carlisle beyond the river. However, Lancaster was my home, and in Carlisle, my longest stay was to be as an inmate of her gray stone jail. A sober, righteous, and busy town, Lancaster—a place to be respected but not loved too much.

Our small house was on the southern fringe of the town where the smell of horses and stables might not offend the ladies as they strolled about the streets. It was built of logs but was now neatly covered with clapboards which Mart Reed had split and shaved from a dead white pine that once had stood in our meadow. The house was set in the center of a small fenced field that served as a horse corral. Our beasts were always friendly, and when someone opened our gate, a horse or two might move toward him; a few found this disturbing, but we three liked it. To the back was a spacious barn that housed grain and fodder for the horses and was a shelter for them in bad weather.

Inside, the house was clearly a man's place, with a small kitchen at one end, the rest of the lower floor a huge living room with a large fireplace. The kitchen fireplace was small and workmanlike, but the one in the big room was a place for giant logs and cheery content. On our walls were fowling pieces, rifles, pistols, fancy bridles, hide ropes, and elk horns. The last we used to hang our hats and caps on. There was a row of sharp axes, a rack of Indian bows and arrows with the beaded quivers that went with them. There was a long, heavy oak table and rush-bottomed chairs. By one window, Mart Reed had set up his sewing bench where he repaired horse gear and worked in leather, sometimes tooling it beautifully. I loved this great room with its smell of tobacco, of leather, and the tang of burning wood. Above was the loft where we slept.

We had supper in our house, after which I bathed carefully in the half barrel we kept for such use and used some of our "soft soap," which indeed almost took the skin off with its suds. Then Father and I dressed in our town clothing. I liked my clean white homespun shirt, but the tightness of my coat across the shoulders and the stiffness of my shoes irked me not a little. There was nothing now of the trader about my father except the bronze of his face and hands.

We walked slowly up the street. Some lights were already on; an old lamplighter was doing his best, but darkness was surely crowding him. Up King Street, we crossed to Anne, came almost to the edge of the town, and to the long building bearing the sign "Horn and Teague."

One odd feature distinguished this building. One part, evidently the dwelling section, was separated from the other, but a roof joined them after the manner of the thing the settler in the backcountry calls a "dog trot." This passageway was closed from the street by a picket gate, and I saw it was neatly flagged with flat stones.

Father and the trader nodded and smiled. For me, I did not like this man Horn with his thin face, his brown coat, the ruffles at his throat, the slim white fingers. He was not a large man, but he did not give the impression of being small. He had no color in his face, but he did not seem ill. To me, he was cold, particularly in his eyes.

Horn came around the counter to clasp my father's hand and give mine a brief shake. "I'm glad to see you, Michal."

That seemed sincere enough. The two men walked back toward the counter, where Horn set out some wine. Our glasses were just filled when the side door opened, and a girl entered. From the way she wore her brown hair loose about her small face, I thought her just a child. Horn's face lighted at the sight of her; the look of coldness fled. "Michal, here is Faith, back from the schools a month ago. Faith, Michal Grove and his son, Peter."

She curtsied and gave my father a small hand as he smiled down at her. Then the same hand rested in mine for an instant, lightly as a butterfly, yet with warmth and softness. "I am happy to meet you. Father talks of you at times when he is not too busy." Now she turned, pushed back my wine glass. "Peter, come to the house for chocolate. These wines are sour. Also, the old friends will wish to talk."

I followed through the door, across the flagged passageway into a room that seemed huge to me. Here was fine furniture, rich mahogany and brown walnut. There were mirrors in gilded frames also a spinet. I caught a glimpse of my lean face and black hair in one of the mirrors. All that pleased was the white shirt. She went into the kitchen for a moment and returned to take a chair and to urge another on me. "There is chocolate, and there is tea, but the water must heat. In a few minutes, we will have whichever we like."

So we sat—she at her ease, but I, who for the last six months had seldom used a chair, felt my weight too great for the spindle-legged thing I was using. She was excited about Philadelphia. "It's a splendid thing, Peter, to be going back. We need surveyors so much, and you can be one quickly." It was evident that she knew something of my father's plans for me, but I did not then get it through my thick head.

Here in this quiet room, the world seemed very safe and sure. Here was peace and a small fire burning against the still, mild autumn chill—a world away from steep trails, from sliding rocks, from men hunting each other with sharpened knives and arrows notched on the strings.

I share one weakness with women—a love of tea. Only, in the woods, we boil it until we have a bitter black brew that can give a tired man a lift. This was mild and yellow. There were small cakes with tiny seeds hidden in them, reminding me of the ones we find in sweet fern; I found the flavor different as I crunched them. Yet they brought to mind for an instant the thick green clumps of that wild shrub on the hillside below Standing Stone.

After we finished our tea, including a second cup for me, she played the spinet a little, a tune very soft and sweet like, it seemed to me, the sound of her laughter. She stopped playing, and I had no idea so much time had passed, but she was standing with her hand outstretched. I had wit enough to come to my feet, to take the small hand lightly in mine and bow over it. "Your father will be waiting."

There was no one about in the store room when I looked in, but somebody was moving heavy things about in a back room. Father had probably gone home. I took my hat from the counter where I had left it and moved toward the door. Idly, my eyes covered the big room with its piles of goods and hides along the wall. Then, suddenly, I felt a prickling at the base of my neck as though cold fingers had touched it lightly. In a corner, on a rush-bottomed chair, was a man's hat. It was black, and in its band was thrust a white goose feather!

I have explained that we Dutch are stubborn. Also, we seldom say all we think. I would not mention the hat to my father, I told myself. He should have seen it.

When I reached my room a little time later, my father was already asleep, but I lay wakeful, thinking of that hat with its white feather. Black hats and feathers were common. Yet I thought of the white man with the Indians back at the Slide. Later I thought of Mistress Wright and her odd warning. But when I slept, I did not dream of hats or warnings—no, rather of slender white fingers on a keyboard and of hair with the brown of the ripe chestnut one has carried in his pocket for a time until it is burnished to a rich brightness.

Despite dreaming, I slept well, for this bed was my pride. Father and I had made it, lacing strong strips of pretty green hide across the frame. As the leather dried, it became taut. Mart Reed insisted it was like sleeping on a drum head, but I liked the thing. It was fine to lie on it in the morning and stretch one's muscles against the give of the lacings.

This morning my eyes opened with the first light. I had learned the business of coming awake with one's full mind, alert and ready. Woods people, whether they be animals or men, must be this way—if they wish to live long. Through the window, I could hear the movement of the horses, then the drum of their hooves which told me Mart Reed would be busy with oats and bran for his feeding. There was the ghost of bacon smell, too. I hoped my father was ready with breakfast. Here at home, there would be pancakes and some of our store of maple syrup.

My bare feet were on the deerskin rug when I remembered. This day I would be on my way to the city. I groaned, all the pleasure of the morning out of me for the moment. I had made a bad bargain or, rather, it had been made for me.

Sitting there, working my toes against the wiriness of the deer hairs of the rug, I puzzled my mind with my father's reasons. Back of me was, for the times, a pretty fair education. Unless I wished to study medicine or prepare for the ministry, a further education seemed as useless as two bells on a pack horse.

Also, it seemed odd that my parent's mind should swing so suddenly to sending me back to the city on account of an Indian girl's open invitation. If I was bound for the devil on account of women, the city was the last place to send me. Surely there, temptation wore a more open countenance than in a smoky Indian village. And this Indian girl had looked much cleaner and less worn than many of the city trulls I was later to see looking out over their window sills.

So—many things moved through my mind while I dressed for town in decent woolen breeches, a white shirt, and long stockings knit by some woman Mart Reed knew. She did make good stockings, almost as strong as linen cloth. I was downstairs, seated before the pile of the cakes I had expected before I settled my arguments with myself.

Most irritating was the fact that my father was in such a mood of satisfaction. He was pleased with his cooking, pleased with my appetite, pleased with what Mart Reed told him of the horses. It was not sensible, to my mind, that a man should be pleased with so many different things.

CHAPTER THREE

AGAIN I SAY that for a man so set on getting his son into the moral safety of a school, my father went about the business in what seemed to me a most leisurely manner. I was satisfied with each hour of delay, being in a vicious mood about the whole business. The morning we had planned to start, we had a late breakfast. Father cleared his plate, got his pipe going, and watched me finish the last of a pile of wheat cakes Mart Reed had baked. "Peter, I have a mind to do a bit of business and some visiting on our way. You will not mind if we are a few days late getting to the city?"

I did not answer, suspecting him of irony, and I think he smiled a little at my silence.

"Mart has to get two horses to Heidelberg. We will take them so he will not need to leave the stock here. I want you to see Ephrata Cloisters and to visit one of the greatest men in our colony, Conrad Weiser. From Reading town, we will go by coach to Philadelphia."

My books, clothing, and the small extras I chose to take with me went into a leathern bag, and my short-barreled rifle, pistol, buckskins, and wood gear went into a long blanket roll. Both would fasten to a saddle. In fact, anything Reed made or shaped would be planned to be fastened to a horse in some way. The old man came out when I swung into the saddle. Father being already down at the gate.

"Peter," he said softly. "Do not be too angry with him. After all—"

Letting me guess at what he had planned to say, he brought something from his pocket and laid it in my hand. It was a beautifully braided watch fob made of horse hair. It needed but a glance to see the colors. He had taken hairs from the tails of all our string so I would not forget the horses. I turned it over and over admiringly.

"Bram," I said softly, "Spur, Blackie—they are all here, Mart." Then I saw a single strand of gray. He had found it somewhere, and he wanted me to remember the old horse at the Slide.

I thrust down my hand and gripped his warmly, then put my horse in motion. When I made the first turn, I looked back and put a hand to him as he stood there watching.

We rode northeastward all that day through a region of small rough hills where boulders lay about as though a giant had spilled them from a bag he was carrying. They were gray limestone, looking much like huge hailstones after they fall into our gray dust in this country. At evening, we came to the house of Justice Galbreath in the great valley that runs from near Reading to Harris Ferry. He was not at home, but we were housed comfortably and well fed.

Next day, we moved eastward up the valley at a slow pace. Well along in the afternoon, we topped a rise and saw beyond a small stream a village with houses built of timbers neatly squared in a mill and set on high stone foundations. To our left and on our side of the stream was a group of three large buildings covered with split clapboards. Back of them were the usual small outbuildings to house animals or tools. We turned into a courtyard and found worn hitching rails for our horses.

As we dismounted, a curious figure emerged from the nearest door-way and approached us. He was a tall man with gray hair and beard. Some sort of long robe covered him from chin to bare feet. His hand was outstretched, and he was smiling. I remember well the warmth and strength of his fingers as he gripped mine, also the depth of blue in his eyes. "Welcome to Zion, brethren. Here we wait for the coming of our Lord. You are doubly welcome, for it is the hour of our evening meal."

"We thank you. Father Conrad, my son and I. Peter, I present you to Father Conrad Beissel. We have heard so much, Father, of your efforts to convert the Indians."

Beissel smiled and answered with an odd quotation: "The Lord shall send the rod of thy strength out of Zion."

My father looked a bit embarrassed. "I wanted my son, who is going to the city to study, to see this place."

Beissel's hand dropped on my shoulder, and he looked down from his great height into my eyes. "Better leave him with us. Here he would learn to deny the flesh and come closer to grace. The city is ever a sink of iniquity."

I glanced at my father, and Beissel loosed my shoulder, sighed, then smiled again. "Young men are daring, having little fear of the powers of darkness."

He led the way inside to a room where a narrow table stretched from side to side. It was flanked with rude benches. No signal was given, but men dressed like our host began filing in. Most of them were bearded; none spoke, but their faces were friendly. Some smiled as they took places with father and me to the right and left of Beissel, who now produced a small tuning fork and struck the table. The pitch established; they began singing.

It was, I believe, the loveliest music I have ever heard. These monks or brethren were magnificent singers with voices clear as bells, and the words were those of the Twenty-Third Psalm. They brought into this long bare room something unreal. Mayhap the singing of the angels is a little like this. The singing finished, Beissel chanted a long grace, then other brethren entered the room, carrying loaves of bread and wooden bowls, one of which was placed before each of us. A moment or two later, a man placed dishes of meat and goblets of wine before father and me.

The bowls were filled with the large beans the Germans call butter beans. They had been boiled with water and salt. Each man had his crust of bread broken, not cut, from the loaves. They ate slowly, savoring each bite. Father and I had taken some of the meat before us. Now, I saw him put his piece back and eat only what the others did, so I did the same. Beissel approved with a smile.

The meal ended with another grace said by one of the brethren. Beissel went with us to our horses and stood with us a little, the breeze stirring his gray hair. "You have come from the mountains where doubtless you met the red men. Our souls yearn to save them from their ways. Do you think we will be permitted to do so?"

Father studied. I think he thought of Shingas in contrast to this gentle soul. Perhaps he thought of the French Black Robes. "That, my brother, will be in the hands of God."

The answer pleased Beissel, who laid one hand on his heart for a moment. Father spoke again. "We go now to visit Conrad Weiser, whom I know."

For the first time, the old man's face lost its look of kindness. With that gone, his face was stern. "Ah, yes. He was one of us for a time. We knew him as Brother Enoch, but he could not deny himself entirely. He could not forget the world, its fleshpots, and its business. We pray that someday he will return."

The kindness had returned when he raised his hand, and we stood there with hats off while he said a short blessing over us. As we rode out of the courtyard, I noticed that father was sweating. We covered a good half mile before he spoke. "I wanted you to see these men, Peter. They are truly holy, but I doubt if the Indians will wait long enough to be won by them. It is odd to find this gentleness and a wild Indian dance within a few days' travel of each other."

It is strange, but so deeply was I impressed by this visit that years after, lying in the corn field at Kittanning listening to that savage dance, I thought for a moment of these gentlemen, their voices raised in the beauty of a psalm. Of course, I forgot them when the rifles began to crack in the greater wildness of that morning.

We passed through Heidelberg, a small village, and a short way beyond came to a huge square stone house set back from the road across a broad yard which was surrounded by a white-washed picket fence. Here were great fields of corn with yellow pumpkins showing. Here were wide barns, half stone, half wood. Herds of cattle browsed. I saw pigs, poultry, and one peacock walking with his tail spread. We could see men at work in the barns grooming horses. The place was more a town than a home, for there were small cabins set close to the main house.

We dismounted at the front gate, tied our horses, and walked in. A man who had been seated on the front porch rose and came toward us.

It is hard for me to tell what Conrad Weiser's appearance was like. Of him, I remembered more what he said than how he looked, for he was a man of great ideas. He was neither tall nor short, a bit stooped. His nose was slightly hooked, and his shock of hair was iron gray. I remember well his huge hands. For some reason, most of the great men I have known have had great hands.

"Michal," he cried. "Welcome, welcome!"

He put his arms around our shoulders and hugged us. "This would be your son, Peter. He is so like you."

He led us to the house and inside, where the whole ground floor was one huge room with a vast fireplace at the end. "Eve Ann," he called. "Here is Michal Grove and his son come to see us."

She came forward from the fireplace, a calm woman with graying hair and twinkling eyes. She was wiping her hands on her apron. "Michal," her voice was a little husky. "It has been a long time. And your son, he is of the same mold. Tell me, have you had supper?"

Weiser beamed. "Best say not. She is ever thus, this wife of mine, thinking of a man's comfort."

Father broke in. "We supped with the Brethren at Ephrata—"

The glance between Weiser and his wife was so sudden that it interrupted what he might have said further. Then they began to laugh and kept at it until Weiser put his arms around Eve Ann to support her. Finally, Weiser mastered himself. "That was most unseemly, Michal, but today we talked of the time I lived there, and we remembered that it is the season of butter beans. To her, I had so often complained at how hungry I was. So, when you spoke, we laughed."

Eve Ann wiped the tears from her eyes. "And my Conrad is such a trencherman. It is not likely he could stop with plain boiled beans. You know, at the Cloisters, they eat whatever is in season; soon, it will be freshly ground corn; in the spring, it is mostly dandelions."

Weiser touched her arm. They seated us at one end of the oaken table. Both carried food to us, and finally, a daughter came in and helped. The profusion was amazing. Here was half a huge ham, a big joint of roasted beef. There was a dish piled high with potatoes that had been sliced thin and fried hard. They crackled when one ate them. Here were wheaten and corn breads, jellies, pumpkin, and apple pies. At each place was set a huge mug of cider richly spiced and warm. When we finished,

Weiser bowed his head and gave thanks. "We are ever more thankful after our bellies are full," he said. "Hungry men do not want to wait over long on the Lord."

The evening at Weiserdorf was most pleasant. Six of the children were at home. "Sammy" was away. "Stayed among the Mohawks last spring. He will be back with the snows," Weiser explained.

We sat before the fireplace telling stories. Then we sang hymns together. Weiser said he knew one that had forty-seven verses though he could repeat but twenty of them. It was pleasant to see how close Weiser and Eve Ann were to each other. Her voice was lovely, and he seemed so proud of everything she did.

Everyone was astir with the dawn, and the family and the working people gathered about the big table. Weiser out-lined the work of the day while we ate. Everything was run efficiently. The meal over, the workmen and the children went about their business, then Weiser, Father, and I went to the broad back porch that looked toward the mountains. He pointed to a distant hill far to the north. "That's Eagle Peak. Once a year, the boys and I climb it so they can learn about the big flat nests in the dead tree. Once, we brought a baby eagle home, but Eve Ann would have none of it."

His eyes twinkled. I had not known she was standing in the doorway.

"Yes," she commented. "Its manner of eating was filthy, nor would it keep its food down as a decent creature should."

We laughed. Weiser drew her out with us and pointed again. "That is the way to Shamokin. The round-topped hill is Rund Kop. Some day there should be a fort there which would make the Shamokin Path safe."

Father broke in. "Conrad, before my son goes to the city, I want him to know a little more of conditions in the colony, so he will know better what the signs of the times mean. This, of course, if you are not going on a journey."

Eve Ann took her husband's arm. "Michal, he goes no more on journeys. All his life, he has served the colony. He has carried too long on his shoulders the worry and danger."

Weiser patted her hair and smiled. "Like Paul, I have fought a good fight. Like him, I have about finished the course, and I am a little weary of Indians."

He studied a moment. "Michal, I grew up in a Mohawk wigwam because of our large family and because we were poor. We came to the Tulpehocken country and loved it. But I have not been my own man since. I have journeyed from Philadelphia to Logstown on the Ohio, and from here to Albany over and over. My friend Shikellamy is dead. The governor wishes me to take more trips; I came from Aughwick only lately."

This we both knew, as did any informed person in the colony. Weiser was known for fair dealing and honesty in Indian villages all over the land. He was the advisor of assemblies as well as savage chiefs. Johnson and Croghan also knew Indians, but Weiser had lived with them. His word on the frontier was gospel.

He rose. "Come, the lessons begin, my young friend Peter."

Back of a fringe of bushes, he had a most curious thing, a huge map on the ground. It was our colony with most of the rivers and mountains shown. There were also flat pieces of wood stuck in as gardeners sometimes mark their rows. I bent and read on each the name of an Indian tribe. On the north were the Iroquois names—Mohawks, Oneidas, Cayugas, Onondagas, and Senecas, each in his place. West of the Susquehanna, he had markers for Delawares and Shawnees.

Then, "It saves explaining," he said. He pointed to the Iroquois markers. "There are the people of the Long House. Johnson, Croghan, and I help to hold them to the tradition that they are friends of the English. The French cannot get at more than New England so long as these people stand firm. In three wars with the French, these people saved the day for England."

Weiser smiled enigmatically at Father, who said nothing but shook his head. The great interpreter went on and pointed to the region along the Delaware River. "That was the home of the Delaware tribes. One way or another, they have been cheated and pushed westward. They have had too much rum. The Iroquois had beaten them in battle, made them women. They could not fight both the whites and the Five Nations. But, I tell you, these people will take scalps for the land they lost."

His voice had risen. "They hang about Shamokin, hoping the Seneca tribe will take up their quarrel. The Shawnees linger wherever trouble is. Back of the ranges, the bulk of these tribes are friends of the French, who will someday loose them. This French and English war will come up the Ohio. The French have made themselves strong at Detroit on the lakes. They will strike at the English colonies on the soft side where English ships cannot help. Friend Michal, this war is ours, in our own province. The Virginians who claim the forks of the Ohio will start the trouble."

He seemed weary now at having talked so much, took out his pipe, and filled it with strong Indian leaf while we studied the map closely. When he had smoke going, he spoke again. "I was at Aughwick. Tanacharison, the Half King, was there. He tried to order the Delaware chiefs about. They listened, but they no longer fear the Iroquois hold on them."

He waved his stick. "This man Franklin thought he had ideas of joining all the colonies, but you cannot join a Dutchman from York colony with a Virginian with his nose in the air and a glass of that green drink in his hand. England wanted to use the Iroquois in its wars against the French. Michal, you know better. We cannot set red men to taking white scalps. An English trophy would look exactly like a French, dried. These English! Three wars and another coming!"

It was plain the old interpreter was nearly done with what he would say. He tossed his pointing stick to one side, tamped his tobacco impatiently with a horny finger as the Indians do. "Mark this well, Michal, and you, Peter. Let the English lose control of the Iroquois, and our America goes in blood and fire and human misery. The Long House lies to the north, a great heavy cloud. Pray God we may keep fair weather. Any day I will sacrifice Delaware interests to keep peace with Mohawk and Seneca. I work for the greater good."

He waved his hand in a gesture that took in the broad fields and the misty mountains in the distance. "It is a land too fair for the feet of war. But war will come, and this time, as I have said, from the Ohio country. There will be long files of painted men bearing muskets charged with French powder, and once more, an English scalp will bring its eight Spanish dollars, laid down in a French post."

"How soon, Conrad? How soon will it come," my father demanded impatiently, and Weiser answered with the promptness of one who has already found his answers.

"Two years. Mark you further—you are Dutch; I am German. In this war, the English will fail and muddle. In the end, we who have become Americans will win the war. We will tame the savages. I mean we of the colonies—Dutch, German, English, Scotch-Irish."

Again father interrupted the flow of talk. "Then what?"

Weiser looked at him a long time, his brows drawn down over his eyes in a frown. Then his face cleared. "You know, Michal Grove, someday this land will be—"

I do not know what he planned to say, but Eve Ann had come to us. She looked at her husband's face a moment, then took his arm before he could finish. "Conrad, our guests will want to taste the new cider. It is now just fresh from the press."

So we moved away, and there was no more said of wars and Indians. It has been my fortune to know some of the great of this colony. Franklin never did impress me, Morris was to mean much to me, but Conrad Weiser was like a prophet out of the Old Book. He made me think of the lines: "I am the voice of one crying in the wilderness." Truly this man, who had been reared in a Mohawk village, had lived until he had become the voice of authority to governors and soldiers, savages, and simple people of our land.

For the rest of our stay, we were visitors, and I delighted in the farm with its great horses that drew loads with so little effort. Here were tremendous wagons to bear in the crops; here was corn, the like of which one seldom sees. It was a prosperous place, well-loved, well-handled, and giving richly of the land's best fruits.

I noticed, while there, two messengers ride up with letters for Weiser. Two Indians came down the Shamokin path and delivered something wrapped in buckskin. Afterward, they sat on the back porch and ate greedily from a platter set between them, dripping grease on themselves and on the scoured floorboards. When they finished, he gave each a small cup of rum and shook his head when they rubbed their stomachs for more.

Weiser furnished us horses to go to Reading, for we left ours in Heidelberg. Here we took the stage for the city, stopping the first night at an inn called "Hare and Hounds," a big building where, from our rooms, we could see the Schuylkill. The place was thronged with guests, for both east and west coaches stopped here for the night.

The wide common room was very pleasant with its bar to one side, rush-bottomed chairs, and oaken tables. The guests sat about drinking cider and smoking long clay pipes, which could be bought at the bar together with fine tobacco. My father liked people, and soon our table was the center of a group listening to stories of the mountains and forest. One man who wore a snuff-colored coat and a stock too high and tight for him, was intent. He finally leaned forward. "Master Grove, you evidently know the mountains. I have caught the name Shingas several times. Have you seen the man? Can you tell us what he is like?"

Father laughed. "Yes, I have both seen and smelled Shingas too often. He is a small, wizened warrior with his hair worn like a white man, and he affects the dirtiest shirt west of Raystown. But remember, he is a leading Delaware chief. He and his fellow, Captain Jacobs, are leaders. Both are crazy about powder."

I looked down at the table, remembering suddenly the warning of Mistress Wright. My father was talking over much, and that had never been his custom except when he was with his friends like John Harris or Croghan. He went on. "Just now, the savages want to get far more powder than they need for hunting. You know it is said they have a lead mine. Both Shingas and Jacobs would barter anything for powder—in bulk—not the small amounts we traders will furnish. Shingas would trade his newest grandchild for a small keg of the stuff."

The stout man nodded. It was my fancy there was a glint in his eye. "I am obliged to you, Master Grove. My name is Judson, a maker of blankets such as are sold to traders like you as well as to stores in the colony. Do you know the firm of Horn and Teague?"

Father was pleased. "Yes, of course. They have outfitted me for many years. It is likely I have packed your blankets over the Endless Mountains for years."

"Endless Mountains, Friend Grove, where are they?"

"Oh," father's tone was careless, "that is the term on the old maps for all the mountains north and west of us. They are almost endless, too. To the north of us, you will see them in the morning only. In this country, they call them Kittatiny or Blue Mountains."

There was nothing for me to do but make circles on the table with the bottom of my cider mug. The stuff inside it was over sour to drink anyway. I watched Judson, a big man and heavy, yet most light on his feet. Under his eyes were pouches that seemed at times to hood his vision. His hands, clasping his pipe or mug, were big and strong and mobile. He puzzled me, and it seemed to me that my father was advertising how much he knew of the hills and the troubles gathering there.

I was glad, in the morning, to find that Judson had left in the west-bound stage, for I felt better rid of him. But the morning was spoiled for me with thinking about how soon I would be in the city.

CHAPTER FOUR

PHILADELPHIA, City of Brotherly Love—I am afraid I did not find too much of this sort of love, though city folks are often kind. However, I did find there keen businessmen. The city is alive with trade, and most of it has to do with ships and sailors. Great masts lifting above the docks are the landmarks of this town which in my day was contained in the land that juts down between the Schuylkill and Delaware Rivers.

When friends seated about woodland campfires ask me to tell of this greatest city in the new world, I say first, to their puzzlement, that as one nears it, there are so many great fields. Then I explain that one crosses fords to get into the town, that the mud is terrible, so much so that travelers leave their carts at inns. Their animals are kept in these fields, which belong to the inns, while the traveler rides a horse into the city, carrying as much as he can on the animal's back.

It was a town of brick houses and brick stores—brick because bricks come from England as ballast on the ships. When the ships are unloaded, the bricks are replaced by grain, or iron, or other heavy stuff. Consequently, bricks are almost as cheap in Philadelphia as in England. In my time, nearly all the business was conducted down near the docks where the market houses stretch for eight blocks.

That day we entered on what is known as the Quelph Road, and we rolled through Germantown between rows of peach trees from which the fruit had been harvested. The weather was dry, so our coach could go right into the city. There was a small belt of woods, then we crossed Race Street, the northern limit of the city, and did not stop until we reached the

Conestoga Inn, which is headquarters for western travelers. I had wanted to go to Clark's Inn because I had a great curiosity about the dogs they train there, dogs trained to turn spits on which joints of meat are roasted. However, in my evil humor, I would make no suggestion to my father.

From this inn, we walked six blocks west, nearly to the limit of the town that way. On both sides of the street, the brick houses closed in. There were narrow sidewalks, but not much of the street itself was paved, though downtown, the carts rumble over cobblestones.

Mrs. Jared Whitmore was glad to see us and full of questions. I had stayed here before when at school. Mrs. Whitmore was about father's age, her husband was often away from home, and she was glad to have someone in her house. My old room was vacant, which pleased me. It was on the ground floor and had a Dutch door which opened to the garden. Here I could have the upper part open to admit air—and often mosquitoes, which never bothered me too much, however. In this room, we deposited my few belongings. Father paid Mrs. Whitmore my rent six months in advance. When she left the room, he gave me a purse heavy with gold and silver. "If you need more, Horn will have it for you, Peter. Don't stint."

Having walked about the room, punched the bed, examined the pictures, father turned to me again. I knew he disliked close places as much as I did. "Well, Peter, I had best be going."

It seems sad to me now that two men who loved each other as we did found it so hard to talk things over. When I was younger, there had been long hours of talk before the campfire. Today we did not mention the Indian girl either to question or to explain. I finally fished a small packet from my pocket. "Please give this to John Harris. He will understand."

He thrust it carelessly into his pocket. "Remember, Peter, if you need more money, get it from Horn."

Then his strong fingers gripped mine, but he released them quickly and placed his hands on my shoulders. For a moment, we looked into each other's eyes. He shook me a little and was about to speak. Then he dropped his hands and, with no further word, walked out the door whistling tonelessly as he went down the long walk. I was glad the gloom of the room hid my eyes.

That was the last I ever saw him.

The school was a drab place, a huge half-empty building that would have made a good warehouse. The furniture in the few rooms we used was simply backless benches. Most of the time, it was so cold our fingers were blue and unfit to write. Our ambitious headmaster was a certain Dr. Smith, but my work was mainly with Simon Grover, a very mild person excepting with such things as inaccuracies in our figuring.

There was one young fellow in the class who was outstanding. Now I might be able, thanks to my father's teaching, to read Latin like a priest, but this young man's power lay in his mastery of mathematics. We all loved to sit and watch him place a problem on our slate blackboard. His figures looked as though they were etched; his lettering was plainer than any print. His name was David Rittenhouse, and he lived on a farm out Kingessing way. It is my notion that we were all proud of him, his wondrous skill in mathematics, and the tiny crow quill pen which he used for his lettering.

Master Grover was patient with me but could not understand my impatience. "There is plenty of time, Peter; no need to do today what can as easily be done tomorrow. Enjoy your studies, do not be a slave to them."

While I studied and slept at the house of Mistress Whitmore, I took my meals outside in the city. So it happened that I knew the whole place well, for I would eat clams or eels down at the waterfront or pork where the country people came in from upstate farms. I liked to see the great ships tied up or coming in until their long bowsprits reached out over the wharves. And the market houses, five of them, pleased me with their array of foods, some strange, some familiar.

But it was the bitter spirit that rode me which got me in my first trouble. Mart Reed had taught me to love horses, and the way these city draymen treated their beasts made my blood boil. It was a cold afternoon, and there was much ice on the streets. I had followed this dray for blocks. The horse was old, bony, drooping. The driver was a huge man who sat perched on the load, plying a whip at each slowing up of the old animal. Presently he turned into a side street. There the ice was worse. The horse was badly shod; it stumbled, came down on its knees, and could not rise, even under the shower of blows.

Today, I could see that brute of a man tied for a while to the black post. He did not see me as I came up over his load. His mouth was open in a curse when I grabbed him and brought him over the wheel so fast that he sprawled on the icy street. With a twist, I snapped his whip short. Then I set to work on him.

He was on his knees, sobbing and sniveling by the time I had enough of it. True, I had only gained a respite for the old animal, but satisfaction was singing inside me. For a moment, I thought of threatening him; instead, I threw what was left of the whip over the housetop and left. The noise of his yelling would bring a crowd in time.

Two hours later, three policemen arrested me a short block from my home. I spent the night in the cold and filth of the Walnut Street jail, and at noon the next day, I was brought, with a dozen others, into a big room where a magistrate in a huge wig presided.

It was something to watch this man dispose of the cases. In nearly every one, the prisoner was sentenced to the workhouse for thirty days, no matter if the charge was profane swearing, or fighting, or otherwise disturbing the King's peace.

Seated there on the hard bench, I was thinking about this king's peace when my name was called. A bailiff touched me on the shoulder with his staff. I rose, walked over, and faced the judge. "Peter Grove, assault and battery on one James Sloan, carter."

I saw that the man I had thrashed was sitting on the far side of the room, and I wanted to smile. Fear and hatred were mixed on his face. He had risen at the call of the bailiff when the door near him opened, and a big man walked in and crossed directly to where I stood before the judge. It was Judson, the man who had talked with my father in the inn. He held a purse in his hand and was smiling. "If your Honor pleases, I just heard of this case. Perhaps you would consider the matter of a fine. I know the young man's father, a good customer of mine."

Judson had an impressive way about him. The judge was listening carefully. He nodded and spoke. "I was about to examine this case, Mr. Judson. It seems there was real violence."

"If your Honor pleases, perhaps a gold guinea to the carter might ease his bruises. Also, I would pay a guinea as a fine." He crossed to James

Sloan, laid a broad gold piece in his palm, and then placed another before the judge, who suddenly banged his gavel on the desk.

"Case dismissed!"

I walked out arm in arm with Judson. When we were clear of the place, he removed his hat and mopped his forehead, though the day was certainly not warm. "Well, Peter, we are lucky this day. The magistrate is a friend of mine. I feared the other judge might be on duty."

"Mr. Judson, I am most grateful."

He raised his hand deprecatingly. "It was nothing. Truly I blame myself for not showing you about the city. I liked your father so much; only the fact that I am busy kept me from knowing you better."

He did allow me to repay the money he had spent. Then he shook my hand warmly and went on. Alone, I went back to my room.

Perhaps I would have thought more of Judson and how he came to know the minute I was in trouble, but there was a most unexpected thing back there where I lived—a white envelope sealed with a small blob of red wax. Mistress Whitmore gave it to me, said a messenger had delivered it, and said there would be no answer.

I turned it over and over in my hand, wondering; then I broke the seal.

Dear Peter:

I am here in the city to spend a few days with my aunt at Number Fifty-Four Pine Street. Perhaps you will call. Both my aunt and I will be glad to welcome you.

Faith Horn

The address was one of the big brick houses just a little off High Street. My impatience spoiled my first attempt at dressing, so I tried again and wondered why I had not thought to buy better clothes. However, I felt that I looked fairly decent when I stood on the small brick stoop and sounded the huge knocker. A servant admitted me, left me standing in the hall until a tall, severe-looking woman entered. She smiled and did not then look grim. She was holding out her hand. "You are Peter Grove? I shall call my niece."

I walked into a huge room with a heavy red carpet that muffled my footfalls. The chairs had twisted and carved legs and arms. There were mirrors in gilt frames like those in the Horn home. I had barely time to look about when I heard light steps, and Faith was in the room.

By her poise, as she came toward me, I knew she was not just a little girl. Her dress billowed about her and her brown hair piled high on her small head made her throat look too slender to bear the weight of it. I did my best to take her hand properly and to bow over it while Mistress Holbrook looked on approvingly. I did not want this woman to think a friend of Faith's was simply a backwoods boor.

It was a wonderful week, for Faith had come to shop, and she and her aunt made me welcome and useful in the carrying of bundles. We ate in coffee houses, and the three of us saw a play. When we visited the docks, I was pleased to show off my small knowledge of ships and shipping. It was my pleasure to point out to them the governor's barge. Finally, our week was over, and Mistress Holbrook and I saw Faith off on the Lancaster coach.

"Faith loves the frontier, but I do wish she would come and live here so she would find a real social life," Mrs. Holbrook said after the coach had left. Then she looked at me sharply.

"Samuel Horn is a cold man. Tell me, Peter, what you think of him."

I did not like Horn, and I remembered the hat with the feather, but I would not talk about my feelings with Mistress Holbrook.

"Truly, I do not know him well. My father outfits with him, and he is considered honest," I said mildly.

"But hard. I'll be bound," she snapped. "Now, come and see us often."

It will not do to tell the whole folly of my falling in with Judson. Suffice it to say we became friends. I saw him nearly every day, for I had time on my hands, being nearly finished with the surveying. We dined together often, and each time he urged me to talk of the frontier. Then came an evening when I was with Judson on a houseboat moored along the bank of the lower Schuylkill.

Two others were there besides Judson, one a fellow who was called Fox and who looked his name. The other one's name was Farrel. I had gone with Judson to see these men, for he said he had business with them.

We talked freely for an hour. Most of the conversation was directed to me, and I talked of trading, of the risks, of the profits, of the way of life out there in the hills. Suddenly Fox leaned forward. "Gentlemen, we have found our man. He knows the woods, the savages. Peter, we want to buy a lead mine from the Indians."

I looked at him. Fox was speaking again. "We'll send this young man to Shingas. He will learn the chief's price. We'll pay it. There is a fortune in this business." He touched my arm. "Enough for you as well, young man."

An alarm bell was ringing in my ears. As surely as though I were following the track of a deer in the snow, I could see the trail leading from the Slide out there by the Standing Stone to this city. I asked my question. "Are you trading with Indians?"

Farrel looked at me, drank from his glass, put it down. "Best say friends of ours trade Judson's blankets with them."

"Charteris?"

Their eyes widened at the name, and they had said, without words, that they would pay Shingas's price in blood and butchery. Wrath seethed in me. For a matter of weeks, I had been used like any gullible fool. Yet, in my heart, I knew they were so set on money they did not care how it came.

Slowly I came to my feet. We watched each other, and one must have read my eyes. His fingers tightened about the neck of the wine bottle. I backed toward the door, opened it, and stepped into the night. None followed; none, I trust, doubted my answer, yet the clash between us had been as real as though weapons had been drawn and blows struck. Mistress Whitmore had a letter for me the next morning. She gave it to me with a smile. This time the sealing was done with spruce gum and a thumb print in it instead of the common wax.

Dear Peter:

John Harris received your package of wampum and explained things to me. I trust my son will forgive his father for wrong thoughts of him. You must know that after our 'marble rolling,' I wanted you out of this country for a season. Now, things look better. Finish your surveying. Perhaps you can come to me soon. Spring is showing in the lower valleys.

Your Father,
Michal Grove

The house was too crowded after that letter. At last, my father understood. I did not reason about the "marble rolling." It was enough that he expected me back in the country with him and that soon.

My walk took me far out along the Schuylkill, where presently I saw a noble stone house set well back from the road. Before, it was a wealth of lawn and evergreens protected from the road by a low wall. On this wall, a man was working, trying to put a big stone in place. I stopped. "Let me help," I offered.

He stood up slowly, a tall man, and thin. His wide brown hat was pressed well down on hair worn loose about his face. A leather apron such as blacksmiths wear was strapped about his waist, and he wore pads on his knees. Suddenly he smiled, nodded, and bent to the stone. Together we lifted it into place. He stood regarding it gravely. "Now, I believe it will remain," he said quietly. "You know, a stone has its place to which it must be fitted truly, or it falls out. There is a hint of spring in my garden; come in and see it."

In a sheltered place, he showed me flowers and explained that they came from friends in Holland. "These are our earliest blooms."

I looked at him doubtfully. He smiled again, the lines of his thin face relaxing. "I mean cultivated flowers; in the hills, the arbutus is budding now."

That was my first meeting with John Bartram, nor did I know then how great a man he was. The next time I came that way, I stopped, and we worked in the garden together. I was ready to leave when he said: "Friend Peter, you will dine with us today. You have worked with me, and the laborer is worthy at least of his food."

We washed at a stone trough into which the water of a spring gushed through a wooden pipe. At the door, a gracious brown-haired woman met us.

"Ann," he said with a smile, "this is Peter Grove, a student and a man who may someday be a mason. Peter, this is Mistress Bartram, mother of my flock and my very best friend." We stepped into a huge room down the center of which was a long narrow table. Mistress Bartram moved to the foot. I wondered at the rows of chairs, at the mountains of bread, the bowls of milk. She struck a small triangle, and they came. It seemed like an army, but there were only six children, the boys looking like their father, the girls much like their mother. Then three men, one Black, came in and took seats. The serving women placed the food on the table and sat down with us. John Bartram dropped his head for a moment, then looked round the table with a smile.

There was plenty of talk, though Bartram spoke most often to the men. He refilled the Black man's plate. "Belton is shy, but his stomach isn't," he gibed gently. The Black man rolled his eyes in pleasure.

Later I sat outside and whittled toys for the children. In other days, when I came here, the pattern was the same—first, labor with the stones, then a fine meal after which I enjoyed the children. This was the first real home I had ever known.

One day I spoke a word and saw a change in Bartram. That word was "ginseng." We had been working on some plants of the common mountain laurel, removing dead wood when I remarked casually: "One day, I want to trade a bit in ginseng."

Bartram laid down his pruning knife and looked at me. "You know that plant?" His question was sharp.

I laughed. "Certainly. It grows by the half acre in the Sinnamahoning country where my father and I hunted."

He dusted his hands against the leather apron and unloosed the pads from his knees. "Peter, we leave for there the day after tomorrow. Be ready."

There was no arguing with this man. Four days later, we were on the great creek with our train of three horses. He had insisted on traveling directly across country; there had been rough going, but he did not hang back one whit. There, beside a tributary stream on which was a tiny natural meadow, I built a small lean-to as a shelter while the botanist admired and measured some of the great pines which are everywhere in that country. Next day, I found a patch of ginseng where the early shoots were just beginning to come forth.

Being late in May, this land was full of flowers; Bartram was like a man enjoying a delayed holiday. He had to see everything, sketch it, measure it, taste the plants and flowers. Ginseng delighted him. "You know, Peter, the Chinese think this root makes them young again."

He turned over in his palm a huge root shaped like the body of a man. "It is my thought that there is here no medicine more than a little bitters for the stomach."

"But," he added after a little, "we may have here a commercial possibility for the colony. Merchants shipped a dozen boxes of this root last year. They want more."

A day later, I showed him a small natural clearing on the side of a hill. The graveled slope was entirely covered with the dusty lavender of wild columbines. Bartram looked. He was a Quaker, but off came his wide-brimmed hat. He whispered softly: "If God so clothe the grass of the field . . ."

While the botanist worked with his plants, I had little to do but catch trout and see that Bartram was well fed with venison, fish, and good cornbread. He did like good food, but he never complained when things were scanty or carelessly cooked. Days lengthened into weeks. I grew careless with inaction.

There was no time during seventy years of colonial wars when a lone man's scalp was safe. Indians valued these trophies for sale to the French and also as marks of prowess. Bartram was busy lifting ginseng plants to take to his garden. I had walked over the hill. As I returned, I saw the savage back of the botanist. He was naked, but for his breechclout, and his hand was reaching for his war ax. It was too far for this gun of mine, but I set the small brass sight against the amulet bag at the Indian's throat. My finger was closing on the trigger when the kneeling Bartram turned slightly, lifting his hands which were full of earth and the plant; then, turning completely, he thrust the whole mass into the Indian's hand. "Hold it," he said.

The Indian was caught. Likely he understood some English; certainly, he understood the gesture. As I walked forward, gun ready, he stood there, his hands full of earth that dribbled through his dirty fingers. His eyes were on me, steady like a snake's. I spoke slowly, gesturing toward him, nor did he miss the cocked hammer of my piece.

"My brother is a runner." Then I pointed toward Bartram, "He makes medicine with plants."

Bartram rose, dusted his hands. I motioned toward our camp and marched the Indian with us. There I gave the native meat and some cornbread, "Eat, my brother. The way has been long."

He squatted on the ground and wolfed the food. When he had finished, I pointed to his war ax. "My brother runs far; his tomahawk is heavy. It would be best if it waited for his return in the tree."

The savage had not even grunted, but he did watch the gun muzzle. Obediently he drew the ax and stuck it into the tree. Then he belched politely and walked off toward the south. Bartram shook his head. "Our Aborigine has wretched table manners. Ann and I had a time training one of our boys who would, at times, belch like that. We cured him."

I laughed. "He was being polite that time. It was close for you, though. Did you not see him?"

His smile was almost like a boy's grin. Then he placed on the ground the small hand lens he used to study flowers. "Lying thus it is a small mirror, Peter. I saw the Indian and his fingers reaching for his ax. My thought was to keep him busy, to get his hands full."

My respect for John Bartram became even greater. I had not guessed the measure of his quiet coolness. Certainly, I would never have thought out this plan. I know now how much I owe this man and the training he gave me when I was with him. He was the true breath of civilization, taming in me things almost savage. While he never told me so, I know he appreciated the fact that I was about to kill a man to save him. Yet I think he valued the glimpse of the wild columbines I had given him more than my willingness to shoot.

May with the yellow tinge on the green leaves was gone; June had come with pretty warm days before we reached home with our pack train laden with specimens. I stayed with the botanist for several days, helping plant specimens and mount others on heavy paper.

It was near an evening when I returned to my room in the city, and Mistress Whitmore was waiting. "Peter, we have been searching for you. This came the second day after you had gone. We could not find you."

The note was not sealed, and it was in John Harris' hand. "Your father was drowned in the river this morning. Come at once."

Mistress Whitmore went out, closing the door softly. I stood there holding the paper in my hand while the shadows came and my world collapsed about me.

CHAPTER FIVE

MISTRESS WHITMORE tried to help me with ready sympathy, but all she could do for me was a promise to send my few belongings to Lancaster. I had no patience to wait for the stage or hire horses. Dressed in buckskins and shod with good moccasins, I walked the fifty-seven miles from Philadelphia to our house in Lancaster from a little before noon to the dark hours of early morning. I stopped a minute or two of each hour to rest and sometimes munched a bit of parched corn.

Our house was empty, the barns deserted. Likely, Mart Reed was somewhere on the trail. Not bothering to undress, I flung myself down on a pile of skins and fell into the sleep of the exhausted, which is so much like death. I woke sometime in the afternoon and went directly to the trading post of Horn and Teague. The trader was back of the counter alone. He stared at me, his narrow face grim and cold. "So—you come a month late!"

I did not wish to argue with the man nor to take the time to dislike him too much. I wanted whatever knowledge he had of the tragedy. "Sir, I have been on the Sinnamahoning with John Bartram for the past month. I had Harris's letter but yesterday."

His face relaxed a little. He picked up and laid down the quill he had been using in an absent sort of gesture. "They tell," he said, "that he was drowned below the ferry. Harris and friends buried him on Watch Island."

I stood listening and thinking at the same time. Then I blurted my question. "He was a strong swimmer. How could he drown in that quiet water?"

Horn half turned, tossed his quill back to the desk top. "I do not know. He was in a canoe with an Indian who reached shore and then ran away because likely he thought he would be accused of killing your father. Perhaps—"

He was interrupted by the opening of the side door. Faith entered, came straight to me, and took my hand. Then she spoke to Horn. "Look at him, sir. I venture he has neither eaten nor rested. Come."

She led me like a child to the kitchen and pushed me into a chair. Next, she wet a towel in cold water. "Wipe your face with this; I'll get you some food."

I had not known how hungry I was until I tasted what she placed before me. Then, I am afraid; I ate like a savage. She sat across the little table, saying nothing but keeping my plate filled. When I finished and looked up, she spoke. "Peter, the last time he was here, he talked of you and his pride in you. Your father loved you greatly. I think he sent you to school to keep you safe, that he feared some great danger and faced it alone rather than risk you. You will go to Harris Ferry?"

Her last word was a question, and I nodded. Speech came hard after her kindness. Fumbling with my cap, I walked to the door; she followed me. Suddenly she was on tiptoe and had drawn down my shaggy head. For one glorious fleeting instant, her warm lips rested on my unshaven cheek. "Go with God, Peter," she whispered, and, as I walked to my home, I no longer felt alone.

When I reached Harris Ferry, the big, heavily bearded Harris met me, his wife standing by. My mind was too engrossed to note the restraint of these people who took me inside the house where Mrs. Harris insisted on giving me food. But my appetite was so poor that I pushed back my plate presently and broke the silence. "Mr. Harris, my father was a powerful swimmer. If an Indian got out, why couldn't he?"

The trader looked toward his wife, and his voice was cold and blunt when he answered. "You have waited and taken your time to be worried. Better go to bed now. Talk can come later."

I stared at him with the same surprise I would have felt had he struck me with a whip. More astonished than hurt, I rose, as did Mrs. Harris. "We have a bed for you, Peter," she said kindly.

In all her natural kindness, she must have regretted her husband's speech, but I wanted nothing more than to leave. The pine thicket where I spent the night asked me no questions, nor did it grudge its hospitality. The smell of the needles, the tiny voices of crickets, and the whisper of the breeze soothed me.

When I came to the ferry in the morning, intent on getting a canoe, there was no one about. Then I heard a call; it was Harris. When he was close, I drew some coins from my pocket and dropped them into his palm. "Canoe hire for the day," I said, and he glared at the coins as if he would throw them at me.

He gulped deeply. "John Bartram came last night. He told us why you did not come. Come on in; he's at breakfast."

Nonetheless, I did not go in but waited until Bartram appeared, his hand outstretched, a smile on his long face. "Though you hurried my breakfast, I'm glad to see you well enough to be stubborn. Why, oh why, Peter, didn't you come to us? Ann packed me off the minute we heard the news, knowing you would need a friend."

I shall always remember him standing there and the grip of those long brown fingers, fingers that could shape a stone with chisel and mallet or handle the fragile stem of a wildflower. It brought me comfort that so great a man would take so much trouble just for me. He was speaking again. "I've told Honest John here of the trip to the Sinnamahoning. It grieves me that I made you late in coming. But your father rests well; death is a peace you are young yet to understand."

We took the canoe I had chosen, leaving Harris behind, though he seemed to wish to come. I saw him, as we pushed off, produce the coins I had given him. It was fair hire for the craft. I was glad he did not seem to know what to do with the money.

Watch Island is a small wooded affair of a few acres. Its upriver point is a headland covered with tall pines. I knew that a woman, a widow, lived there, but I had never seen her. I only knew that she was Swedish and that her husband had been killed by Indians within the past two years. Her name, I remember, was Benson.

She met us at the small wharf—a tall, strongly made woman who wore her yellow hair braided and wound about her head as had Mistress

Wright at the Blue Goose Inn. Her face would have looked young had it not been for its deep lines. Her voice was low-pitched, calm. Bartram stepped out, held out his hand. "I am John Bartram, Madam. This is Peter Grove, whose father you had the mercy to lay at rest."

The woman's face softened and came close to a smile. She beckoned. "Come, I'll take you there."

It was a lovely place where soft shadows ruled, yet where the sun could shine through on bright days. Needles had sifted down on the mound of raw earth, softening it to the sight. There was a small wood headboard with the name "Michal Grove" burned on it.

I did not realize for a while that I had been left alone under the pines beside the place where he was sleeping. It was as it had been when I was a boy and waited for him to wake so I could ask my questions. I remembered that he would sometimes smile and not answer my queries, so I would work out the answers myself.

Presently this mood passed. I sensed the fullness of my loss, the sureness that I would never hear him speak again. Then something happened. To me, it was as real as the pines about me. It was a voice that I did not hear but which made me understand. "Peter!"

What was it? Challenge? Warning? I had no way of knowing.

Bartram and Mistress Benson had been looking at her garden, and he smiled as I came up. "I have told our hostess she is a better farmer than many of her race down on Tinicum."

He dusted his fingers and knees from long habit. I have more than once heard that he had been caught making this gesture when he came from the Meeting House.

Mistress Benson looked at me a moment. Then—"Michal Grove was with my husband in the hills two years ago when he was killed, Peter. Wait."

When she emerged from the house, she was carrying a small cloth-wrapped parcel. She spread the contents on a bench. "Your father's small ax and tinder box are with him."

Bartram looked at us, but I nodded, knowing the frontier custom. Here were a few coins, perhaps a dozen and amounting to a little over a pound sterling. There was the small bone-handled clasp knife that

Thomas Cresap had given me. My initials were cut deep in the handle. My throat tightened when I thought of his carrying it with him, perhaps to remind him of me when his hand went into his pocket. There was also his sheath knife, the end of its bone handle carved in the shape of a dog's head. One thing more, a soiled handkerchief with a comer tied. Kneeling, I opened the knot and found a small gray pebble.

Bartram and I studied at it. He touched it, shook his head. "I have no skill with metals, Peter."

With the point of my clasp knife, I scarred the pebble until a bright line showed. "Lead," I said. "Lead."

That tiny piece of metal shocked me, wrenched my memory back to things I wished to forget—the Slide, Judson, the warning of the woman at the Blue Goose. Perhaps this small stone was a hint as to why my father had died. I could not believe he had drowned.

When she saw the pebble, Mistress Benson disappeared into her cabin. When she rejoined us, it was to show another stone like the one in my palm, only larger. It, too, had been scratched with a knife. "My man had this in his pocket when he was killed. Michal Grove buried him, brought this back to me." She rubbed the stone slowly with her toil-worn thumb.

I could not think of anything more to say until Bartram walked down to the landing; then I turned to her sharply, my voice low. "He did not drown. Was it a knife or a hatchet?"

She stared at me with wide, startled eyes. Then she spoke slowly. "No one else must know. It might start war. There was a small, old Indian with your father. It was a knife."

"Shingas?" I questioned sharply.

She shook her head gravely and answered in a level monotone: "I did not say."

I said nothing to Bartram as we paddled back, nor did I wish to talk more that evening.

Harris pressed me to stay at the Ferry after my good Quaker friend had taken his departure the following morning, but I wanted to get back to Lancaster and talk with Mart Reed. After that, there would be the high hills, the trail, and a chance to see Shingas.

I came to the Blue Goose about early candle-lighting time and found the common room thronged and managed efficiently by Cooney, with Stouffer at the bar. Passing the barns, I saw many horses in the pens. The crowd meant traders. Mistress Wright was away on a visit, Cooney told me quietly when he served me the bread, cheese, and ale which I carried to a table. Seating myself, I noticed two men near me at a corner table. Both were big, blond, and quiet. In the corner behind them stood two long rifles with powder horns and war bags hanging from their muzzles. There were glasses on the table before them, but they were more than half full.

Bread and cheese finished, I leaned back in my chair and watched the crowd. Eddies of smoke drifted from pipes; men lounged against the bar. In one corner, a fellow in buckskins was patiently dancing by himself as though practicing. Presently a big man in a soiled linen shirt open at the throat, his shock of hair pushed back from a flushed face, swung around, put his back to the bar. Suddenly he wheeled, pounded the bar. "Cooney, quick, liquor! I jest seen a ghost!"

Cooney slapped a bottle down before the man, who poured and downed a huge drink. Then he turned and started walking directly toward me. Now he was at my table, leaning forward, his breath in my face. "Sonny," he roared. "You scared me."

I looked at him. He was pretty drunk and had made so much noise that others were looking at us and moving forward until I was the center of an arc of men. "Yessir," he grunted. "Fer a minute, I thought old Michal Grove was back, him that got what was coming to him in the river."

It is my misfortune that often, when I am most angry, I grow quiet. Murder sang in my ears as my temper mounted. I laid both hands on the table, palms down. The big man beckoned. "Looky here, men, I ain't Fred Parr if this man ain't the spit of Michal Grove, damn him."

With one shove, I drove the table against his knees, staggering him off balance into the ring of men. Then I was over it, driving into him, a blind mist of temper shutting away everything but his broad surprised face. Again and again, I hammered my fists into that face, seeing the blood leap as I struck home.

But the ring of men gave back; he was clear, and he rushed. My temper did it. Too angry to make the right move, I was swept off my feet and went down on my back. Mouthing oaths, fingers crooked like talons, he was coming down on me. I rolled to one side and twisted. My moccasined heel went home on the side of his face, sprawling him on the floor.

He scrambled up again. "I'll snap your eye strings fer that, you—"

His rage choked him. He was slavering like a wild dog. The men were yelling. "Go to it, Parr. Give the cub hell!"

I could see the blackened nails on the hands he held half open, but I was cool once more. This charging business is only dangerous to the man who does it. Parr swept forward. I dived under one thick arm, snatched at it, and swung it over my shoulder. He screamed like a stabbed hog as the arm snapped, and he was flung full length on his back. This time I was on him, hammering his face. He was breathing like a spent runner. I grabbed him by his hair and ears and pounded the puncheon floor with his head. "You swine," I gritted. "You said he got what was coming. What do you mean?"

His eyes opened. "Naught, naught—I heard—" he panted.

One more slam of his head, then I wiped my hands on the front of his foul shirt, came to my feet, and slipped my knife from its sheath. The men were lined against the wall. I balanced the weapon in my hand. Behind me, a soft voice spoke. "You want to kill him, best take him outside. Spoils the floor—"

I wheeled and understood why Parr's friends lined up. The two men who had sat in the corner stood, rifles cocked and pointed. "Take your time. Ask them other fellers."

I walked down the line. "Anyone know what he meant?"

They shook their heads, eyes on my knife and on the rifle muzzles. No one spoke. Cooney stood behind the bar. Stouffer had replaced a huge mallet under the shelf.

"Well," the rifleman stepped forward. "Guess we'll leave. This place stinks of polecat."

He motioned to me. The other man and I were outside when our spokesman waited in the doorway a moment. Then he drawled. "Best not follow. That always makes me kinda mad. My name's VanCamp."

I saw the look of understanding on the faces of the men. The name carried weight even with this rough crew. Certainly, they took his advice, for no one followed us for the few miles to a dense pine thicket where we made our beds—mine being made of the blankets they shared with me.

"I'm Mose VanCamp," the big man told me. "My partner's Dan Pence. Cooney told us you're Peter Grove and that you look a lot like your Pa. Anyways, you're kind of a hellion in a barroom fracas."

Both men were instantly asleep, but I lay for hours listening to their breathing and thinking. What had Parr meant? Why had he hated my father? What was there about the small lead pellet in my pocket?

Finally I slept.

CHAPTER SIX

MORNING CAME fresh and lovely with a gentle breeze that moved the tips of the pines against a background of cloudless sky. For a little while, we lay relaxed. Then, with a flip of his long legs, Pence threw off our blanket and came to his feet in almost the same movement. I had no food with me, but my new friends seemed to have plenty. We ate leisurely and talked. I told them of my father's death. Pence filled his pipe. "Me and Mose heard about that a little after it happened."

VanCamp busied himself stamping out the remnants of our fire, stamped the ashes from his moccasins, then made his comment. "I don't figure that Parr knowed more than he said. He's just an ornery bastard. Folks say he works at times for Hugh Mercer down country. You sure worked him over bad. Where'd you learn that?"

"My father," I said, busy tying my moccasins. Then I looked up at the two men. "Tell me, is there some story about him?"

They looked at each other. VanCamp did the talking. "Folks say powder is getting to the redskins pretty fast. They blame the traders. I never seen your father. Do you know Charteris or a man named Horn?"

"Yes, Horn's a trader in Lancaster. He outfitted us. Charteris is some sort of Shawnee half-breed," I answered.

For a moment, I wanted to tell these men the whole story about the Slide, but I held it back. VanCamp was nodding. "Yes, Charteris is thick with the Quakers. Pence and me don't work that country. You ever hear of a lead mine?"

My fingers touched the small pebble in my pocket, but I shook my head negatively, sure that it would be best not to talk. A little later, we parted. I was going down to my home; Pence and VanCamp were bound for York.

Mart Reed was at the house, the horses in the feedlot, and he heard my explanation as to why I had been so late coming after Father's death. "I figured it was something like that. For a spell, I was coming to hunt you up—but he was gone—what was the use?"

Reed had changed. His upstanding hair looked less jaunty; the lines on his face were deeper. He had aged, and there was an air of defeat about him. His pipe alight, he said: "Sit down, Peter. I'll tell what I know. It was this way—we lost our pack loads, never mind how. Well, we picked up some buckskins at that town—"

He looked at me sharply and continued, "Well, we come to Harris Ferry. I kind of wanted to get the horses back home for a rest. Your father said he wanted to stay awhile at the Ferry. Harris took our skins. There was some Indians about; there always is there. Next I knowed, he was dead. What I can't figure out is how they got him in a boat. I was down at the island. That woman didn't know anything."

He tapped out his pipe. "The horses is all right. You figure to go on trading?"

I did not know, and I did not answer at once. Reed went on. "Your father let me put my savings in the horses. Now I own seven outright. I figure you'd better go up to Horn and get your father's money. There's a couple of reasons why I think it'd be better to trade elsewhere."

Money—so far, I had not thought of it. I still had some which my father had given me that day of our parting. Besides, I had sold a few pounds of ginseng through Bartram and had the money for that. Yet there must be funds somewhere. My father had said that if I ran short, I should go to Horn. Many traders acted as bankers for their customers.

Another thing bothered me—Mart Reed's statement. It was seldom that he spoke ill of anyone or expressed a doubt of a man unless he was not good to horses. Yet he had offered his mild suggestion that we should trade elsewhere. There was just one thing to do—see Horn and have the matter cleared.

The trader was in the big room busy with a number of men who were outfitting, so I dawdled about until the customers finished and Horn was free. Then I asked the question about Father's affairs. He was extremely civil and smiled when he answered. "No, he never banked with me to any great extent, seldom more than he needed to outfit again. Let's see."

He drew a huge leather-bound book from a shelf under the counter, opened it, and perched his steel spectacles far forward on his nose. "About three hundred pounds less a few shillings. That is about what I expected and according to his custom."

I frowned in my bewilderment. The sum seemed quite small. It did not seem possible that my father should spend a lifetime trading and not amass more than enough to make another trip. "Do you know if he had investments elsewhere, Mr. Horn?"

He seemed to study for a moment, but his reply was disarming. "No, your father and I are Dutch. We fought in the old wars together, and we were associated a long time, but I know little of his affairs. Shall I give you this money now?"

"No," I said. "I was thinking of Reed, who wants to go trading again."

Horn closed his account book and returned it to the place under his counter. This whole interview was most natural, but I kept thinking of the hat with the feather, of which the chair in the corner reminded me. "Trade is risky," Horn was saying. "England and France will fight again. The war will be in this province. It will come up the Ohio."

I thought of Conrad Weiser, of my father. All these men who knew expected war, and in Pennsylvania. Now here was Horn saying the same thing. He crossed his arms and leaned forward over the counter. "It's this way. Trade with the Iroquois might be all right, but that business goes into New York. The English keep a jealous grip on such business, and it would be hard to make a start up there. Besides, everybody is touchy about the people of the Long House, afraid of getting them against the English. Do you understand?"

I nodded. It would be entirely possible for a slight accident to set a tribe against all white people. A careless or greedy trader could manage that easily.

"Now the Delawares and Shawnees—some hang about the village of Shamokin trying to get the Senecas' sympathy, some get in here, quite a few reach Harris' place. The bulk of them are over the mountains, and the Delawares are angry. They remember their place was down country, that they were cheated, that they were bullied by both Iroquois and whites and could not find peace until they moved to strange hunting grounds."

He waved his hand. "Shawnees—you can always find them where trouble is. No wonder their very name means 'wanderer.' Always someone is driving them out. So, Peter, west of the mountains, the tribes are in savage humor. A trader might find business; he might find death or robbery. It is a poor time for that business except for a man who is well-known, one with whom they have done much business like Croghan or Cresap."

I interrupted, "You really expect war then?"

He nodded. "There will be war until England and France settle for all time who shall rule in America. There is room for both in this land, but there is not the will for both to live together. If I were you with your education, I would go into surveying."

Suddenly I blurted at him, "Do you know a trader named Charteris?"

His answer was prompt. "Heard of him often; he's part Shawnee. His father had a post on the river, but I do not know the man."

He was not in the least disturbed; anyway, I was taking a poor way to get at the truth. Most anyone could wear a feather in a black hat if he had the hat and the feather. Actually, I wanted to kick myself for going at things with boyish directness. In such a humor, I strode back to my dwelling.

Reed was happy to see me, for he had news that pleased him. John Harris wanted loads taken to Philadelphia. When I explained about the money, he seemed satisfied but not greatly concerned. He was more interested in horses than any other property.

Two evenings later, I called on Faith, who answered the knocker and was glad to see me. "Come in, Peter."

She was dressed in a soft gray gown that made her look like a Quaker, except that she did not wear a cap, which would have hidden the beauty of her hair. We talked of the weather and of Philadelphia. Finally, she came right out with this remark; "You are troubled, Peter, and not thinking about what we are saying. Is it about your father?"

I nodded. "'He was murdered. Faith, not drowned."

She listened closely while I told her all I knew, then agreed. "I believe my father thinks so, too. He and your father have known each other so long."

I could not tell her of other things like the Slide and the soft gray pebble in my pocket.

"Just one thing, Peter. Don't brood; get to work. Take out a pack train or do some surveying. I was lost when Mother passed until I busied myself. Don't think too much; it will not bring him back."

On my way home that evening past the rows of brick houses, I thought little of her advice, for I was remembering the softness of her hand as she gave it to me when I was leaving, also the shine in her hair. I felt guilty that she occupied so much of my mind when I should be grieving.

Candles were lit in my house when I reached it and opened the door. There were Pence and VanCamp looking very much at home. I cried out with pleasure. "Wait, I'll set out some brandy. Too bad Reed wasn't here to do the honors."

VanCamp raised his hand. "Never mind. Dan and I don't drink overmuch. We stopped to see if you'd go along."

I took a chair, faced them. "Sure," I said. "Do you mind telling me where?"

VanCamp shook his head. "Don't promise that easy. Listen—there's always Indian trouble. I can't tell you jest where Dan and I fit in, but a band of Mohawks slipped down over the Blue Mountains. They killed a man and his wife and carried off a little girl. Four or five days, they'll be crossing the Wyalusing Flats. We're to stop 'em."

"But there's no war. Mohawks are friends," I said.

"Hell," VanCamp sneered. "You got a lot to learn. Scalps is eight dollars in any French post. It's better money than beaver trapping. Anyway, that band's not to get home."

I sprang up, began to take off my town clothes. Presently I was dressed in buckskins and was making up a pack. I put in a second pair of moccasins. Pence gave his approval. "You'll need 'em. We got nearly two hundred miles to go."

"Yes," VanCamp cut in, "and we'll have to waste part of a half a day with those old he-sows at Shamokin."

Bright dawn found us north of Harris Ferry. We did not go as the crow flies but followed the river. Level going was better than beating our hearts out crossing ridges. In the long night march, I had time to think things through. After all, this wasn't my business. It was restlessness that sent me out with these men. True, I could call it duty, but it was partly because they seemed to want me, and lately, I thought I had found some who did not care too much to have me about.

We slept the first night five or six miles south of the Seneca village of Shamokin, having made a tremendous march after very little sleep, but we were three big men carrying little besides our weapons. Next morning, we breakfasted with appetites like wolves, almost finishing what provisions we had brought with us, though we did hold back our corn meal and parched corn. Before mid-morning, we were coming into Shamokin.

This, I knew, was one of the most important Indian villages in the colony, and from a hill, we could see how beautifully situated it was. Before us was a great piece of flat land. To the north and east was fair river coming in between high hills, then widening to contain a small island before it joined the other wider branch that comes down from the northwest. Across the main river, a huge hill lifted itself, its face forming sheer cliffs hundreds of feet in height.

From our vantage point, we could see the village contained about fifty houses which were half wigwam, half bark. Some lodges showed on the island. This was the village of Shikellamy, friend of Conrad Weiser. He was the Seneca who had ruled the Delawares and been a friend of white men. However, at this time, he was then dead, and his sons were a drunken lot. Moreover, the Delawares were getting tired of Iroquois dictation. Men like Shingas and Captain Jacobs, with the promises of the French in their ears, would be hard to bully. Seneca rule among the Indians in our colony was getting shaky.

We came down our hill and entered the place. It was the dirtiest Indian village I had ever seen, and the largest. A host of dogs, all with mangey backs, hung about us, snarling and fighting among themselves but yet not daring to attack us. Over the river bank was a litter of bones and some dead animals, and over everything was the reek of decaying fish. Flies were everywhere. Naked children scuttled into the houses as we went swinging along, and several squaws leered at us from open tent flaps.

We passed the usual ball ground, now deserted of players, to where, before a larger house than the average, sat a dozen men, all old, enjoying the warmth of the sun. We presented twists of tobacco which passed around the circle. They tore off chews. Two of them filled pipes that gurgled when they lit them. We seated ourselves at the gesture of one who seemed to be some sort of chief. VanCamp spoke. "We are bound for the Sinnamahoning—ginseng."

The old men looked about at each other and grinned lewdly. One spoke a few words in their tongue; then, they all rocked back and forth in silent laughter. Their spokesman pointed a finger at VanCamp. "Your squaw now tired of you? Now hunt man-making root."

Of course, I knew the reputation ginseng had among settlers and savages, how it was supposed to promote strong manhood. Dutifully I joined in the laughter at VanCamp's supposed infertility. The chief tapped himself on the chest. "For us, maybe ginseng. For you, no ginseng. Our young men need our women. But, maybe for much tobacco—"

His grin finished what he considered either a proposition or a joke.

They were still cackling among themselves when we rose. As an additional present, we gave them about a gill of priming powder, which pleased them a great deal. We went out of town on a good swinging stride. Pence was fed up on his visit. "Every damn thing in that town is rotten, even that old backside's brains. Why does an old coot think such lousy stuff?"

VanCamp merely grinned at him, and I wasn't going to waste any breath in argument. I would need all I had to travel with this pair of iron-muscled men.

We turned east at the first large creek coming to the river and marched through a succession of narrow valleys. Later we killed a small deer, dressed it carefully, and cooked most of the meat. From now on, fires would be a danger. Then we inspected our weapons, going over them with the greatest care.

Both men approved my short rifle and the pistol, which fired the same size ball. With their oil stone, I sharpened my father's knife and my ax. Theirs already had razor edges. We carried extra flints, each a small pick for the pan of his rifle, each an equal share of the food. VanCamp spoke soberly. "Remember, if a man gets hurt, can't travel, we leave him. Better lose one than three."

From now on, we were exquisite in caution. We lighted no fires; we stopped at the crest of ridges, studied the land for long minutes. Once, we came across the ashes of an old fire and inspected it carefully. Pence thought it a good ten days old.

Yet, for all our caution, we did not find the war party—it found us! A rattlesnake did the business. VanCamp was ahead, Pence next, trailing his rifle. I was last. It was midafternoon, and I was pretty tired. There would come a time when I could out-travel these men, but I was not yet hardened to it. The snake struck from the coil it had taken when VanCamp passed by it. Perhaps it had aimed at Pence's leg, but it hit his gunstock instead. I saw the two yellow spots of venom and involuntarily cried out my warning.

Neither man ever chided me for that bit of folly. The human voice carries far in the quiet of a forest. Yet, it made little difference. Pence killed the snake with a blow of the brass-bound stock. Then he wiped the blood from it on the ferns. We stood looking down at the writhing serpent.

There was no chance to raise a hand or a weapon, for they were about us too soon, ten nearly naked, sweating savages. Each man wore the remnants of his war paint, which they had not freshened. Each man's scalp lock was braided. Some wore feathers; one had a woman's comb fastened in his greasy scalp lock. The broad bands of white along their cheekbones gave them the air of uncouth, unholy owls or strange creatures coming into the sunlight from foul caves.

There is nothing gentle about the Indian's way with captives. The brave who had snatched Pence's rifle glanced at the priming. Then, without warning, he felled the woodsman with a blow of the barrel. A greasy-looking buck took VanCamp's weapons, looked at them, then spat full into the captive's face. I caught my breath and expected to see VanCamp leap on the savage, but his face did not alter by a muscle. He stared ahead while the spittle ran down and while they snatched his arms back of him and tied them with rawhide thong. As a further refinement, they twisted the straps that tied us with a piece of stick to make them tighter and to make them cut into our wrists.

The one who tied me up kicked me forward so that I was closer to my friends and so that they could fasten the three of us together. They edged us forward, poking us with gun barrels. As we walked, they searched our pockets, getting my flint and steel, VanCamp's pipe. Pence's jew's harp, about which they seemed as puzzled as small children.

Their camp was in a forest glade not two hundred yards from where they had captured us. There, tied to a tree like any little dog, was another captive, a small girl. A thong was knotted about her thin neck, and her arms and legs were crisscrossed with scratches and welts. She stared at us with vacant eyes. It was plain that she was broken in spirit and nearly dead from abuse and starvation.

Our captors squatted on the ground and gobbled the meat and corn taken from us. One tossed a scrap of meat toward the girl, who snatched it up and worried it as a dog will. I saw VanCamp's eyes turn toward her several times. Pence was looking a little better; his wits were returning after the savage blow. The Indians got to their feet, belching. They had not given us a scrap of food, nor did we get any for the next two days.

We filed out of the woods and climbed slowly to high, flat country that stretched away interminably. There was plenty of timber but very little underbrush. The Indians set a good pace, but it was easy for us to match them. When night came, they tied our arms and legs about a small sapling. The only relief we had from the thongs was when they loosed them for this purpose.

By the second night, we were nearly famished, but the little girl had been dragged along most of the day and was in a desperate condition. When she had dropped, she had been kicked to her feet by her captor. Now, stopped for the night, she fell into a small pitiful heap. Her owner kicked her without result, and I saw Pence writhe. The Indian next to him saw and poked him sharply with a stick.

They had killed two grouse on the march by throwing sticks. After pulling some of the feathers off the birds, they toasted them lightly over a small fire. A handful of entrails were flung to the child, and her claw-like fingers fumbled the filthy stuff, and half carried it to her cracked and sore lips.

When he had finished his portion, the girl's owner wiped his fingers on his dirty shirt, rose, belched loudly, and walked toward his captive.

He grunted, snatched at her hair, and partly raised her from the ground. She dropped when he released her with little sign of life. It was all over in a moment. His tomahawk flashed down; then, he ripped off the pitiful little scalp.

Oddly, of the three of us, it was VanCamp's stoicism that broke. His powerful body lunged forward against his bonds. Veins stood out on his corded neck, and his lips were drawn back from his teeth in an animal snarl. If I had seen that terrible fury on his face and known it was directed at me, I would have been afraid whether the man was tied or not. One of the savages leaped up and brought the flat of his ax down on the tawny head with terrific force. VanCamp collapsed.

At noon of the next day, we reached a good-sized stream. Here they located a canoe in the bushes. In its prow was a store of corn which the savages divided carefully. There was also a skin-wrapped flat bottle which the chief, the man who spat in VanCamp's face, put in his war bag. Two of the warriors left us here, likely to work the canoe upstream.

That night we camped under a spreading oak tree, and our captors did a strange thing, something I was to see again on the Sinnamahoning. Each man struck his ax into a limb and stood his gun against the tree. Weary and hungry as I was, I could sense an impatience among the warriors. There was much jabbering; their fire was sketchy, and all the food they had was a moldy-looking piece of venison and a little corn.

We had been squatting on the ground while they ate. Now they did a careless job of tying us up. The man who did it kept turning to see what the others were doing. He had some trouble with knots and slashed the thongs impatiently, but he had us tied at last in the usual way. I would not have noticed had it not been for the look in Pence's eyes. The warrior had dropped his knife, and VanCamp's broad moccasin now covered it.

The reason for impatience soon became apparent, for the chief produced the skin-wrapped bottle and delivered a fairly long harangue about it. Then he drew his knife and scratched the glass carefully. He was dividing the liquor into portions. Each brave kept his beady eyes on that flask as it went around, watching lest someone get more than his share. It went around twice. Then the chief smashed the bottle and handed the pieces about so they could lick the last drop from the fragments.

We had marched long miles that day. The Indians had had two drinks apiece, and in a few minutes, they were sleepy. One by one, they gouged out places in the ground for their hips, wrapped their blankets about them, and slept. The fat warrior who had killed the girl sat by the fire. It was he who would keep watch.

Hanging there in my withes, I could smell the rancid odor of these savages. The firelight flamed up, died back. My mind was wandering. I was back with Mart Reed and his small horse, Bram. I thought of Faith Horn and her bright hair, of my father. I had forgotten all about the knife under VanCamp's foot until a faint stir roused me from my lethargy.

There was just light enough to follow what he was doing. He was sinking down, trying with his tied hands to reach the knife under his foot. The warrior at the fire rose, yawned, walked over to Pence, slapped him smartly in the face, and went back to his place.

Perhaps an hour passed, time that seemed like a month. I knew Van-Camp was free. The Indian at the fire was asleep. He had rolled over on his side and was snoring. I could see VanCamp come to Pence's side, knew that the two men were free. Then VanCamp's lips were close to my ear. "Quiet."

My hands swung clear at his quick slash. I felt the cold blade of the knife against my ankles. He was up again, whispering. "Rub your ankles!—careful—no noise!"

On that night of the Wyalusing Flats, what there was of boy in me passed away. No one could have looked on the murder of that child and ever felt pity for an Indian again. Not ten feet from me, eight of them were lying. I rubbed my ankles, my wrists. I had no desire to escape. What I wanted most was to punish these snoring devils.

We moved to the heavier shadow under the tree, and Pence handed me our three guns and my pistol. I fumbled and primed them. VanCamp whispered again, "Pence and I, hatchets. You, the guns. If any get away, we lose our hair."

It does not seem possible that three men, starved for days, beaten, pushed about, would have attempted the desperate thing we did that night. Yet, none of us would have left without it. I had the guns beside me, my pistol through my belt. VanCamp and Pence edged toward the warriors, and I saw the axes come up gleaming in the faint light, then sweep down.

In all the fighting I have seen since, I have not heard this same sound, though I have seen war axes work in battle. But this was alone in the quiet of the forest, a sound between that of breaking a stick and an ax blow against a small hollow log. I fired a rifle as a warrior gained his feet.

There is no describing what happened there in the thin moonlight, nor is there any telling how long it took us. I think I fired three times, but we had killed three at the first attack. Some of the braves were up. The chief caught VanCamp's wrist. For a moment, these big men wrestled, then the savage screamed, tore loose, and ran. VanCamp's tomahawk, thrown with all the force of a powerful arm, caught the man in his broad back. He sank down. I fired once more.

"Good," VanCamp yelled. "That saved our hair."

It was all over. A few minutes before, we had been three tethered captives marching toward a torture post. Now our captors lay dead about us. I was suddenly ill, desperately so, and leaned against a tree, retching until I felt I would tear in two. Pence clapped my shoulder with a bloody hand, "Let it come up, Peter. I was sick after my first fight."

Once I had vomited, I did feel better and helped while we gathered, all the corn the savages had. Then we wrecked their weapons. VanCamp took the scalp of the child from the dead warrior and wrapped it carefully in a piece of buckskin. We dragged the bodies together in a heap. As an aftermath, Pence scalped two of them and hung these trophies on a tree to indicate how we scorned these warriors.

Hours later, and miles away, we slept.

By the second morning, we reached the place where the child had been murdered. The pitiful little body was just as it had been left. We washed it carefully, wrapped it in good buckskin, put the little scalp with it and buried it at the base of a great pine. Then we stood about, three Dutchmen, and said the Lord's Prayer in English because we knew the child sleeping there could not have understood it in Dutch.

"One thing, Peter," VanCamp said later as we swung along. "You'll have to use the ax; you can't see to prime a gun in the dark."

Pence grinned. "And his hair'd look just like a Delaware's in a Mohawk lodge if the gun failed."

We did not travel south but west, having the Sinnamahoning country in mind. None of us felt that our work on the Flats would go unnoticed. The men who had left in the canoe would tell of captives, and the woods would swarm with Mohawks.

I have always loved this Sinnamahoning country with its pines, its natural meadows, and its bright streams. There we loafed, ate, and dug ginseng, some of the roots being as large as my wrist. In the evenings, we talked. One of these evenings, Pence looked across to VanCamp, who was puffing his short, evil-smelling pipe. "You tell him, Mose."

VanCamp stood up, then ceremoniously, in the Indian fashion, he blew puffs of smoke to the four compass points. "Peter, Governor Morris has some watchers in these hills. He can't send troops, for that would start a war. But when the Indians raid, he sends us to raid back. We're Morris men. We watch the Connecticut people because we think they arm the Delawares. That's why we're here. We was sent."

I leaned forward to speak, but VanCamp stopped me with his raised hand. "Peter, likely your father was a Morris man. Anyway, we know about the Slide."

Pence threw aside the stick on which he had been whittling. "Morris is in a hell of a fix with Quakers holding back while the Delawares sharpen their knives. Then there are traders shoving powder, whiskey, and more knives to the red sticks."

I nodded. Things were taking shape in my mind; Charteris, Judson, my father. Things fitted. "Somebody's making money out of this dirty business."

Both woodsmen nodded soberly in agreement.

Three weeks to a day, we walked into the village of Shamokin again. It was just the same. Old men sat in the cleared space. We showed them our great store of ginseng, and they poked the stuff with dirty fingers and accepted some of the finest roots as gifts. No Indian would have gathered such a quantity as we had. Perhaps we had an alibi. Anyway, this village was ruled by the Senecas; the dead men up on the Flats were Mohawks.

CHAPTER SEVEN

PERHAPS IT WAS a reaction to the grim business we had carried on north of Shamokin village, but we had gone less than five miles south of it when Pence indulged himself and us in a little risky comedy. He was leading as we swung along in our customary single file. Now he signaled by putting up his hand. When we had seated ourselves, he spoke, his voice very serious. "Boys, I'm kinda tired of walking with all this nice river going just our way. My moccasins is thin."

We looked at him without comment, and he continued, "Now there's one thing had ought to be done. There was an old bark sweat house back there in the village with a lot of dead brush piled on it. The thing had ought to be burned. Then our old friend, him that wanted to lend us women, would be glad to let us have that canoe we passed. He'd be tickled."

He stood up smoothly. "Peter, I'll leave my rifle. Let me have your pistol. Gimme about an hour."

What VanCamp might have said could have been interesting, but he held his tongue and only shook his head a little. Pence disappeared into the brush.

"Nothing to do," VanCamp muttered, "but he's up to devilment."

It was nice waiting in the sun; I dozed, then slept until VanCamp roused me. "Come."

Pence was down there on the river, seated in the stern of a big canoe. He waved us into it with a grand gesture. The frail craft leaped at the powerful thrust of his paddle, and nothing was said until we were around a bend. Then he explained, "Well, the sweat house burned. They was so pleased everybody ran to the fire just like they do down Lancaster way. I didn't want to be a bother, so I just stepped into this canoe and came away. Them Senecas is nice folks if you treat 'em right."

I looked back at him; his face was serene, his lips puckered to start whistling. Sometime later he spoke again, "Them Senecas don't build too good a canoe. One thing they get in a hurry and use pine pitch 'stead of spruce gum, so you kinda stick to their boats 'till enough greasy Indians have rode in it and oiled up the pitch. Now, this here boat's still a bit raw."

For all the comedy, Pence and VanCamp were careful when we abandoned the craft at evening. It was beached where a current might have carried it had it been drifting. We erased all signs of our occupancy and brushed out our tracks in the sand with branches. Pence even took the vine rope that had fastened the boat back of the village and rubbed the end so that it looked chafed.

We slept that night snug enough in a drift of leaves, and by mid-morning, we were half a mile from Harris Ferry. A man worked away vigorously in a field. We recognized John Harris. He was unfeignedly glad to see us, coming forward with a roar, having thrown his hoe over his shoulder. "Glory to God, here come our three Dutch bulls again, back from chasing only He knows what up-river."

He led the way to his home and showed us a place to drop our packs. VanCamp did the talking for us. "John, first off, that Shamokin place stinks. Better sell what land you've got up there. Then get Morris to clean the place up."

Harris laughed. "Mose, Morris'll build a real fort there someday when he can get some money out of that penny pinching, sweetness-and-light Quaker assembly."

He poked a pack with his foot, and Pence opened it to show the store of roots. Harris stared, then tasted a piece of root, spitting it out directly. "So that's ginseng," he commented. "They say a Chinaman will sell his wife to get it."

"Will you handle it?" VanCamp questioned, and Harris shook his head.

"Don't know about prices. You boys get it to Philadelphia. They'll handle anything down there."

We trooped into the house at Harris' invitation and ate with the family. Harris sat at one end of the long table, his smiling wife at the other. Here was all the plenty of colony days; meats, vegetables, sweet cider, crusty cornbread. None of us talked. I was sitting beside Harris and helping myself from a dish when my sleeve fell back, showing the half-healed scars made by Mohawk thongs. Harris' quick eye saw. "Rough country, up river," he commented dryly.

"Fact is," VanCamp answered, "we had to tie up Peter nights. He wanted to dig roots by the light of the moon."

Mrs. Harris missed no part of the interplay, but the others continued eating stolidly. At the table, we agreed that my friends would go to Lancaster and send Mart Reed up to me with the pack train. In the meantime, I would be a surveyor and run Harris' lines.

The next few days were pleasant indeed. I liked the open air and the work with compass and chain, and Harris was most pleased to get this work done. One evening we sat in their home talking. Harris thrust his big hand into his pocket and produced some coins, which he placed in my palm. "You got off on the wrong foot, Peter, and paid for a boat. Emma and I want to talk to you." His voice was a little grim.

I held the coins in my palm for a moment, then placed them in my pocket, for I really had no quarrel with these good people. Anyone might have misunderstood. Harris took plenty of time in getting his pipe lighted. Mrs. Harris laid aside her knitting. I became conscious of a fragrance in the room. She smiled. "You smell bayberry in the candles."

I nodded but noted that the unused fireplace was filled with sweet fern. The homeliness of this room was soothing.

"First," Harris announced, "your father told me why he sent you back to school. It wasn't the Indian girl; he wanted you out of the backcountry."

Harris let that sink in. "Worst is, I ain't sure what he dreaded. He wasn't afraid on his own account. I figure he was puzzled and didn't want a reckless boy mixed in things."

I ignored the slur to my youth and questioned. "What do you think it was?"

He shook his head. "I'm not sure, but somebody is getting powder to the tribes. There's talk about a lead mine, but that was old when I was a boy. One yarn is that your father ran powder. We know that's a lie but mebbe he pretended to, to get on the inside."

Mrs. Harris broke in now while I was thinking, "There's more. John and I don't want you to take to the woods like other Indian killers. I hate to mention the Colemans, even VanCamp and Pence. I wouldn't want my boy prowling like a killer wolf. It just ain't right for a boy who had a good father."

Now I leaned forward and drew back my sleeves so they could both see the scars of the Mohawk withes, and I spoke quietly to keep from hurting this good woman too much. "I can forget these and how I got them, but I saw those hellions butcher and scalp a little starved child. All the wrong she did was to grow too weak to keep up, and so they killed her with a hatchet. I make no promises about woods running."

Turning to Harris, I asked: "Do you think the Connecticut people are running powder? Do their canoes pass here?"

He grunted. "Do you know something, or are you guessing?"

When I did not reply, he spoke again. "I can't believe white people'd help savages much."

I leaned back, thinking. Connecticut claimed the northern part of our colony under her sea-to-sea charter. I knew settlers were pouring into the Wyoming country, but it scarcely seemed possible these people would help savages, much as they disliked the people of Penn's colony. Yet the powder we destroyed at the Slide had come downriver. Among these New England people might be an unscrupulous trader.

Harris was talkative. He went on in the same vein as had my father, Conrad Weiser, and Horn. "War's coming. The Delawares are bitter about lost land and think the French'll help them. Their chiefs, Shingas and Captain Jacobs, are palavering with the Frenchies even now."

I agreed with a nod. "But, our business'll be keeping the tribes back of the mountains."

"Washington scares me. He was sent out there to warn the French off from their new posts and blockhouses and to claim the land belongs to Virginia and the precious Ohio Company. We know the land's Penn's but

Governor Dinwiddie is land hungry, and so's Washington. Mebbe he'll say something that will set things off. These days you've got to call even an Indian dog 'Sir' or start trouble."

Mrs. Harris had heard enough; she spoke decisively. "It just can't be. Wars don't settle anything. Them poor folks in New England got the brunt of the old wars, now it'll come to us. Why do men fight anyway?"

"Because women can't and won't," Harris answered almost roughly.

I rose and went outside to the edge of the bluff and watched the fireflies a little. Here and there, candlelight showed in a cabin. One light near the river shone over the dark water. Here on our side were the lights of peaceful homes, but the far shore was a mass of blackness, unreadable, menacing. Over there were the answers to the questions that troubled me. There was a fever in me to find those same answers no matter how dark the country into which I might be led.

The Harrises had not gone to bed when I re-entered the house. I had another question for John. "Tell me truthfully, was my father a poor man?"

Both glanced at me sharply, then at each other. Mrs. Harris spoke first. "He was Dutch, a good trader, and always thrifty. No, I would not have thought him poor." She turned to her husband. "What do you think, John?"

He answered roughly with a question to me. "Well, you got what he left. Do you think it much or little?"

"Three hundred pounds, John," I answered, "and Reed owns the horses."

He stared at me, then said almost involuntarily, "Why, he'd clear that on a single trip."

That was all he would say. When I reached my room in the loft, I was not so sure all my problems lay out beyond the river. There was the question of money that might have been left to me by Father. It scarcely belonged in the backcountry. There was also this matter of a pair of brown eyes, of chestnut hair, and the hint of laughter in a voice. Faith Horn did not belong out there. As I dropped off to sleep, it was with the feeling that I must begin to do something about settling problems.

Mart Reed, accompanied by Scott Stouffer, the son of one of the men at the Blue Goose, came the next day. He was in good spirits and explained what was in the packs; he had a new idea. We would do a wholesale business, that is, carry goods to traders like Croghan and Cresap. It seemed a good idea to me, for I did not love haggling with savages. The following morning we were off for Cresap and Old Town, with every pack bell jingling and Stouffer happy, being full of Mrs. Harris' corn cakes.

Captain Cresap was the ancient enemy of the Penns. Under Lord Baltimore, he had fought a bloody little war, trying to force Penn's people out of the lower counties. Deserted by his patron, Cresap lay in a Philadelphia jail for a time, a sharp come-down for the fiery swordsman. Disgusted, after his release, he had sought the high Blue Ridge country. Not so far inside the Maryland line, he had built his post of huge two-storied log buildings. About them, his workmen had built their places until the whole was a town. Slaves tilled his fields; helped about the post. Cresap had an eye for defense. About the central buildings was a good wall of native limestone, inside which was a flowing spring. Cleared fields offered no cover for the approach of savages. Old Town was a strong place, especially when held by this lion-hearted old man.

Cresap was glad to see us, shaking me by the shoulders with hands still heavy and powerful. His thick, iron-gray hair dropped to the shoulders of the white shirt opened at his corded throat. He rumpled Mart Reed's thatch of up-standing hair, slapped our boy on the buttock, and even chucked little Bram in the ribs, at which she showed her teeth. "Peter, Peter, I *am* glad! You are Michal again in the saddle—black hair, gray eyes. Tell me, son, do you—

I smiled, being sure of what he was about to ask, and drew from my pocket the small knife he had given me so long ago. "It was in his pocket, sir, when . . .

He stopped me by taking the small tool gently in those big fingers more suited to a sword's hilt. "Poor Michal," he said softly with the suggestion of a break in his voice. "I knew he carried it, Peter, for one evening when we talked, he took it out to whittle. Mayhap he wanted something of yours in his hands, for he loved you. I had thought it lost in the river."

When he passed the knife back to me, his voice held an unvoiced threat. "Could we but know what that small bit of steel does."

"I do know, Colonel Cresap. It was a knife in the back; a blade struck in by Shingas!"

His eyes were suddenly two deep wells with meaning drowned in them and unguessable, but he spoke a warning. "If you kill this chief, Shingas, think you the Delawares will keep the hatchet buried? It would mean war. The times are too troubled even now."

He mused a little to give me a chance to speak, but I said nothing.

His mood changed suddenly, as though he had drawn a curtain over the serious things about which we had talked. His face lightened; he took my arm. "Come, Peter. I have such a wonderful thing to show you."

As we went, I could not help noticing how well kept things were. Everything was in its place—no crumbling in his stone walls, no loose chinking between cabin logs. All was in order, as old soldiers like to have things.

The fur warehouse was a big building of heavy logs above ground and stone walls below. Cresap unlocked the huge padlock on the door and let the sunlight into the interior where peltries were stacked high. There it was, in an open place, a small brass cannon of the swivel type but mounted on light wheels. Cresap patted it proudly. "I shall not tell you how I came by this thing, Peter. There are ways, and I am not dishonest. I have craved such a piece for many years. My blacksmith made the carriage. See, the wheels are high enough to handle well, but yet strong. He used the best hickory."

He patted the breech again affectionately. "For a good meal, there goes in first a pint of powder, then the same measure of lead slugs. Lacking lead, we can use old nails, bits of iron, or a handful of sound pebbles. This is the way of it. The stone wall will check an enemy, since it is a bit too high for easy vaulting. We leave the gate wide open, but, with luck, as the enemy rushes, we meet him at the gate with a blast from this."

It was hard to leave the place when our business was finished. We had heavy loads of both furs and deerskins, far above the value of the goods we had traded. Cresap wanted these sold, the money left in Philadelphia, the city he had once called a "fine Maryland town." He also entrusted us with a bag of gold pieces to be placed there. It was certain he expected trouble on the frontier.

High up here in the hills, there was a tang in the air that told us summer was well on the wane. There was a hint of haze on the ragged line of blue mountains to the west. Cresap came out and stood by the train, the morning breeze stirring his gray hair. "Peter, you are a young man and will not heed, no more than I would have done at your age, but it's this man Charteris."

I grinned down into his worried face. He shook his head. "Mind you, son, I'm saying nothing of dead horses in the Juniata with small kegs on their backs, kegs that might have held powder. Charteris is loose, he and his Shawnees. He spoke your name to me."

"Yes," I said, "he is the man with the feather. He is the drake of the flock with a feather curled up on his back."

Cresap grinned, then sobered.

"Yes, he is a dandy, with a love of white shirts and women, but the man's a bad one. Remember, his father had a post below your Lancaster town. He had Shawnees with him. Wherever this man rides, the Shawnees are with him."

He looked around cautiously, then added a word: "Your damn Quakers think Charteris is great stuff. They trust him. He is a fine trader, a peacemaker. I tell you, son, I'd liefer give the first bite to a rattlesnake. Only a damned fool will take chances with that man."

I leaned from the saddle to grip his hand, then clapped heels into my horse's ribs and joined our string of a dozen pack animals now filing into the timber. Despite my bravado, I knew well that Charteris was bad medicine—a half-breed, smooth, cynical, dangerous. The French valued him for his hold on the Shawnees, the Quakers for his hypocritical ways when among them. Cresap would not have mentioned the man without reason, and I was puzzled.

A pack train moves slowly, and ours was heavily laden. At Reed's insistence, we stopped three days in a mountain meadow to rest two horses that were not in good shape. From there, we moved in the direction of the old Raystown Path. Presently ahead of us was a deep defile through wooded mountains, but to the left, a narrow valley reached northward toward Aughwick. We had debated whether to take the defile or swing north and go by Aughwick. Now, decision was snatched from us. A rifle cracked, my horse pitched forward and, falling, I saw the bloom of powder smoke up on the hill.

Desperately I fumbled for my rifle torn from my hand in my fall, but Reed had fired already. Other shots came, and a second horse went down. Reed swung his lead horse to the left, leaped off, and with a stick managed to turn the entire string in that direction which dropped the animals over a steep bank. In less than a minute, he had our train out of the zone of fire. He came back and crouched by me. I fired at a boulder that looked like a shelter. A savage sprang into view and started to run. Then Reed fired again, and the man pitched forward and rolled down the slope.

For a moment, it had looked pretty bad; two horses down, both of us under fire, and the boy so frightened that he could do no more than to hang on his horse. Now our train was safe for the moment; we had killed one of our ambushers.

Presently we moved from our shelter without drawing fire and climbed slowly up the side of the ridge. One walked while the other covered him. But we found no more of the attackers.

"One dead Injun ain't enough for two horses," Reed growled.

We scouted about for a little, then Reed was impatient. "Peter, follow the ridge. I'll go after the train."

When I reached the spot where I could look down behind the low hill that hid our horses, my eyes caught a sight that sent me down the hill at a full run, for Charteris had been too smart for us. We had played into his hands. One savage had Stouffer back against a rock and held a knife against his stomach; another had our packs on the ground and was busy rifling them. Charteris stood watching, the hat with the feather on the back of his head, his rifle ready. He was watching the path over which the train had come.

My rifle shot tore the gun from the half-breed's hands. My pistol accounted for the Indian who held the boy. The other savage swung round plainly thinking two men were firing. He never saw Mart Reed, who shot him down with as little compunction as he would have finished a snake.

Charteris was running, and I was loading my pistol as I ran after him. He stumbled, fell, and I pounced on him, my fingers in his long black hair. There wasn't a great deal of fight left in him because his arm had been broken by my shot. I half dragged him back to the others, and he lay quietly enough while we finished re-charging our weapons.

One savage was dead; the other must have been merely stunned, for he was moving his head from side to side. I had a good chance to study Charteris' face with its broad nose and flaring nostrils, its heavy lips. The whole was as full of menace as that of a rattlesnake. The man was dressed in the finest of buckskins, and a white linen shirt was open at his brown throat.

We tied the pair back to back to a tree after I had put a rough splint on Charteris' broken arm. He made no sign of pain, but his lips curled in derision at my show of mercy. We found their horses near and took two of them to replace our own dead stock. Reed returned to the place of the attack to get the loads. In the meantime, I looked at Charteris's bullet wound again and did a better job of bandaging it with my handkerchief.

Reed joined me; then he bent to examine the lashings and drew them a little tighter. As he bent forward facing the half-breed, suddenly Charteris spat full into Reed's face.

Always a quiet man, Reed wiped his face with a bunch of grass, then he moved so quickly and ruthlessly that I could not have stopped him had I chosen to do so. The flat of his rifle stock smashed home on the outlaw's face, knocking the man senseless.

"Peter," he said quietly. "One of us had ought to kill that beast."

With the train ready to move, I did not know what to do with our captives. Certainly, we could not burden our pack horses with them, and we did not relish the job of watching prisoners. Reed made the decision. We stripped the pair of them and made a bonfire of their clothing. Then we tied them back to back with rawhide thongs. It might have been kinder to shoot them; certainly, it would have been wiser could we have looked into the future.

"Some time till they get out of the woods," Reed said dryly. Stouffer was still too scared to say anything.

We said nothing about our adventure when we reached Harris Ferry, having come over the mountains from Aughwick. We had lost nothing and led one extra horse. Charteris had been beaten at his own game that had left so many dead traders in the shadows of the mountain ways.

I was surprised at our profits. We had done no direct trading. Yet I had over a hundred pounds sterling after paying Reed and the boy. Reed smiled at my satisfaction. "It's a good life and business, Peter. We have the horses, the open road, and a good living."

On our road to Lancaster, we stopped at the Blue Goose to leave the Stouffer boy with his father. It was most pleasant to sit at table with Mistress Wright and see her bright hair piled high on her head and to watch the roundness of her arms when her full sleeves dropped back. Reed, however, was ill at ease. When we were on the road once more, he commented: "I do not like that woman. She should not run a tavern. She is too smooth, and there's something in her eye—"

I threw back my head and laughed; he did not finish, but it was quite plain there was more on his mind. He rode grimly and once spoke almost sharply to little Bram when she snatched a mouthful of browse from a tree as we passed.

In my house, I had a small task left, and a pleasant one. For months I had the thing in mind and had worked at it in odd moments, gathering here and there bits of bone, odd fragments of wood, colored pebbles. Each of these I had shaped into a bead. With my knife point or with the frizzen pick that went with my rifle, I had made a small picture on each after the Indian fashion. Here was a small quartz stone from a Sinnamahoning stream, here a laurel bead from Tuscarora Mountain. There was a walnut one from Raystown. An Indian woman at Harris Ferry had drilled the beads as only a squaw can, and I had them neatly strung on strong linen thread.

Faith Horn was alone when I came, and that pleased me. She cried out in pleasure when I presented the string of beads. I explained the small pictures as she leaned forward over the counter, her bright hair close to me as I pointed.

"Talking beads," she said, running them through her fingers. "Peter, wherever you go, make a bead. Sometime we will have a history of all you have seen and done."

Perhaps she had said it thoughtlessly, but the fact that she had used "we" thrilled me. I leaned forward, took her slender wrists in my hands, being sorry they were so large and brown. Her face framed in the looseness of her hair was very close, her lips were parted a bit. But she shook her head. "No, Peter."

She came around the counter. The beads were about her throat. I raised her one hand to my lips, and she smiled. She touched the other to my shoulder lightly. "You see, we must be very sure. Not yet—"

There is small wonder I did not stop to see Horn. I was too elated. I strode back through the town, my head in a cloud. The world was a wondrous place. Lancaster was a fine town; the mud puddles in the street were good to keep wagon wheels from drying too much. Our humble home was a beautiful place. Little Bram met me at the gate. I walked on into the house with my arm about her neck. Reed stood in the doorway smiling. He spoke dryly. "For a dour man, you seem to have found good weather. Come in; I have baked a pie for us."

Next morning I was on my way again. I had plans, and there was a man I must see beyond the first mountains—George Croghan. He was an Irish Protestant, who had come to Penn's colony and risen rapidly. In New York country, Sir William Johnson was the big man; in ours, it was Croghan. Already wealthy from the trade, he owned literally square miles of good land. He knew Indians; they trusted him, and if some of them did not, they feared him. To him, they brought their furs, their troubles, their news, and their appetites for whiskey, which he gratified sparingly. Now he would be at his post, Aughwick, the place of counsel in the Trough Valley beyond old Tuscarora. He could tell me what I wished to know.

The Great or Kittanning Path runs from Philadelphia westward, crosses the Susquehanna at Wright's Ferry, then winds northwest taking the easy way through the mountain gaps, passing westward through Aughwick up the valley of the Standing Stone and, finally, to Shingas's and Captain Jacobs' evil town on the river a little over a score of miles from the Forks of the Ohio itself.

I crossed the great river at Wright's Ferry and traveled fast, using this path and lying up for the night in a thicket beyond Sterrett's gap. Beyond that place, it was all forest, but the path was so much traveled that, in places, it was trodden a foot deep in the soft forest floor. I was moving fast as woodsmen go, part walk and part trot.

Like Cresap, I had not seen Croghan for a long time, and he seemed as glad to see me as had the older man. Somehow they resembled each other, though, of course, Croghan was the younger and more lighthearted. Both men were powerfully built; both had the direct, searching eyes and strong handclasps. Croghan was less bitter about colony affairs. His welcome was cordial, but he asked no questions.

We spent the evening in the great common room where men gathered from up and down the small valley. Most of the talk was of war, but the feeling was that what happened beyond the Loyal Hanna River was Virginia's business. Only one man seemed to disagree, a giant of a fellow in buckskins black from wear.

"Friend," he said, "if they fight out on the Ohio, the savages'll come into our mountains. There's a lot of Delawares and Shawnees right close and all honing to collect any kind of scalps jest so there's hair on 'em. Me, I'll hole up like a bear. I seen enough redsticks in Kaintuck."

Croghan spoke softly, close to my ear. "That was John Findlay, long hunter. He's been everywhere. There's no fear in him; he is just talking."

Later, Croghan and I talked for a long time. I told him about my father, but he had heard the whole story. Then I asked him about the money. "You're sure he didn't buy lands?" he asked.

I shook my head. "But, I'll try to find out in the city."

He laid his hand on my knee. "How about Shingas?"

My eyes must have registered my surprise that he should know the thing that troubled me. He went on speaking softly. "He has killing coming to him, has had for many years. But he's a Delaware chief. His death will set off a frontier war. It will be an excuse. Too bad a tree don't fall on the old sinner."

He rose in agitation, walked halfway around the room, and returned. "Peter, your father was one of my very best friends. I don't want his son to loose the whirlwind. Don't be fooled; the fighting—another bitter war—it's just across the mountains. You'll get your chance."

His face was grave. No one could have doubted his earnestness. Croghan knew Indians and the white men of this frontier. He knew how savage a war between such men could become. Now I changed the subject and asked about ginseng.

"It's a good trade, Peter. The place for it is north—Sinnamahoning, Wyalusing Flats."

He looked at me intently, and I rose. He smiled a little, and his voice was soft. "Piles of dead men can't be hid. But, it is Pence and VanCamp the Mohawks want. You'd be reasonably safe on the Sinnamahoning. It might have been a hornet's nest for you."

CHAPTER EIGHT

IN THE EVENING, as we talked, it had seemed all right for George Croghan to know about dead Mohawks on the Wyalusing Flats. But in the morning, I was not too sure. The way news flitted through the wilderness was always a matter of annoyance to me. Croghan would get his news from Indians, who would carry the same news to other Indians, and I did not covet a blood feud with Mohawks. Besides, there was the matter of two dead Shawnees. I kicked the blanket off my bunk impatiently.

George Croghan, Thomas Cresap, Conrad Weiser, each seemed to know as much about me as though I had written each a ten-page letter once a month. Croghan had even assured me, from the vastness of his knowledge, that I was safe on the Sinnamahoning.

Outside the building, having sluiced my face and neck with icy water, I was busy at my teeth with a sassafras twig when I remembered another thing. It was this everlasting talk of war. Each held forth gravely on the spark that might touch off the struggle. I knew little of British or French kings, of their times and seasons for war, but I was suddenly resolved to go a little distance west to see for myself if these dangers were really there. I bit off the end of my twig, spat away the raveled fibers of wood.

A few minutes later, without having said a farewell to Croghan, I started in the direction of Harris Ferry. An Indian boy was hunting crayfish; I stopped to ask him about the path over the mountain; then I turned south of east until I stood on the first foothill, the one we call Blacklog.

Looking back, I wondered how George Croghan had ever found so beautiful a place, and I envied him a little. There were flat lands for corn, a bright stream, and to the west grandeur of hills and mountains that almost bar description. Except for our own Great Island country, this Aughwick, the old council place, is the loveliest spot in the hills. But Croghan had no business being so proud of this place—he did not make it.

From Blacklog, I turned north and kept off the trails until I reached the Juniata not far from where they later built Fort Granville, and from there, feeling sure I was now safe from idle curiosity, I went up the river on this most lovely September day nor did I leave the riverside until I reached a gap in the northern hills. Through this, I reached a country of tumbled hills and the small village called Chicloon. Because we bought so many deerskins at this place. Mart Reed used to call it "Leatherton."

Indian villages change little, but the sunlight today improved this one. I noticed that they had built a cribwork of logs about some of the lodges and had stuffed grass in it. Likely they expected a hard winter.

Squaws were getting in corn from the fields. A few men faced the ball ground, but no one was playing. These old men seemed to remember me and plied me with questions, as Indians will of their friends. There was no word of trouble or of my father's death. Presently, after I had passed around tobacco, I showed them a big ginseng root which I had brought for Croghan's inspection.

"Is this root found here?" I asked when they had handled it and sniffed at it.

One old man grinned lewdly and spoke, "It is scarce, but Powder Horn is young and full of pith. No need root to see Mikwah."

I grinned obediently at the supposed Joke, but I do not like Indian humor, which is likely to be either dirty or cruel. Besides, I did not want this old man with the sore eyes to remind me of what he thought might interest me.

Indians share their information. Probably every member of this band had heard of the trouble between me and my father within a short time after it had happened. Further, Indians are quick to find a motive for any action. They reasoned that I had not come trading, that I had no relatives here; therefore, there could be but the one reason—the girl in the bark lodge.

Presently I walked down to the playing field and idly cast a pole at the rounded stone that lay there. Several times I did well, but one needed an opponent to give some spice to as poor a game as this. I walked to the cornfield and looked at the ears; then, I was interested in the log cribbing of a house. Of course, I knew I was fooling exactly nobody, yet I went through subterfuges until I was down by the stream. A capful of wind brought the smell of the village to my nostrils; I turned to my left and walked rapidly up the brook until I saw the small bark house in its hemlock setting.

I had come quietly and stood staring at the skin curtain that farmed the door. If I would get information anywhere in an Indian village, it would be from a girl like Mikwah. I knew enough about the frontier and these forest people to be sure of that Presently, fingers thrust through the skins and drew them aside. She was standing there, her rounded arm raised, a touch of a smile about her mouth. Dressed in a white buckskin shirt and a bright woolen skirt, she looked well against the forest background. "So," she said softly, her voice purring. "You come back, see Mikwah."

I had not known she could speak English so well. She went on. "This time Peter does not want to buy a shirt, perhaps . . ."

I smiled and shook my head. "No, I want to talk. Maybe Mikwah will help me."

She looked at me a bit doubtfully, then she sat down on the moss cross-legged, and I sprawled before her. "My father is dead." I stopped and drew a gold piece which I laid on her knee. She listened intently when I told her how he had died, but not who killed him. "I have come to Mikwah for word about Shingas."

At the name, she bristled like an angry cat. "He is"—she seemed to search for an English word to express her feeling, then spat on the ground. "Listen, Peter. Two years past, Mikwah had a husband like you, young. Shingas came to our lodge, look at me. Then he take my husband far north to fight. By and by he come back, say my warrior die in big river. He tried to buy Mikwah."

She twisted her shoulders and spat on the ground again. "He comes to this village." Suddenly her eyes widened, she leaned forward and pounded my knee. "Maybe he will come tomorrow. You will kill Shingas for Mikwah."

I explained that I might want to kill Shingas but that it would start a war for a white man to do away with the chief. She seemed to understand and suddenly had another idea at which she leaped to her feet. "You show Mikwah. Get a good way, she will kill Shingas. Maybe he come to this lodge, what will she do?"

"You might be killed."

"Mikwah not afraid."

I studied the problem. If the girl did kill the chief, she would lose her own life—unless she did it defending herself. Of course, she would have a knife.

"Have you a gun?"

She shook her head, and I had an idea. With a knife, she could hope for little against a warrior known for his knife fighting. I rummaged in the pocket of my hunting shirt and produced a small but large-bore pistol. She took it with a pleased cry, and I saw she knew how to handle it. Then her face went sober. "No powder," she told me, and I realized that a squaw could not get it.

This time I searched in my pack and gave her my extra horn. Then I showed her how to load the weapon. I completely forgot that my initials were carved on the horn. She promised faithfully that she would use the weapon only in defense and also that she would tell me when Shingas appeared in the village.

For the rest of the day, we visited. Her talk was of the forest, and I liked her ready laughter. I spent the night in the village and the following day visited with the girl again. It was the third day when she returned from the village that she told me Shingas was there. As I hurried toward the council place, a boy met me and said in English: "Shingas, he want to see white man."

I took time then to place my rifle and pack where I could get them in a hurry. My knife and hatchet were in my belt. I sent another gold piece by the boy to Mikwah.

The chief was seated in solitary splendor before a lodge a little distance from the playing field. He was unspeakably dirty, and his eyes widened when he saw me. His hair was tied in two braids with snakeskin and hung down in front of his shoulders like a woman's. His face was a mass of closely set wrinkles so that it looked like a worn glove. He waved grandly to the ground for me to be seated, and I did so, being careful to choose the upwind side, for he smelled to high heaven.

"Shingas know boy with white eyes, Indian hair—Powder Horn."

He went through the business of lighting his pipe with punk.

"Shingas knows that I am not a boy." I looked into his eyes, and there was no fear in me, only eagerness. "I, with white eyes, am favored of Manitou. I hunt the Sinnamahoning. I see in the dark. Where did Shingas see me before?"

"Croghan," he grunted. Then: "Shingas needs powder. You trade him some."

I wanted desperately to slap his wizened face, but instead, I replied civilly enough. "Shingas must get his powder from Croghan. So the white fathers say. It is a law."

He did not like me. I doubt if he liked anyone. Now he drew his knife and picked up a twig which he whittled like a white man. I wanted to taunt him more. "There is talk, along the big river, of war. What does Shingas, friend of the French, say?"

Of course, I knew that I was insulting him. One does not ask an Indian chief the direct question. Around the lodge to our back came an Indian dog. It was miserably poor as such animals always are, and it moved with a cringing manner bred of a lifetime of cuffs and kicks. I doubt if in its short life it ever had a full meal. Shingas watched the animal, not answering my question.

It was all very quick. I did not know the poor animal was in the reach of the old beast. His wicked knife flashed. The animal dropped to the ground with a gasping howl, then gained its feet, trying to run with its entrails dragging. Shingas sat still, a satisfied grin on his face. Blood hammered at my temples. Shingas was very close to death at that moment. He was cleaning his bloody knife in the sand.

Then I exposed a secret. Between my shoulder blades, I carry a sheathed throwing knife as my father taught me; the cape of my hunting shirt conceals sheath and weapon. My hand flashed back; the heavy blade flicked over my shoulder and struck the poor dog at the base of its skull, ending its misery.

Shingas's face was a thunder cloud. I retrieved my knife, returned, dropped to one knee before him while I wiped my blade in the sand. "Shingas is a great chief. He is a killer of dogs. He does not know how to use a knife well."

I paid no attention to his anger, but I talked while cleaning my blade. His dirty fist clutched the haft of his own weapon. "Shingas thinks he will slay the white man with the white eyes. Then red coats will come. They will hang Shingas to a tree, so he chokes slowly and is dead."

I leaned far forward close to him. "Listen, Shingas. I have strong medicine. I see Shingas on the warpath. I see him dead in the water, choking on his own knife with which he slays dogs."

Some men were coming. I rose, pointed the knife toward the chief, and warned, "I do not like to be followed. If this happens, I will fool those men who follow me, come back to cut a long slit in Shingas' belly so it will no longer hold corn. Manitou will have his spirit leading the dogs."

I thrust the naked knife into my belt, turned my back, and went for my pack and rifle. Yet, as I walked away, I had a feeling of coldness in my back where a knife could be driven home. It was easy to believe Croghan's statement about Shingas. "Dangerous as a tromped rattlesnake."

Clear of the camp, I felt pretty cocky, for I had just rubbed things in pretty hard on the most dangerous man on the frontier.

Since that time, I have learned a great deal of caution, but then the wine of the fall season, the whisper of danger made me step wide. But, for all my bravado, I did not return to white man's country by the usual routes. An arrow makes a bad hole in a man and a bullet could reach me from any convenient thicket.

When I did get back to Harris Ferry, I was still pleased with myself. I had not learned much about coming war, but through Mikwah I had met and bearded Shingas. It might be that she would shoot him some-day. Pretty generally, I had had a good time.

Mart Reed was at the Ferry and content to carry goods for Harris or Philadelphia, but the ginseng idea was strong in my mind. If I hurried, I might get out a good load of the root before the ground froze. So I stocked my pouch with corn meal and parched corn, took my small brass kettle and a little tea, together with some dried meat. As an afterthought, I had the blacksmiths shape me a small, light pick from an old tomahawk.

Going upriver was a matter of speed. I was traveling light and stopped very little excepting at Great Island, where I admired the good land held in the huge bow of the river.

Near where the Sinnamahoning enters the river, I went inland a fair distance to a place of dense thickets. Here I labored for two days building a canoe. When I had finished, it was plain the thing was not beautiful, yet I was proud of it. The beam was wide, the bottom thick. It would carry the load I would find. It was easy to hide it, and the evidence of my work in the thick young hemlocks.

That same evening I killed a small doe and the next day, dried most of the meat over a bright fire. I knew it was not the best way to cure meat, but I did not want smoke to show too freely. With food at hand, my canoe ready, I set to work digging ginseng.

Those two weeks passed rapidly for me in that wild and beautiful country. I dug roots until I was weary. In the evenings, I watched the game come down to drink. One night I saw a huge moose. The small people of the woods were everywhere—the rabbits, the foxes, and the squirrels. In this time, I gathered two great piles of the roots. Of course, I could not dry them, but I did put them in the sun for what it was worth.

It was getting colder. There was no point in remaining longer, so I packed two huge loads downstream and got the canoe ready to launch. When evening came, I lashed my bundles fast and slipped out on the quiet river. Once, before I reached Great Island, I had to stop and wait for daylight to help me get over some bad rocky stretches, but most of my traveling was at night. It was eerie business slipping quietly along with no noise but the gentle lapping of the water against the gunwales. When the moon was high and bright, I crouched down so that the boat and I looked like a floating log.

John Harris was amazed at my load when I reached his post and quick to advise me. "Get that to Philadelphia to Mordecai Lewis. He has ships in the China trade. I'll spread out the roots a few days so they won't be too damp."

While I waited, I took his compass and did a bit of surveying for him, but I had time for thinking, and most of it was about Faith Horn. I promised myself great things. First, I must have large holdings like Harris, acres of grain, fat cattle grazing. There would be a stone house about which John Bartram would advise me. The time passed pleasantly.

In the common room, the talk was still of war. John Findlay was back from far-off Kaintucky. He said the new British general would need pack horses. He was here to earn money.

When the January thaw opened the roads, I hired horses and took the road to Philadelphia, stopping at Lancaster for some of our animals and asking Reed to return the ones I had brought. In Philadelphia, I stabled my beasts at the Tun Tavern but was careful to lock my roots in my bedroom. I chose the Tun for they told me Mordecai Lewis frequented it to keep in touch with sailors.

When I came downstairs, I asked the man at the bar which of the company in the big room was Lewis, and he grinned. "He's over there and likes to be let alone. Best not bother him."

Lewis was a man of heavy brows and a bulbous nose which jutted over his mouth in a manner suggestive of a ship's prow. His hat was on the table, exposing his shock of closely clipped iron-gray hair. His big voice rumbled when I stopped at his table and accosted him. Instead of speaking, I flung a large ginseng root before him on the table.

"Where'd you get this?" he growled.

"That," I said dryly, "is my business. Will you buy?"

"This port shipped fifty-seven boxes of the root last year, a little short of one ton," he muttered. "How much have you?"

"Come upstairs," I replied.

When I dragged out my sack from under the bed and poured the roots on the floor, he whistled in amazement. "Great stars," he rumbled. "It is not quite dry enough to ship, but I'll take the lot. One pound colonial currency a pound."

I tumbled the roots back into the sack angrily. "I'm not a complete fool just because I run the hills. I want to go into this business, but my hair won't be risked for measly colonial currency. It's one pound sterling, sir."

He snatched a large root from the top of the sack, bent it in his big fingers, turned to me. "Sold, you damned highwayman. Now get you back to your infernal hills and get me more."

He jerked open the door and bellowed for a scales which was produced for him. We found I had a round ninety pounds of roots, and Lewis had one of the hotel servants carry the bag to his nearby warehouse. When we were alone, he opened a huge strong box. We put the roots in it. Then from another box, he produced ninety golden sovereigns and one Spanish doubloon, which he placed on top.

"That," he pointed to the top coin, "is your retainer. Bring me all the stuff you can get. Don't waste time with furs; they are often poor business, and they always stink."

Next day I had several errands. The first was a visit to the land office, where I was told politely that no parcels of land had been purchased by my father except for our home in Lancaster. "Just one heavy buyer up your way now—a man named Horn, but his holdings are well up on the Susquehanna."

My second errand was the purchase of a gift.

The gold in my pocket made fine music on my way home to Lancaster, and Mart Reed was delighted when I showed it to him. "That makes nigh to seven hundred pounds, Peter, and it's clear money. You are doing very well."

I turned over most of it to him to deposit in this new counting house in Lancaster. Just now, I was impatient and in no mood for money talk.

I felt no foreboding that evening as I walked through the snowy streets. Horn was busy with customers. When he had a moment, I asked if Faith was in.

"Yes, she is in the house." His tone was civil enough, and I went outside and sounded the small knocker on the front door. In a moment, I heard the light tap of her heels, the door swung open, and her clear voice said: "Come in."

She had not seen me clearly; now, she stepped back. I drew from my pocket my gift, a silken scarf that matched the rich brown of her hair. The clerk had told me it was wondrous fine and had drawn it through a ring as proof. I laid it gently across her arm as she closed the door.

It was evident she had been seated by the fireplace, for there was her chair and small sewing table. Now she turned the scarf over with her slim fingers. Her voice was cold when she spoke; so were her eyes when she looked straight into mine. "Peter, you left some beads out of that necklace."

I stared back at her. She went on. "There should be one for a pile of dead bodies on the Wyalusing Flats, another for a squaw named Mikwah, and a third for powder furnished savages."

There was nothing I could say. She held the scarf between thumb and fingers as if it were soiled. "Take it to Mikwah or some tavern woman. I do not want you here again with a foul mind and bloody hands."

Many things rushed through my mind as I faced this cold, angry girl. I wanted to take her slim shoulders in my hands and shake her until her anger passed. But of course, I did nothing and said nothing. I thrust the scarf into my pocket and went out into the night.

Anger was in my blood like a fever. I tramped that night for many miles and hours and did not know I was weary until I saw a light shining in a window. Of course, I was out of Lancaster, and as I approached the lighted building, I saw it was the Blue Goose Inn. Inside, Cooney plied me with liquor, then finally helped me up to bed.

There is not much I remember about that night, but I had been desperately cold. Then I was warm again. A hand was stroking my hair; my fumbling fingers found the soft body of a woman. A dim light burned on the dresser. By it, I saw the yellow hair beside me on the pillow. Now my strength came upon me as the Good Book says of Sampson, who loved strange women. I drew her warm body close under the feather tick that covered us.

We talked a long time in the morning, and she wheedled from me the story of Faith Horn, of my doubts of her trader father, and my quandary as to what I should do about my father's death.

"What I don't understand," I stormed, "is how she learned that I gave a powder horn to an Indian girl."

Mistress Wright smiled slowly, for it was she who had come to me in the night. Her smile was like the heat that rises from flame. Her bare, rounded arms were up as she braided her yellow hair. "You are a simple man, my Peter, and have forgotten a man named Parr whose arm you broke in this house. He is telling the tale of an Indian girl who was found dead and upon her was found two golden coins and a full powder horn with your initials on it."

I stared at her. She added a word. "Cooney heard him tell the story. He went to Lancaster six nights ago."

The casement window opened at my push, and the cold air rushed in against me. Mikwah was dead; how had she died? My hands ached for a corded throat, for something to hurt and so appease the devil rising in me. By the time I had eaten a little, then taken my departure and walked back to Lancaster, I was quieter. Mart Reed watched me quizzically while I changed to buckskins.

"Mart," I said. "I'm going to the Ferry; maybe I'll see if there's a ginseng market in the Connecticut country. Maybe . . ."

I couldn't think of anything more to say but, as I was leaving, the old man said: "I wouldn't take the road by the Blue Goose, Peter. The other way—"

I whirled in such anger that I interrupted him. To this day, I am not sure he smiled, but he did finish: ". . . is better traveled."

He might have meant anything by that remark and probably did.

CHAPTER NINE

JOHN HARRIS had the faculty of always being surprised and glad to see me when I came, and today was no exception. Having shaken my hand vigorously, he urged me into the common room, for the air was sharp. The big place was warm from the log fire roaring in the chimney. Before it sat a man in the uniform of the British army.

"Sergeant Robbins," Harris spoke cheerfully, "this is Peter Grove, one of our young traders."

The massive Sergeant heaved himself to his feet. It was evident that he had been drinking heavily. He looked me over from moccasins to the crown of my head. I admit I was not a prepossessing figure with my buckskin breeches, my brown linen shirt, and worn fustian coat, which Mart Reed had mended with buckskin.

"Oh, yes," the officer mumbled. "Hold up your right hand, my man, and take the oath."

I looked at him. My evil humor had not left me. "John," I said to Harris, "this turkey cock is drunk. Why don't you put him in the stable?"

The Sergeant's mouth opened; he tried to say something but hiccoughed instead. With the flat of my palm, I shoved him. He dropped limply into his chair and let his head sag forward, too drunk to resent my action.

"What does he want, John? Why should I hold up my hand?"

Harris looked at me in astonishment and some horror.

"Peter, the Sergeant is recruiting for the war—"

"What war?" I demanded. "They had a fuss last summer out at Great Meadows, but that was Virginia's business."

Harris was amazed at my ignorance.

"You have an education, Peter, and should know the big war has started."

"I've been busy," was my reply.

Yet I was surprised. I had lately been in Philadelphia, in Lancaster, and had heard nothing. But I had been mightily occupied. For so long, I had been told that war was coming that, now it had come, I had failed to give it attention.

Harris explained. At last, England was ready to settle this matter of who should rule in America. A large, trained British army was being sent to this country. It was led by a General Braddock, who would take it to the forks of the Ohio, capture the French fort there, and control that country for England. Two other expeditions would move against the French in the northern regions along the St. Lawrence, and the British fleet would prevent all reinforcements to the French. Braddock was to be the supreme commander in America. He was a great general, and the army coming a powerful thing. No French force could stand before it. I jerked my hand toward the drunken sergeant. "Men like that?"

Harris looked at the fellow for a little. "He came to us two days ago. He eats like a starved Indian and drinks all the time, paying with a kind of voucher that I hope is good. He is the recruiting officer."

"Anyone enlist so far?"

Harris spread his hands and shrugged his heavy shoulders.

"Careful, John," I said; "that was a French gesture. They will have you arrested."

He grinned; we turned toward the bar. Then he thought of another thing and was suddenly excited. "They want to enlist three thousand men from this colony. England is sending chests of gold and silver. They want to buy everything—grain, meat, wagons, horses."

I leaned against the bar. This was the thing I had heard so long from men like Cresap, Croghan, and others. Yet, I had lived with the idea so long that the realization did not seem real. My mind flashed back to the powder business. Even that which we destroyed at the Slide had been meant for this. English ships had so hampered the French that they could not get enough munitions through to arm their savage allies. So Shingas, Captain Jacobs, Charteris, and others had bartered for the thing with which they would destroy the frontier. Lead they had, powder they must buy.

I remembered Findlay's prophecy: "They'll come boiling over these mountains." He had meant if the English lose. Harris was voluble. "Peter, with what you know of surveying, you could get a good place in this war. Maybe you could be a captain like Hugh Mercer down there on the Conocheague."

I snorted, for I knew something of Mercer. He hated the English, for he had fought with the Scotch army at Culloden. Trained as a doctor, he had ambitions to be a military leader. Rumor had it that he was friendly with young Washington, hoping through him to get in with the set of rich Virginians. He was now a Justice of the King's Peace down on that creek that waters the Cumberland Valley. On the side, he still practiced medicine and dispensed drugs.

"John, I'm interested in ginseng. I've got so many private wars I can't undertake another for the sake of an English king. Hugh Mercer—"

He interrupted me. "You're partly right, Peter. You've got Shingas, him of the dirty shirt, then Horn. Do you know a fellow named Parr?"

My face must have told him enough. He nodded. "I see you do. For a young fellow, you're doing well in the enemy line. Parr left here about an hour before you came."

He pressed me back when I started for the door, and his hand was like a pretty good-sized ham. "The fellow already has a bad arm. Besides, he's one of Mercer's bug tits. Don't be a damned fool, Peter. This powder story he's telling is bad, particularly so if the savages get loose in these parts. It won't help beating Parr again."

"I had not meant to beat Parr this time," my voice was grim.

Harris nodded. "That is what I thought, that you did not intend to beat the man."

He strode across the room, wheeled, and returned, stirring the roots of his beard with the stem of his pipe. "It's your Dutch temper. I know we sit and talk, and you want to act. Things puzzle you. There's your father's death, then his money and property. There is also this devilish powder running. Time will set you right if somebody don't kill you or you them.

Emma and I loved your father. We do not wish to see his son slitting throats in border brawls."

I looked down at the bar top, worried a splinter loose with my thumb nail, then, rising, smiled ruefully at him. "I'll promise to lay off Parr this time if he hasn't gone further than I heard."

I have explained that news travels far and fast on the frontier. Now this village about the Ferry was a confused place. Travel was heavy. Some people were coming out of the backcountry, unwilling to remain and face the hazard of an Indian war. They said it was the same way down at Wright's Ferry, where the road went down toward Virginia. But the lure of British gold was in the air. Many venturesome men were coming west. Braddock would need thousands of horses, almost as many wagons, probably many pack trains.

One thing was evident; there was little feeling for this British war. Scotch-Irish, Dutch, German, none of us had much sentiment in the matter. It was Virginia's and England's war. If they wanted to fight the French, we would feed them and transport them—at a price.

John Findlay reappeared after a quick trip into Virginia, and he was crammed with news. "Braddock's at Alexandria. He's got two regiments with him, a slue of big guns and sailors to manage them. He's got hard money, equipment, horses and his own bevy of whores."

His speech was greeted with laughter, then another man challenged. "Don't forget, he wants to raise men in this colony. How many of you woods colts'll take the king's shillings?"

A general hoot of derision was his answer.

"Let Georgia and Virginia fight their own damn wars. But, if there's money to be made, we want our share."

Findlay voiced the opinion of the crowd.

Toward the middle of March, I left the Ferry. I wasn't interested in war, and my dreams had pretty well collapsed about me that evening when Faith had turned me out of her house. I had no regular employment, no one to whom I could go with my troubles. So, I went north along the river, telling myself I would go to the Connecticut settlements about a ginseng market. But, I did not go. Instead, I lived like a bear in the mountains north of the Ferry, spending lonely nights before a campfire and equally lonely days just tramping about.

Finally, I went downriver to the trading post and found John Harris vastly excited. "Governor Morris himself was here and asked about you. I didn't want to tell him you was just gallivanting about up-river because you was too mean to live with folks and was likely just hunting trouble."

"What does he want?" I demanded, incredulous that the governor should ask about me.

Harris snorted. "Does the governor of this colony tell me what he wants with a lantern-jawed, stubborn young Dutchman who won't stay put ten hours at a stretch? Get you to Lancaster and find out. He's at Gideon Shippen's house on Queen's Street."

I certainly never would admit to Harris the speed I used in getting to Lancaster. There, in my home, I dressed carefully in my very finest town clothes. Then I presented myself at the Shippen house, a red brick affair with a knocker shaped like a dog's head on the front door. A servant answered the summons and stood looking at me for a moment.

"Tell Mr. Shippen, Peter Grove is here."

The black man shifted his huge feet, moved to close the door. "Ef you wants Mr. Shippen on business, go round back to the office."

My temper is short; I had hurried a matter of thirty miles to get here, and I was not going to argue with a servant. So I thrust the door back violently and stepped inside. Coming out of a room into the wide hall was a middle-aged gentleman dressed in sober brown, even to the lace at his wrists.

"What is it, Andrew?" he asked the Black man, and I stepped forward.

"Sir, my apologies. My name is Peter Grove. Governor Monis left word for me to come to him, and I have hurried here from the river country."

Smiling, he came forward with an out-thrust hand. "My name is Shippen. Andrew has been sending people away today because so many would bother the governor. He is anxious to see you. Come."

A big man sat by the window with a long clay pipe in his fingers. There was no mistaking this shock of black hair, the bulbous nose, the small mouth with thin lips. This was Robert Hunter Morris, one time chief justice of both New Jersey and Penn's colony, and now our governor. I knew he had been a great lawyer. He entered office as governor under many handicaps. His was a Quaker Assembly; also, his was a troubled time on the frontier. The Quakers would have nothing to do with defense, with raising troops so long as their own scalps were secure.

"Your Excellency," I apologized, "it was my loss to miss you at Harris Ferry."

He looked at me, his eyes seeming to be sheltered in dark caves under his heavy eyebrows. Then he laid down his pipe, extended a huge hand. "That phrase was nicely turned. You favor your father mightily, Peter Grove."

He was smiling. "Your father and Horn, the trader, were men whom the King did not like well—something about the old war in which they both fought the English before they came to this country. But, it was my pleasure that they both made their homes in this colony."

"Sir, if I can be of service to your Excellency—"

"Any healthy young man can be of service, but Van Camp and Pence speak well of you, and they are hard to please." He motioned. "Lock the door."

I did so, and he gestured me to a chair. "You have seen my two men in their hunting. It is evil business, but these are evil times. You are young, better educated than either of these, alert to the frontier. Braddock is marching. Have you asked yourself what will happen if he fails?"

I stared at him. It had not occurred to me that this great expedition could fail. My answer was lame. "Why, then the Indians will come over the mountains—fall on the settlements—but Braddock should not fail."

The governor laughed mirthlessly. "Yet he is British. In my position, one must accept the fact that he may—fail. I must have men in the mountains to watch, to wait, to tell me news as truly as do Pence and VanCamp along the Iroquois frontier. I have enemies who will mislead men, like Charteris, perhaps Mercer. There are two Indians to watch, Shingas and Captain Jacobs."

He tapped out his pipe, then suddenly, his eyes bored into mine as though he would read my thinking. "It has been reported to me that you have been furnishing powder to the savages."

It was surely impossible for one man to know so much. Had he been different, I would have answered him defiantly. Now I tried to tell him how I had left the powder. I talked like a schoolboy summoned by the master. He stopped me with an upraised hand. "They tried to blacken your father also, Peter. I know about the Slide. Your father was my man in this region."

I sat stunned while he rose. Now I understood things not clear before, perhaps why my father had sent me back to school. Here was the reason for the Slide, for other things. It explains the pattern of his death.

Morris' big hand was on my shoulder. "You are to go on with your father's work. Be as close-mouthed as he was. Even his son did not know. Michal Grove was a rare man."

He strode about the room, came back before me, and pointed a long finger. "If Braddock fails, if the savages come, if things turn desperate, I shall buy scalps. I tell you, Peter, a bounty on scalps will drive every red man far from the sight of a Penn's colony pine tree. Yes, worst to worst, I'll buy the scalp of every stinking Indian who meddles with the peace of this colony."

There was savagery on the broad face like a cloak. Here was a man to fear and also one I could love for the kindness in his voice when he spoke of my father and for the warmth of his hand when it gripped.

"Listen," he admonished as we parted, "you are to watch; when we've shot our last bolt, let me know. Then we'll buy dead savages at a price to make beaver trappers rich."

I walked through the streets of Lancaster town that day with my head up. I thought of Mrs. Harris and her hopes for me. Something had led me to that quiet room. I had been puzzled, confused, lacking of purpose before. Now I knew what I must do, and the challenge sang in my veins like new wine.

Mart Reed was excited, for he had word of the wages to be paid for men and horses to transport the army's goods through the mountains. Even pack trains were needed. Braddock was on his way through Virginia, his men raping and stealing as though they passed through a conquered country. His officers, in their arrogance, outraged the men who knew the frontier. "Forty shillings a hundredweight," Reed declared. "I'll take a wagon, use Bram for riding, six horses to the pulling, not four."

He was so eager that I helped him get ready, and I have been so glad since that I had sense enough for that. The wagon was light but very strong, its body caulked like a boat and, over all, a linen top. The tires were broad. Beneath the coupling swung a small keg of mixed tar and tallow to grease the hubs. An ax and a shovel rode in pockets of leather; chains were coiled about the bolsters. Reed had a good outfit. Now he wanted me to ride with him to the British camp, and I could not refuse him.

We went by way of Wright's Ferry and swung southwest to Frederick, where the main Virginia road goes west, and there we began to have our first difficulties. People would not put us up for the night or sell us fodder for our teams.

"Damned Britishers," was their word as they turned us away, sometimes setting their dogs at us. There was no sympathy for us because we were out to help the expedition.

"Hope the redsticks get a lot of their hair," one surly farmer commented. His sheep had been slaughtered in his pasture field by uniformed soldiers.

"It's a big army," another told us. "Couple of thousand men. There's sailors with big cannons, lots of prime horses. Got their own whores along with 'em. Chests of hard money, lots of liquor."

I remembered with amusement Findlay's story of the army. These frontier people saw the same things. The washerwomen and camp followers had established the reputation of this army bound west to fight the French. We came up to the expedition at Cresap's place, Old Town. Cresap found a chance to talk with Reed and me. I was glad to tell him his money was safe in Philadelphia, but he did not seem to care about that. He was worried and lamented. "Braddock's a damned fool. Provincial officers won't serve under him. Washington's the only one, and he is just an aide, and he with the grippe. Rides in the wagons most of the time."

But Reed was happy at once because an officer admired his outfit and wanted to buy Bram. Not that he would have sold the little mare any sooner than he would have his right eye. But he liked to have her admired.

The vast camp was a miracle of precision with orderly streets in a tent city, big guns together, each covered with its tarpaulin. It was wonderful to see this city which was able to march through the wilderness.

Cresap walked with me a short distance the following morning. Just as we left the cleared area, a horseman approached. He was riding a big chestnut as only Virginians can ride, and he pulled the animal up a little as he passed, touching his hat with his crop to Cresap. I had a chance to see the lean face, the deeply set gray eyes. Cresap looked after him, then turned to me. "That was young Washington. Maybe it's he that should lead that army, not that old British coxcomb."

I came out of the woods near McDowell's Mills and found George Croghan there and, in an evil humor, strange for him. "They sent that horse-headed St. Clair to boss our building a supply road for Braddock. If he'd change his linen as often as he does his mind, he'd be a sight for a ballroom. He's threatened to bring British soldiers to make these woods-men work. You just figure how that'll go down with the Scotch-Irish or Dutch, either." He grinned at his last word.

That was a good bit of complaining for George Croghan in one day and a fair index of how unsettled the minds of those men on the frontier had become. I was depressed and kept thinking of Governor Morris's words, though, of course, I voiced none of them.

Croghan had turned away, now, he came back. "I'll join Braddock in a couple of days to keep his Indians in line. If Braddock gets himself licked, the redskins'll boil through these hills."

A few hours later, I got myself in a better humor by catching three large trout from a brook. Spring was bright about me, fresh and strong. I found some leeks, broiled my fish, and with cornbread made an excellent meal. With a full stomach, some of my depression left me.

CHAPTER TEN

FOR NO BETTER reason, excepting that I might see Faith from time to time on the streets, I came back to Lancaster. I told myself that I would write a long letter to Governor Morris, but I never did.

Lancaster was a town that kept itself well informed, having its newspaper, *The Leader*. Besides, the coming and going of many traders and the traffic that flowed through the town on the way to and from Virginia brought all sorts of news and rumors. I spent much time in Demuth's tobacco store, in the big hardware place, and in taverns, listening to the talk and trying to keep abreast of what was really happening because I felt Morris might expect this of me.

Our big inland town had an interest in the war but felt it was Virginia's business. The other wars with the French had left this colony alone, and the same thing was expected of one now brewing. There was no feeling that England could lose and the concern of Lancaster was with supplies and business.

About one thing, though, the town was indignant. It was felt that the British force should have moved through our colony, which could have furnished supplies—at a price. But Braddock had landed in Virginia and was marching to save the Ohio Company from bankruptcy. Therefore, food, wagons, and horses moved west, but the young men did not enlist in the British forces.

But, being in Lancaster and never seeing Faith irked me sorely. There were times when I felt I must swallow my pride and go humbly to her door. But her word had been so final, and she had held my gift as though it was soiled. Again, I felt I should see her father about my own parent's business.

Here and there, I picked some little word about Horn. He was out of the town most of the time and was taking long trips upriver. His daughter usually rode with him. One man claimed that he knew Horn was buying a great deal of land now that little or no fur trade was coming out of the forest.

Then it happened. I was coming into Duke Street with my head down and nearly collided with a tall young officer in the uniform I had seen at Old Town. By his side, slim, straight, bright-haired under her bonnet, with one small hand on his arm, walked Faith. Neither saw me, for which I was thankful.

Three days later, I saw the notice in the Lancaster Leader. The copy was a week old. "Samuel Horn of the trading firm of Horn and Teague announces the engagement of his daughter. Faith, to Lieutenant Charles Orme of His Majesty's Forty-Fourth Infantry. Lieutenant Orme is now on the recruiting service in the colony."

For days I loafed about our house, empty now of Mart Reed, no horses being in our stables. What I had read hurt. I was stunned by the finality of the matter. Publicly now, my Faith belonged to another man. I did not belong here; my place was on the far Sinnamahoning or in the country back of Aughwick, where Governor Morris had the right to expect me to be.

One afternoon as I sat on our small porch smoking my short pipe, which I had carved from a laurel root, a man came down our street. There was no mistaking the uniform—it was Orme! He entered our gate and did not close it, which was not according to custom, and came forward with the confident step these British officers use. His uniform was immaculate; lace showed at his throat and wrists. It made me understand those washer-women with Braddock—I mean the lace. A slim sword swung by his side.

I did not rise nor greet him. He produced a handkerchief, touched his lips with it, then wiped his hands. I thought of the statement that British soldiers were not supposed to soil their hands with ax helves. "My man," his voice was high pitched, but it was the condescension in it that angered me, "they tell me you are late from General Braddock's camp."

He had made a statement; there seemed nothing to say in answer. He continued, "Since I am the ranking member of his Majesty's forces here in the village, it was your duty to report to me."

I noticed that his a's sounded like e's, also that he called our town a village.

"Two things, my man," he went on. "Report to my inn this evening; I wish information. Afterward, you can be my messenger."

So far, I had not spoken a word, but anger nearly choked me. He bent forward, stared sharply at me. "You are, of course, British?"

"God forbid," I said fervently. "I'm Dutch."

My anger passed. This thing before me, in its uniform of bright colors, lace at its wrists, powder in its hair, was funny. I honestly tried to hold it back, but I could not. I threw back my head and laughed. Twice I tried to choke it back. He stared; then, his face became red with righteous indignation.

"Sorry," I gasped. "I could not help it."

Next moment he leaped at me, and his rush carried me and my chair to the floor. He snatched out his slim sword. I did not know if he wished to beat me with it or run me through.

The lieutenant had his due meed of courage and willingness to fight, but he had not followed pack trains through the mountains, nor had he ranged savage hills with Indian killers, nor had he been trained as my father had instructed me. Yes, he used his hands, but his face was soon such a mess that I took mercy on him and threw him solidly. The small sword was at my feet, so I turned him over on his face and laid on the blade where it might do the greatest good. Finished, I broke the thing and hurled the pieces over the house.

It was beastly business, I know, largely prompted by jealousy, but, after all, he had come to me, and he would have beaten me to a pulp had he been man enough. From his point of view, it would have been kinder on my part to have killed him. In time he rose and limped slowly away.

Just at my supper time came old man Kreiner who had been town constable for many years. He approached, carrying a long Deckard rifle and a rolled paper in his other hand. Coming to the porch, he regarded me quizzically. "Are you Peter Grove?"

Very soberly, I answered him. "Yes, Mr. Kreiner, I am the same lad you taught to tie a trout fly. I have two of them still."

His face lighted with the hint of a smile, but he sobered instantly and waved his paper. "This here is a warrant for one Peter Grove for assault on the person of one of his Majesty's officers."

I looked straight at him. He grinned. "I read that most as good as you could, Peter," he added.

Presently he sat in the chair I offered him and allowed me to lean the rifle against the side of the house. Then I read the warrant with all its legal verbiage. It did say I was to appear before Squire Wickersham in the jail office to answer a charge of assault at six o'clock that evening.

My old constable friend needed no urging when I told him I was frying some ham for my supper and that he must eat with me or I would not go back with him. In a short time, I had the meat frying and a journey cake in the ashes. We sat down to a good meal, and Constable Kreiner ate like an old wolf while I told him hunting and fishing stories. I told him of a great turkey I had killed near Aughwick, of a trout that nearly took my last fly. He dozed over his pipe while I washed the dishes.

We walked side by side to the jail. The big rifle got into the old man's way, so I asked his permission to carry it for him. We went through town, he strutting proudly, I carrying his weapon, waiting his command to use it on myself.

Squire Wickersham was punctual, but, to my chagrin, the room was crowded. The Squire even wore his judicial wig.

"Your Honor," Kreiner announced, "here is your prisoner."

I handed the old man his rifle, and a snicker passed round the room but was quickly repressed as Wickersham struck the desk with his gavel. "Peter Grove," he addressed me. "We have known you since childhood. Now you are accused of a flagrant breach of the peace, an assault on the king's officer."

He drew down his heavy brows; his wig slid back a little showing a fringe of his gray hair. "Such an assault could be punished by a fine, by a prison sentence, or even by death, depending upon the gravity of the assault and the condition of the person assaulted. Also, it depends whether the said officer was on duty when the crime was committed."

I nodded, "Yes, Squire Wickersham."

"Are you guilty or not guilty?"

I cleared my throat. "Truly, I did a wicked thing, but this man's laces and manner tickled me until I laughed. Then he, sir, assaulted me—within my own dooryard. We sparred a little; then, I threw him to save his face from further battering. Finally, Your Honor, I did spank him for his childishness. Truly I did not lay violent hands upon him."

Wickersham scowled, but the corners of his mouth twitched. "Not violent hands," he roared. "What do you mean?"

I looked about the room. "Some here have seen me wrestle; I have been among some violent men. Had I laid real hands on this popinjay, he would have needed God's care."

There was nodding about the room. People here knew something of my strength.

But the Justice roared, "Guilty or not guilty?"

"Guilty, Your Honor."

"Then, Peter Grove, you have made a laughingstock of one of our country's defenders in uniform. You are sentenced to pay a fine of one shilling and directed to take an extended vacation into the backcountry where your peculiar talents may be useful."

After a burst of handclapping, Wickersham cleared the room, then leaned forward to me. "Peter Grove, you have raised a hornet's nest. Get out of Lancaster for a few weeks. I thought Morris wanted you there."

I looked at him for a long moment. Slowly he drew down one eyelid a little. I shook hands with him, gave him his shilling, and left.

So I went back to Harris Ferry pretty pleased with myself. However, I had an uneasy feeling that I might have brought chagrin to Faith. Besides, my week or so of dawdling meant that no news had been gathered on the frontier.

Braddock had started west well on in June. That is, he had left Old Town. There had been little definite news from him since. I stopped briefly at Harris Ferry, then had a man send me over the river. This was the eleventh day of July. A mile along the trail, I saw a horseman approaching and waited. His horse had been cruelly ridden; the man himself hung to his saddle with his hands. "Braddock's killed," he called to me, and I took his bridle. He wove back and forth in the saddle. "Whole army's licked, killed, running."

I swung the man from the saddle, dipped some water from the brook, washed his face and wrists. Then I gave him a drink. Presently he was better. I led him and his horse to the Ferry and blew the horn for a boat.

Once we were over the river, a small crowd collected and followed the messenger and me to Harris' common room. There we gave the man whiskey. All gathered around while we questioned him, and gradually we had his whole story.

Braddock was beaten, dead, and buried. All that fine army had been put to rout somewhere near Fort Duquesne.

Only Washington's courage and skill had saved those who escaped. What was left of the invincible army of the king was getting back into Virginia as fast as frightened legs could carry them.

"Mind you," the man declared, "Dunbar was in reserve with a lot of the army, but when Braddock's men came up, they joined the running. The Indians got scalps, the big pay chests. The army burned wagon loads of powder; they buried the dead officers and drove wagons over their graves. I'm for Lancaster."

Harris fitted the messenger out with another horse. He left in a few hours.

The crowd had stood in stunned silence. No one had really thought Braddock could be beaten. It was such a splendid army. I saw a woman raise the point of her apron to her eyes. Men stood gouging small holes in the ground with the toes of moccasins. To us, it was as though a mountain had crumbled, exposing the plains to fierce winds. I remembered the rank on rank of red-coated soldiery, the great guns, the camp followers. Mostly I thought of Mart Reed out there somewhere in the chaos of the rout.

Governor Morris's words rang in my ears now: "If Braddock fails." This man with the heavy face and shadowed eyes had the Scotch gift of second sight. I had been told to watch. There was work for me in the hills.

Two days took me to Aughwick, now empty of the vibrant personality of George Croghan. The people there had heard the bare news of defeat and were not wasting time. Their stockade was finished. A good stock of ammunition was at hand. As an extra precaution, they were digging a well inside the palisade. There was plenty of food and fodder for cattle. Croghan had taught his people well.

From Aughwick, I went south to the valley of the Cumberland, as we call it, though creeks drain it and not a river. McDowell's Mills was strong enough, a good post. This was a well-settled country with smoke from chimneys seldom out of sight. I passed the small schoolhouse where Master Whitehead taught a dozen or so children in the summer because winter weather blocked the roads and trails. On the whole, it was a beautiful land, which later I was to see empty. To the west was the blue barrier of the mountain. Beyond that would be Shingas, Captain Jacobs, and the black post at Kittanning. From that country might presently come the forces of the devil.

In six days, I was back at the Ferry with few details of what had happened. That same evening John Findlay came. He had traveled far, and we waited patiently until food and drink restored him. He seated himself on the bar in the common room. People crowded about; women stood at the open windows looking in. Candles guttered along the walls with winging clouds of insects about them. Findlay looked older; there were lines on his face. He began his tale. "First, the march was too slow. Braddock would march, stop, build roads, send back for more equipment. It seemed as though he tried to slow things. There was a power of swearing that the general didn't do. Red Sticks hung about in the brush and got a scalp now and then. They got plenty of washerwomen and their men friends who visited in the brush."

I was close to Findlay and impatient. "Mart Reed," I questioned.

"Gone," he answered shortly and turned to the crowd. A man passed him a tankard of ale. "You know how I said Braddock was always sending back? Reed went back for another load; his horses were fast. It was mebbe five miles. He'd lost a horse, and little Bram was hitched. I saw the whole of it. There are big hills out that way, steep drops of a couple hundred feet right off the road. Reed was coming round a bend fast. Wasn't any soldiers for miles. I was across the ravine. A feller shot from up the hill.

Reed stood straight up; his weight swung the reins—team, wagon, and all went over. Reed died with his horses."

I had no word to say; neither had these people about me who knew Reed well and remembered his kindness to animals and men.

"Feller that shot was white, I'm pretty sure," Findlay continued. "Anyhow, he wore a feather in a black hat."

My nails dug into my palms. If I had only killed Charteris that day! I saw faces turn toward me, questions in their eyes. Among these people, such a death demanded an answer.

"Didn't hit the feller with two shots, but we did bury the team and Reed together there at the foot of the hill under a little landslide. He's with his horses." Findlay swung around, drained the glass of whiskey Harris held out to him, shook his head. "I ain't too clear about it all. There was a lot of bad blood in that army. The column crossed a little stream, crossed it again. They hit us up front, Indians and some French. Then they swung round us, front and left. It took just one big yell, a couple of volleys, and them redcoats was shooting into each other, screaming and milling like sheep. Them British officers held their nerve; they ain't easy scared. But the men shot them. I was back of a tree. The general was riding hell out of his horse, pounding at the men with a big sword. His horse went down. I seen a big Virginia feller raise his rifle. I didn't hear it crack, but the general doubled up.

"Then there was a mess of running, shooting, hearing them red devils screech. Some had blood running down their arms from ripping off scalps. Washington got us clear. They killed his horses, but he managed to get us brush fighters into the timber to cover the retreat. He was everwhere at once. If he didn't get that army stopped at Fort Cumberland, it's running yet" Findlay stopped and mopped his face.

So that was the story. The might of England had hurled itself at the French and Indians, and now the frontier was wide open. The savages would be confident. They would come on the settled land like locusts and destroy. I thought of lonely little farms back in the hills and of what might happen. If only, as Croghan and others had said, "they hadn't sent us a damn fool for a general."

Mart Reed was dead. Charteris had killed him. Restless, the next morning, I started back toward McDowell's Mills.

Five miles out of that place, two horsemen rode up to me and stopped. "You're Peter Grove, ain't you?"

"Yes, what of it?"

The second man answered, "Hugh Mercer wants to see you. He heard you was down this way lately."

I knew Mercer's home was less than a mile away, and I remembered how Morris had catalogued the man as a possible enemy, so I walked along until I came to a lane leading up a hill to a big clapboarded house with a deep front porch. On a post was a sign: "Hugh Mercer, Justice of the Peace."

My rap on the broad paneled door was answered by a call to enter. Mercer sat behind a desk. He was a fine-looking man though a trifle thin of body and face. I judged him not more than thirty years of age despite his long record as a soldier and physician. He had an air of keenness about him like a good hound which has found a track, but I did not like the man any better than I liked the dark coat, the white stockings, and the silver buckles on his shoes. He was a dandy of sorts. Now he laid down his quill and leaned forward, the lace at his throat falling gracefully forward. "Peter Grove, eh? We have been looking for you."

"What for?" I demanded as he picked up the quill again and dawdled with it.

"Powder," he answered bluntly. "Powder to the savages."

I set my rifle in the corner, walked to his table, and seated myself opposite him, and he did not like me that close. "You will tell me all about this," I advised softly.

"Trading men found a squaw—dead. She had two gold pieces and a full horn of powder. On the horn were your initials."

Again I found the pain of knowing that Mikwah was dead, and I suspected how she had died but could not be sure.

"Your trading man was named Parr, who has a sore arm, Mercer. If I find that he killed Mikwah, he will pay for it the next time I see him. As for the powder business, you know it is plain foolishness."

His face showed anger. "Listen," I said. "A man who will take Parr's word will listen to Charteris and any others of this unholy border crew." He opened the table drawer and produced the powder horn, I snatched it from his fingers and rose. He whistled shrilly.

Two men ran in the door back of Mercer. He turned to them: "Tie him up. We'll see how a stay in Carlisle prison will improve his manners."

I grinned into his angry face. "No," I said. "Indians may be over these mountains any day now. Today I cannot bother with jails."

The two men leaped at me, but I smashed the powder horn over the head of one and tripped the other, so he lost interest in the whole business. Then I seized my rifle.

"Mercer," I threatened, "you know something about this powder business, I think. If I ever catch you or that stinking lap dog, Parr, in anything suspicious, they'll be needing a new king's justice in these parts."

Outside in the cool air, I was disgusted with myself. Governor Morris had given me a place on this frontier and a responsibility, and here, I was engaged in another quarrel. Each way I turned, it was conflict—Judson in the city, Parr in the Blue Goose, Orme in Lancaster. I was in a mood to go into the forest and hide. I must make it my business to avoid personal quarrels if I would be any use to the big man with the searching eyes.

My swing north showed the people busy on their farms. The com was fine; potato tops were turning brown in small fields; pumpkins showed plump in the corn rows. Often I stopped to talk to farmers and found them undisturbed.

"Them Indians won't cross the mountains," one declared. "Besides, what hev I got that a redskin'd cross them hills to get?"

"Your hair, brother. It's worth eight dollars laid down in Duquesne, and that's the price a savage pays for a musket. Cut loopholes in your house, get more powder, a spare gun," I urged.

He laughed. "Can't shoot so well anymore. Guess I'll leave the fighting up to John Armstrong. I'll feed a war, but somebody else has got to fight it."

There was some logic in his conclusions. I was glad for his confidence in Armstrong. God knows there was need now for some anchorage of trust. This tall, thin, stern Scotch-Irish engineer and soldier, John

Armstrong, was the natural leader of these Cumberland people. I knew he was a friend of Governor Morris and in his confidence. It had been reported that Armstrong had been trying hard to get munitions. If any man could make these farmers fight, it was this same man.

But to me, as to others, it still scarcely seemed possible that Braddock had failed. I remembered those long rows of tents, the hundreds and hundreds of horses, the bright uniforms, the arrogance of the soldiery. Now every Indian on the frontier would hold a red uniform in derision. The French would be confident. Already word was coming through that the expeditions in the north were bogging down. Munro and his men had been massacred at Otsego when they surrendered to Montcalm. The frontier was open. For hundreds of miles, savages could look down on farms and villages and plan where to strike and burn and carry away captives. Weiser's word that we must win this war ourselves was coming true. Surely England had used her best and failed.

CHAPTER ELEVEN

NOT MUCH over a month after Braddock's soldiers had run screaming from the battlefield beyond the mountains; the war came home to us along the great river. Hostiles struck in the lovely Penn's Creek valley forty miles north of Harris Ferry. Fifteen settlers were killed or carried away, and the savages were still ranging the country, searching for more victims.

John Harris had the message early in the evening; by the gray of the morning following, thirty of us crossed the Juniata a full fifteen miles above our ferry. Harris had worked like one possessed, getting men together and equipping them generously from his storehouses. We traveled better than trained soldiers and by mid-afternoon reached Middle Creek and were just ten miles from the scene of the killings. At the stream, Joel Blaine, a farmer, was marching far up ahead and did not stop at the creek but waded across. A gun cracked from the brush on the far bank, and Joel went down in a heap. Two painted warriors darted into the open to take his scalp.

Harris killed the first with a rifle shot, and somebody with a pistol dropped the second, for we were close. Then a volley from the timber wounded John Grant, who sank slowly to his knees, clutching his stomach.

"Cover!" Harris yelled, and we dropped behind trees, stones, and brush and, from our vantage points, poured a withering fire into the brush on the far side of the stream. Half an hour later, we went over, covered by riflemen.

John Grant died that night. He lay with his head in Harris' lap. The dying man was uneasy. He had been a person of real piety. Harris understood and bent his head. Softly his heavy voice repeated the children's prayer:

"Now I lay me down to sleep;
I pray the Lord my soul to keep—"

The ghost of a smile crossed Grant's face; then, he was dead.

One can never describe the details of an Indian raid, but we found ten white people dead along the creek—four men, the others women and children. A baby had been impaled on a picket; a boy of six or seven had his head split to the neck. A girl of about ten had been shot. It is impossible to tell the condition of the bodies of the adults. All were scalped.

Near one of the cabins was a dead cow. Her belly had been ripped open, for intestines trailed back some little way on the ground. A huge piece of flesh had been sliced from her hip. The trailing intestines made me think of Shingas and the dog.

Shortly after we arrived, some of the settlers appeared. They had fled downstream and had taken refuge in a stone barn, but there had been no attack on them. In all, there had been about forty Indians, but one body had gone east, another back toward the west.

Harris, who looked a little puzzled, was standing near me as he listened.

"All right, John, I'll follow one crowd," I offered.

He nodded. "But we haven't enough men."

Dan Pence was in our crowd; so was Coleman. I called them.

"This'll be enough, John."

One of the settlers stepped forward. He was a tall, wiry, redhaired young fellow. "Name's Solly, Tom Solly. They got Grandpap; let me go along."

Fifteen minutes later, we left the main body, traveling light and fast. We swung up through the country and crossed the river near where the Bradys lived later. We did not ask questions about that canoe we borrowed, since we were pretty sure the trader, Derr, who lived there, would have passed the Indians over. None of us had too much regard for him.

We had supper at a cabin a good fifteen miles up-country. Our host was a man who said his name was Ettwein. His wife was a little, scared-looking woman. Somehow we didn't trust this Ettwein. Up in this country, many of the folks looked toward the Connecticut settlements, and they had no feeling for anybody down our way; besides, this was Iroquois country. They didn't want any part of this war with Delawares and Shawnees.

We ate with the door wide open and with our rifles across our knees. Pence did the questioning.

"No, ain't seen no Indians fer the past week," was the reply.

I saw the wife look at him, but he stuck to his story. Of course, it was possible that he had not seen the war party; we hadn't scouted enough to be sure how close they came to this place.

"See any white folks?" Solly asked.

The man did not reply. I spoke softly. "My friend, there may come a time when you'll be more ready to talk."

I put a small silver coin on the table. Coleman and Pence pouched what was left of the cornbread and the bits of meat while the woman looked on. They knew this business, and Solly would have to learn to eat fast and to treasure even broken food.

Two hours later, we struck the trail and knew we were going right. So far, we had traveled in the direction we felt the war party would take, now we knew. However, there wasn't light enough left to examine things carefully to determine how many warriors were ahead, but we felt better not to have missed the quarry.

Except for mosquitoes, we had a good night in a hemlock thicket. Solly was uneasy at first, but fatigue claimed him finally.

In the morning, Pence killed a grouse with a stick, we cooked the bird in a hurry and were on our way in good time. Again we would not waste time following actual tracks. My idea was that the war party would get to the Sinnamahoning, then up the First Fork until they reached the great trail, which runs east and west, and finally to Kittanning. On the way, they would tempt any Senecas they might meet with their fresh scalps, and a scalp meant something. It would buy a trade musket. My main concern was whether the party had any captives.

Presently we were in the open country east of Great Island, and we pulled back to the ridges to escape observation. There we killed another grouse and a rabbit and had a really good meal.

We were now sixty miles from the village of Shamokin and as much more from Harris Ferry. A hard march of twenty miles brought us at evening to the great bluffs where the Young Woman's creek comes into the river. We white men call it the North Bend, and here is a favorite Indian camping ground.

At dusk, we knew we had come up with our quarry, for we saw the light of a fire. Leaving Coleman and Solly, Pence and I slipped down the ridge until we could see the fire built in the center of a cleared space of perhaps an acre area. I could not see any white people. Some of the Indians wore coats; once, I thought I saw a white woman, then realized it was a warrior who had on a woman's dress.

Pence laid his hand on my arm, whispered softly, "Let's get back."

He had seen the same thing. These Indians were uneasy; there were at least four sentinels watching. I whispered to him. "How many?"

He turned to me; I could see his eyes. "Great God of the mountains, there's a good thirty."

"We won't tell Solly," I said. He nudged me in the ribs, and we slipped away.

Coleman, Pence, and I knew our only chance to attack the party was when the warriors felt there was no pursuit and so were off guard. Here they were edgy, watchful. We must follow, watch and strike when the chance came.

The Sinnamahoning is a wild blue river coming out of timbered hills, running over rocky ledges, kicking itself into white spray in rapids. It is big water, as large as the Susquehanna into which it empties at the place we call Keating. I have explained that we did not follow a trail. In this country, one follows the river and leaves it only at certain places, for the hills reach for the sky, and it is bad going. We felt reasonably sure that these braves were going to Sinnamahoning. From there, a few miles would take them to Canoe Place, from which they could drift down the Allegheny River to their home country, making a big show of themselves as scalp takers before any other Indians they might meet.

We cut the trail when we came to the great creek. Pence examined it a bit. "I agree, Peter, they're making for Canoe Place. They'll go down the French River."

Now we detoured, getting back on the hills. It was coming evening, and presently on the breeze, we found the spicy, heady odor of a wood fire. Pence looked at me. "They're camping!"

When it grew more dusk, we could see the faint spark of their fire below us and to the right. Solly seemed nervous.

"This is it," I announced. "We'll rest and eat. I'm tired."

Stretched on a bed of pine needles, we ate some cold meat, and a handful apiece of corn meal washed down with spring water. We lay there for a good two hours after full dark before I rose. Coleman was already standing, leaning on his rifle and looking down to where we had seen the light. The stream was a good friend; the sound of its brawling hid any noise we may have made as we came down the ravine.

Now that we were close, we saw it was a big fire, the light shining out on the main stream. We drew back a little, and each man went over his weapons. I checked Solly's and, remembering my first reluctance to use an ax and knife, gave him my pistol. For the rest of us, the main thing would be edged steel.

We slipped closer. There were no sentries, just one huddled figure close to the fire. He was awake because occasionally, he coughed. There was no doubt the Indians had given up all thought of pursuit. At the edge of the clearing was an oak tree with one long out-stretched limb. On it hung bits of clothing and pouches; tomahawks were struck into it here and there. A stack of guns leaned against the trunk of the tree. Most of the braves were already rolled in their blankets. We were sure there was not a captive in the crowd.

Pence looked at me. "Give the orders, Peter."

I wondered at this, for he and Coleman had been about Indian business a long time. There was no chance to talk to Pence about what Governor Morris had said, but I felt sure he knew and that he regarded this as my show.

"Solly, your job is to throw every gun into the creek. You get two with your gun and my pistol—that's your part." I grinned at Coleman and Pence.

"Mebbe they're Senecas, but I didn't come this far to go back empty. You fellows just wade in."

We crept closer. The old brave sat by the fire, his blanket drawn up about his head. He coughed almost steadily for a time. All the others were rolled up in their blankets. I started counting but stopped. No use, five or ten or fifty, we'd hit them. No raiding party must ever feel secure.

A cricket started his everlasting chirping. The old warrior stood, looked about. His face was sharp in the light. He was old, all right, too old for a hard-traveling gang like this. Then he rolled himself in the blanket and lay down close to the fire.

The sound of heavy breathing, the cricket, the sleepy chirp of a bird somewhere in the trees—that was all. The fire became less bright. A wisp of breeze brought the Indian scent to my nostrils. I touched Coleman's arm, found it tensed.

We moved forward, Solly clutching the pistol, the rest with axes ready. Coleman brought his ax blade to his forehead in the swordsman's salute.

I cannot tell just what happened there that night in the firelight on the far Sinnamahoning, but we had an accident to start. We came into the camp through thick bushes, and a warrior was rolled in his blanket at the very foot of them so that Pence tripped over him and fell sprawling. The old man who had been coughing sat up. I saw his mouth widen for his yell, then, while yet on his knees. Pence brought his ax down. The man dropped into the edge of the fire. Solly had forgotten about the guns. I leaped to the tree, grabbed an armful of them, and dragged them to the stream. With both hands occupied, I saw a warrior leap toward me; then, the boy's pistol flashed. I remember that there was little sound but of grunting and of blows.

A savage flung himself at my legs, and my vicious kick was just in time to stop him. I had missed some of the guns, and now a shot tore the ax from Coleman's hand. There was firing from outside the circle of firelight, and we would be good targets. Coleman snatched the woman's dress from a dead warrior, gestured toward the brush. I caught Solly by the arm and gained the shadow. From there, I fired the last shot and saw a warrior plunge into the creek. Pence and Coleman pressed beside me and waited until I was ready to fire again, but the warriors had had enough of us for the time being. They had scuttled into the safety of the darkness.

We wasted no time. Coleman told me afterward that he thought we had no chance at all, but there have been times since when I have been far more frightened. They call the little stream now after my name; I mean the one that flowed through the camp and into the Sinnamahoning.

A hundred yards from the camp, we took to the water. The wading of a swift stream in daylight when you are in a hurry keeps one busy, but now it was dark, our muscles dragging from the sharp action through which we had passed. Yet, in an hour and a half by my figuring, we had reached the mouth of the creek, and before us was the wide water of the main river.

We skirted its bank for perhaps a quarter of a mile. Here a broken ridge of rocks thrusts up across the moving stream. I have crossed here since, but in daylight and then with effort. Twice this night, I went in over my head; once I was rolled over. We were nearly across when we faced a six-foot jump over wild white water. All of us cleared but Coleman. He pitched his rifle clear, but he fell in with his fingers clutching the rock at our feet. It was Solly who flung himself prone, his hands going out over Coleman's struggling shoulders and clutching the man so he could drag him to safety.

We did not stop but climbed the high ridge south of the river with all the speed we could muster. Beyond this crest, we found a pocket in the rocks, and there we built a small fire. By its light, we drew the charges from our wet rifles, dried the bores, and reloaded. I think all of us felt better when we were able to defend ourselves again. Coleman lamented the loss of his ax in the fight, but somehow in all that wild melee, he had found and brought away something—four small willow hoops on which the braves had already stretched scalps for drying. There, close to the mountain top, we buried these under rocks.

All of us were bitterly tired. We put out our fire, went on until we found a drift of leaves against a rock, and there slept like dead men until the sun roused us to a fine morning with air as clear as if wind-blown. And now we had fun, though we were a little shocked at the commotion we had caused.

"Half the Seneca nation is over there," Pence said when we looked down and across the river from our ridge.

Two or three war parties were following the river like hunting dogs. I caught glimpses of other Indians pretty well up on the ridge on that side. If we had not crossed where we had, they must certainly have flushed us and finished us with little trouble.

The rest was just walking until we came to the path that leads southward from Great Island. We killed a deer, ate hugely, then pressed on until we reached the Widow Smith's mills at the mouth of White Deer Creek. She was glad to see us, and we spent the evening with her and her large family after a huge supper of vegetables and pork. She watched us eat while she smoked her cob pipe. She was disgusted with a small fort being built near her mill.

"You boys never seed such a damned thing. They build where the savages kin set on the ridge and shoot down inside the stockade. My Clara, who ain't three yet, would know better."

Pence left us a day later when we crossed at what we now call McCall's Ferry. Coleman left a few miles farther down, bound eastward on an errand of his own about which he did not feel like talking. Solly went with me to Harris Ferry.

For long days I had walked and fought. Danger had blown its breath into my face. I had lived for what I felt and saw, shutting away all else so I could be alert. Now, my mind went back to Faith. I thought of the gleam of her hair, the sound of her voice. It was like the strike and grip of great hunger. She was to marry a popinjay. After all, I had no right to think of her, yet all I wanted was to see her again.

CHAPTER TWELVE

LANCASTER TOWN would carry on business calmly though the greater part of it were on fire. That is my considered judgment after knowing it under frontier conditions. Just now, its main interest lay in a small new fort to be built on the edge of the town, for the construction meant business—horse and man hire, nails, bolts, hinges.

The Legislature of the colony had roused at last, though much of what would be done was still talk. Forts were to be built along the mountain barrier. Each was to be garrisoned by soldiers who would patrol the land between. Regulations were set up for enlisting troops. Some were to be regulars, some militia, and the third type rangers, in which class I would fit once I returned to the woods.

My house was empty and cold, with the mice in charge. There was dust on the equipment that had been Mart Reed's pride. In the shed was Bram's stall with her special halter hanging there, but the little horse was dead with the man who loved her. The whole place made me think of death. In desperation, I resolved that I would see Faith.

The knocker on her door clattered, but it seemed no louder than the hammering of my heart when I heard the sound of quick light steps coming. She wore a dress gray as a Quaker's, and there was white at her throat.

"Peter." For the word, there was joy in her voice, but the coldness followed immediately.

"Will you come in?"

This was civil enough. Taking heart, I followed her inside, and we talked of the weather, of Mart Reed, and a very little about ginseng business. My eyes were wandering from long habit. The man on the frontier or on the Indian trail who does not see everything presently will see nothing ever again. So my quick eyes caught it, a glimpse of her small sewing table. On it was a box, and on that, the travel beads I had fashioned before many a campfire.

Presently I rose. The beads gave me a sort of courage I had lacked before. I wondered what she would say if beads were added to mark the battle on the Sinnamahoning or the dead along Penn's Creek. We were near the door. "I wish you much joy in your marriage, Faith."

She caught her breath, and I saw her small white teeth catch her lower lip. There was color on her face. "I thank you and shall pass your word along to Lieutenant Orme when he returns from Canada, where his regiment is stationed."

Suddenly I seized her shoulders. She looked at me with no fear in her wide brown eyes. I was desperate to say something, but my lips refused to frame words. I wanted to draw her warm body close, to own her. Her lips parted, and a gleam had come to her eyes. Then her hand came up and slapped me hard across the face. "Go back to your Indian and white wantons and paw them. If Lieutenant Orme were here, he would run you through for this," her voice was furious.

I raised my finger to my cheek and touched the place where she had struck while wild rage sent its gusts through me until I trembled. "If your lieutenant ever again draws his cheap sword on me, I'll make him swallow it. Don't let him ever cross my path!"

Recklessly I seized her shoulders, swept her close. It was my thought to crush her lips with mine, but, instead, for just a little, I let them rest on her forehead as I might have done to a child. Then I wheeled and went out.

Coming humbly to this house of Horn and leaving it in anger had become a pattern to me. So was the long savage walk to still my temper, which followed it. Tonight, as I strode along with my gun in my hand, I blamed myself bitterly for behaving like a spoiled child. My father had wished me to grow to be a gentleman and that I had compromised by becoming a fool.

Again my feet, rather than my judgment, found the Blue Goose where Cooney was working in the kitchen over a great pile of dishes. He grinned and jerked his shoulder. "She is in bed. Go to the bar, I'll call her."

Mary Wright knew how to welcome a man. She came down the stairway with her hair about her shoulders. She was dressed in the loose gown she wore in the mornings, and her bare feet peeped into sight as she walked.

"Ah," she cried. "It is our Peter, back from the wars."

She was warm and fragrant in my arms, and her fingers rumpled my hair as I held her.

"So," she said softly. "He still wears his hair."

I seated myself on the settle and drew her to my knee, but she rose almost immediately.

"Law, Peter, this will never do. Let me show you to your room."

She led the way carrying a candle, so her sleeve dropped back from the loveliness of her rounded arm, and dutifully she showed me a small room and set the candle on a chest of drawers. Then she gave me her lips for a goodnight kiss. "Good night, Peter."

Her bare feet made no noise on the skin rugs as she left, but I followed. At the door of her room, she stopped and stood framed against the candlelight. Her voice was very cool. "If there is something else, Peter, I am afraid you will not find it. You have too much trouble in making up your mind."

In the darkness of my small room, I took stock of myself, and what I found was most unflattering. What I was, a woman like Mistress Wright would have no trouble learning. Yet, after a little while, I slept.

It was either the dog's barking or woods habit that roused me to faint morning light in the room and a nipping chill in the air. I slid naked from the warm bed and unbarred the window. The light was not yet full. The narrow fields of the inn property stretched back to thick woodland. Here and there was a stump left. I was about to return to the comfort of the bed when my last glance caught them—five figures coming from the woods. Even in this light, I saw the feathers in their scalp locks.

I leaped into the hallway, caught up my rifle, pushed its muzzle through the window.

"What is it, Peter?" I did not turn at the sound of her voice.

"Indians. In the field."

One of the figures stepped ahead. They were about a hundred yards from the inn when my rifle pitched its orange fire. The leading warrior went down, rolled, scrambled off on hands and knees.

"Here." As I drew back from the window, Mary Wright thrust another rifle into my hands. I fired again and winged a second. She had my rifle reloaded in a moment, and its discharge brought a ragged volley, but they were running for the timber, dragging one with them over the snow. Evidently to the attackers, two men were firing from the inn.

I watched for long minutes. There was no movement. Later I would go out there and look things over. I believed there was one dead, two wounded. Suddenly behind me was a ripple of laughter. I wheeled.

Mary was standing there wrapped in that same dressing gown with one hand holding it closed at the throat. With the other, she held my hunting shirt. "Oh Lord, Peter. It is just now I saw how funny you are there at the window dressed for your first birthday. Here it is morning, and you fighting with no stitch to your back."

I slid the shirt over my shivering shoulders while she bent over in her laughter. "Truly, I will remember a fine maid who loaded rifles. If she wore more than her hair, I did not see it," I said. Then I caught her to me and hugged her hard while she shivered and stroked my hair.

"You do like me, Peter, me, Mary Wright, whom you think a bad woman because—"

I stopped her lips with a kiss, but she went on when she was freed.

"I am not a girl with brown hair and lordly ways who will have naught to do with a man who fights with the savages. Nor do I love red-coated officers and the big words—"

I shook her gently, but when I released her, I could see that she was crying softly.

Cooney helped me search the hillside. We found blood, as one will when tracking a wounded deer. I was pretty sure this party would not strike again nor stop before they crossed the river.

Harris was jubilant when I reached his place. At last, the Quaker assembly had broken down and was actually about to build forts everywhere. I stayed with him a full month, doing more surveying and helping with his accounts. Then word came that a company of Rangers was to be raised and put on patrol.

"That's my idea.," Harris claimed, though I doubt if Governor Morris realized it. A week later a letter came for me, very impressive with the great seal on it, but the note was simple enough.

Dear Peter:

John Armstrong will have the ordering of the new patrol. It is my wish that you enlist in it, but he will detach you on my service when necessary. Keep alert. If ever you see that man—(Here, a name was carefully scratched out. The note continued:) then good sighting to thy rifle.

GHM

I would not tell Harris of the contents of the note, though he was curious, but it made me feel again the presence of this man with the huge head, the pursed lips, and the vision that went beyond all eyesight. It was fine that there was a man like this to serve.

John Armstrong welcomed me at McDowells Mills. He was a tall man with an amazingly cold eye and a hooked nose that made me think of a bald eagle at first until I remembered the picture of Julius Caesar in my Latin book. He had big, powerful-looking hands that made the pen he was using seem a small thing. He greeted me abruptly. "I've heard a great deal of you, nor has it been all good. Part of it is amazing adventure. Tell me—"

His head came forward; his eyes attempted to master mine. "Have you ever been in a place called Wyalusing Flats?"

I smiled at him. "Colonel Armstrong, I do not remember."

He smiled in turn, showing strong yellow teeth. "All Morris men are like that." He leaned back in his chair and tried again. "Up there in this place you do not remember is a small grave. A short service was said there by three men, each handier with a war ax than with a prayer book. There is also a story of an Indian girl named Mikwah and a horn of powder."

I stood up and faced the man, angry clear through. These cold-blooded Scotch-Irish of the Conocheague country made me sick. Nor would I listen to this one any longer. "Sir, I am not yet a soldier. I am a free man. You and your tales can go to hell. Take with you another of your glib people, one Hugh Mercer."

The door was open in my hand when he seized me by the shoulder with a strength that amazed me. He was smiling. "I was testing what they say is a 'devlish' temper. Truly I am going to hell, in this case, an Indian village. It may be that I shall take Hugh Mercer. Assuredly, I shall take a stubborn, stiff-necked, young Dutchman named Peter Grove, who has a grudge against a chief who wears a dirty shirt."

"Shingas," I growled, but he kept on smiling.

"Yes," I said, "I would even go with Mercer for a chance at him." I liked Armstrong now, went back, and took the chair he proffered.

"There are some men I want for the company. There is young Breck, a boy named Solly, and John Coleman. Your patrol will run from Aughwick to the Great Island. Tell the men they'll get six dollars a month; they find their rifles, but powder, lead, and blankets will be furnished."

The Colonel was abrupt. After closing and locking his door, he returned to me. "First, before you go north, you are to lead me and Lieutenant Potter to where we can see this supposed lead mine country. We start tomorrow."

Three days of hard traveling found Armstrong, young Lieutenant Potter, and me in the hills above the twisting valley of the Raystown Branch. We were there for hours while the wind played with loose snow. Armstrong studied the land through a small telescope.

"Well," he said closing the glass, "we've come this far; we must look about more."

Potter grinned. It was easy to like this young officer, for he was an excellent woods traveler and most cheerful about the business of camping and content with simple rations. We crossed the stream on ice, went up it a mile or so, and climbed the mountain they call Terrace. Here we seemed on top of the whole colony. In every direction, the snowy land dropped away, miles on miles of tumbled mountains with here and there clumps of pines looking like giant's coats flung down on a white floor. To the north and west, we caught glimpses of the Juniata. Armstrong used his telescope again. At his question, I pointed out where the Kittanning Path ran through the mountains.

There was no trace of Indians on the mountain, but we did find a curious thing in an open place where, with the snow gone, might be a ledge of rocks. Here, to the out-thrust branch of a small oak were tied lengths of horse hair, the other end being held down by a stick until each strand was tight. We looked at it and wondered. When the wind was sharp enough, this device might give off faint tones.

"No," I answered the unspoken question of the two officers, "I never saw the like before."

I was to see one other of these devices, but I never learned what they were or why they were made. But there are many things in Indian life that I do not understand and for which I care even less.

We swung off the mountains to the east and cut no trails—no signs of tracks, even of game. At our evening campfire, Armstrong was positive. "I don't believe the savages are working a lead mine. I doubt the whole mine business."

Back at McDowell's Mills, Armstrong first put me through a long catechism about the lead mine rumor. He kept insisting that there was no such thing, and I saw no very good reason to argue with him. Then he wrote a long letter to Morris in which he doubtless expressed the same opinion.

In the winter, these Scotch-Irish people about the Mills had many parties, and I had a good time. Nobody had ever bothered to teach me to dance, but I liked to watch and listen to the fiddler. I had never been with young people my age in a social way, and I learned to like the parties better than the dances because they were more intimate. One of them was a "snitching bee," where we peeled and quartered apples, then, using a big needle, strung the fruit quarters so they could be hung up and dried in the chimney. There were forfeits in this business, and the girls usually had to pay with kisses. I noticed with surprise how willing they seemed to pay their debts.

These were a devout people. On Sunday, we all went to church and worshipped with a long prayer and a still longer sermon. I am afraid I did go to sleep several times, but after all, I am Dutch without the same worry about hell which these folks seemed to have. But I did like the way they sang their hymns in the manner of a battle song. They were a fighting people, whether the enemy was a red Indian or English whom they had fought at Culloden.

Armstrong's cook passed on a receipt that I have had used in my household—turkey stuffed with chestnuts. It is better than roasted bear paws or the meat from behind the eyes of an elk or other large beasts. But I could not drink the raw com whiskey on every table. It was strong and rank enough to use to clean a gun fouled with poor powder, though I never found a Scotch-Irishman who would waste his liquor in so foolish a fashion.

CHAPTER THIRTEEN

THE WINTER of 1755/56 was about as severe as our colony could ever expect. We had everything from deep snows to sleet storms that froze on the trees, so that game starved. There were crusts on the snow that would let a man walk a few steps, then plunge through. I saw drifts at places in the hills a full twenty feet deep. There were days so cold that trees would crack like rifle shots. I know a lot about the weather, for through it all, we Rangers enlisted by Armstrong prowled the hills like lean and hungry panthers. Some of the men with me were my friend Solly from Penn's Creek, John Coleman from the upper river, and Thad Breck. It was we four who traveled the upper country from McDowell's Mills to the Great Island and east and west from Harris Ferry to Aughwick.

Through wind and snow, we traveled and earned our stipend of six dollars per month with blankets and powder furnished. We used little powder, but our blankets often stood between us and death in the bitter cold that winter.

Armstrong was a driver. He made me use what surveying skill I had to plot the mountain region until he knew the land as well as I. We would sit in his office and plot and plan. One day he pointed his pen at our map. "A fort goes at Granville. There is a good ford and crossing."

I remonstrated. "It's too close to the tribes. Shingas will take it."

"Aughwick's closer," he countered, and I nodded.

"Yes, but Croghan's there. He can muster forty rifles. Shingas will never tangle with George Croghan." I spoke with conviction.

Armstrong's beak of a nose went up in derision. He shook his quill at me. "Croghan may be Croghan, but I'll put Brother Bob at Granville. He'll hold it."

Early in April, Armstrong directed me to report to Carlisle and gave no reason. Occasionally he could be most military, and then he was always exasperating to me. I did not care very much for Carlisle. To me, it was a solemn place from the grayness of the stones used in their houses. The jail was of the same stuff. I found the town thronged with provincial soldiers and from them learned that the governor was in town, also the Commissioners and George Croghan. A half hour later, I saw Armstrong himself wearing his best uniform coat.

Monis was traveling on other state business, but he took time for a short conference with us in a big stone bam with sentries set before the door to keep away the curious. Croghan had brought an Indian dressed in a calico shirt and pretty respectable trousers. He presented him. "Governor, this is Jo Hickam, a Delaware. He works for me, and he has something to tell."

Morris nodded gravely, and Croghan motioned to the Indian to tell his story. "I go to Kittanning. Captain Jacobs there." He held up his fingers. "One hundred forty braves, mebbe thirty prisoner. I go to Logstown. One hundred braves, lots more prisoner."

Morris leaned forward, addressed the savage. "Jo, do the Delawares go to the Six Nations for help?"

Jo nodded. 'Ten men go Shamokin now. Get powder. Get knives, hatchets."

Morris' lips tightened. "Gentlemen, a fort must be built at Shamokin. We'll have eight posts in all west of the river. Armstrong has my plans for the summer's work."

With the Indian outside, Morris faced us grimly. "Men, I've reasoned with the Assembly, but they are blind. British forces have been defeated wherever they attacked. We are very close to being driven from this colony. If the Six Nations come down, we'd better make our wills. It's like holding back a mountain torrent with outspread fingers. The savages come through; we must make them afraid, strike them in their homes.

I've one plan left, one arrow in my quiver. If I use it, every dead Quaker will turn over in his grave. But if the time comes. I'll use it."

His fingers went into his waistcoat pocket, produced a purse, and from it some coins. He held them up. "In the interim, I shall privately pay these twelve guineas, British gold, to the man who will bring me Shingas' scalp wrapped in a piece of his dirty shirt."

We all guffawed; then Croghan and Armstrong went to Morris and whispered. The governor held up his hand. "The price of Shingas now is twenty guineas. Croghan adds another eight!"

Going north after the conference, I came to the cabin of a man named Hudson, halfway between Fort Hunter and Shamokin village. Hudson had a fine small farm set in a cover of the hills where the soil was rich and deep. Two miles above his place, the river ran over rocky ledges which break the water into foam. We were smoking together in the evening. He was thoughtful; now, he spoke diffidently. "Grove, I got a queer question. Does a whip-poor-will ever call over the water?"

This man was a farmer, not a woodsman. I studied while he took a splinter and relighted his pipe. "I don't know, but I don't think so. Why do you ask?"

He puffed out a cloud of smoke. "Two evenings ago, I was upriver late near where the rocks are. A whip-poor-will cried close to me on the bank, and one answered from out on the water. It happened twice, so I wasn't mistaken."

What he said chilled me, but I didn't want to warn him unless it was necessary. There was already too much panic.

"Well," I said, "maybe one of those birds flew out and landed on a rock. You know night jars aren't the best fliers." I don't think he was satisfied, but he did nod his head.

"I did know they set down when they holler."

At daybreak, I was opposite that stretch of white water, for I suspected a war party. It was a rough-looking piece of water consisting of twisting channels and occasional half-exposed rocks. I studied it a long time. Finally, I saw way out what seemed a stick above the water. It might have been the limb of a tree caught and held submerged.

Five miles downstream, I ran into Coley and Solly, who were bound north, and I told them Hudson's story. Coleman listened closely, then spoke softly.

"You say that was two nights ago. Well, the morning after Hudson heard his bird, a man named Swinehart, his wife, and baby was butchered eight or ten miles down river *on the other side*. Hudson's birds was Indians crossing!" We detoured Hudson's farmhouse and hurried to the place of white water. With Solly armed with our three rifles, covering us from the bank, we worked our way out in the water. Coleman, who had grown up on the river, showed his skill here in finding rocks so we could wade forward. The stick I had seen was a marker showing a ledge where a rough piece of stream could be crossed only by jumping to the right place. No one could have set it there but Indians.

We worked back to the bank, secured a length of grapevine, and went out again. With Coleman tied to the vine and I holding, we managed to set that stick at exactly the wrong place. He who jumped to it would strike not a rock but a deep channel of fast water.

That finished a while before noon, we loafed the remainder of the day. We planned to spend the evening here. It was possible that the war party had re-crossed and gone home; again, it might have remained over there in the hope of more plunder and scalps.

From where we watched, we could see an object the size of a man on the far side if the light was right. Just about the time deer come down to drink, Coleman grabbed my arm hard and pointed. Three tiny figures had come to the water's edge on the far side. Each of us looked to his priming. Solly and Coleman carried long-barreled rifles that would do well at long range.

The figures were slow. Perhaps they were waiting for others. The party might well have been larger. But no more came, and there was just about enough light left for them to cross if they were coming.

We had no doubt they were Indians, and they were very deliberate in all they did. Each carried a long pole, and they finally edged into the water. At best, this crossing was dangerous business. As they came closer, we could see they were burdened with heavy packs, likely the spoils of their raid. They kept bracing themselves against their poles and moved slowly. Solly nudged me. "They're tied together."

It was true; they were tied as men sometimes are in the high hills to protect against a slip. This was heady business, watching these savages coming closer and closer to where we had changed the marker. I could picture the scalps at their belts, the horror they had brought to that lonely cabin. Coleman was speaking softly. "Take the upper man, Solly. I take the next; Peter, the man downstream."

"You mean the one with the toppy?" asked Solly, referring to one brave's headdress.

"Hell," Coleman swore, "you can't see that good."

Solly snickered softly. The Indians were now at the bad place. Coleman edged forward; he was breathing as though running. "God," he whispered. "I must see."

The leading Indian did not hesitate but balanced himself, drew his staff from the water, and jumped. One long scream sounded over the tumbled water. The man's plunge tore the others loose from their slippery stand. All three, burdened as they were, were in the water.

We did not move for long minutes. Three men had just died out there in the river, but they were of the locust folks who would destroy our land and people. Suddenly Coleman clapped his hand to his mouth. Out over the water went the hideous gobbling war cry of the savages. It rang and rang, coming back as an echo. To me, it was as though cold fingers were laid to the back of my neck. For my part, I had rather shot those warriors in battle, but Coleman rose. "That's the way I like to wash my Indians, all over and just once," he smiled cynically.

It was pleasant enough to follow the hills and streams when one had companions like these two, but for the main, I traveled alone. Many a time, I sat alone before a tiny hidden campfire. The person always in my mind then and before my inner vision was Faith. I would recall each turn of her small face, the determined chin, the richness of her voice and smile. Over and over, I reminded myself that the hope bred of seeing those travel beads on her table was futile. In the daytime, I was alert with my mind on the forest, on my mission. It was the nights that troubled me.

On this trip, I came down by way of Shamokin and was surprised and delighted with the progress being made on the fine new fort. There were men strung all down the river as far as the Ferry itself. All of them were busy getting stores up the stream or guarding or doing other things to further the big project.

Harris had a Black man, Stacy, whose job was entirely with the horses, and he was as fond of the animals as Mart Reed had been. The second morning after I came to the Ferry on this trip, he saw me, and his face lighted.

"Master Peter," he told me, "I got something fer you."

He hurried to his cabin and returned with a tiny parcel well wrapped in foolscap paper which he placed triumphantly in my hand.

"What is it, Stacy?"

He grinned and rolled his eyes. "Dunno. Man and lady rid through here. Man was little and sour. She was young—with a smile. When he went inside, she ask did I know Peter Grove, and she give that there to me fer you."

There was only one couple that would answer this description, and my fingers trembled while I tried to open the parcel. The paper finally dropped, and Stacy snatched it up. It was blank, but clumsily, I dropped the thing which the wrapping had contained. Again Stacy retrieved. There, on his wide black palm, lay a large brown wooden bead like those of the travel necklace. I took it reverently, turned it over and over, then I saw. Scratched in tiny letters as if done with a needle were two words: "Be Careful."

Stacy stood with a wide grin on his face. Absently I reached in my pocket and handed him a gold piece. He stood, shifting from one foot to the other. "Nossir, Master Peter. Gin I used it, they'd say I stole it."

So I gave him all the silver in my pocket and went away with my treasure. No one but Faith could have sent me the bead. While I did not know what had prompted her, it comforted me. Perhaps she was warning me, knowing the dangers of my living. She did not want me to take chances. Even if she deplored the savagery of my work, she was concerned for my safety.

I walked down the great valley of the Cumberland that day to report to Armstrong. The sun was bright, the day fair. I did not care if every Frenchman this side of the ocean was hiding behind the blue reaches of the Tuscaroras. The world was mine. I carried a talisman that made me invincible. I bore the gage of the lady of the bright brown hair.

CHAPTER FOURTEEN

IN THE CRITICAL summer of 1756, the cloud of defeat hung heavy over the English colonies in America. True, Sir William Johnson had defeated the French leader, Dieskau, at Crown Point, but the great Montcalm had turned the tables by taking an English fort and then failing to restrain his Indian allies from massacring his prisoners. And, Johnson had led, not English regulars, but American fighting men, farmers, and fishermen from New England. In the great river basins of the St. Lawrence and the Ohio, not one English fort or home was left.

In Penn's colony, we had built many little forts and then failed either to garrison them well or to equip them adequately. The Indians came over in small bands, avoiding strong places. They fell on lonely farmsteads like the devouring locusts, which leave little but destruction behind them. These raids crossed the Susquehanna and were striking deeper and deeper into the so-called "Improved Pennsylvania." Discouragement was the pattern of the day.

Down in the Cumberland Valley, a preacher had used the text: "And there came out of the smoke locusts upon earth; and unto them was given power."

John Armstrong heard about that sermon and talked grimly to the pastor for frightening the people. "A couple more fool sermons like that," he said, "and you preachers won't have a congregation left west of the Susquehanna."

I was on my way south to report to Armstrong, and toward evening of the fourth of August, I stopped on the last foothill to look down over George Croghan's excellent post at Aughwick. There were some new things. A palisade guarded a way down to small Fort Run, and something which I took to be a cannon gleamed near the main gate. But, what surprised me was the throng of people in sight down there and the number of cattle grazing in the meadows.

Croghan was very cordial when I met him in his big common room. He threw down his quill pen and gripped my hand in the impulsive way he had. "Welcome, welcome."

I gestured to the outdoors. "What's going on, so many people here?"

"We're just forted up," he said grimly. "Guess you haven't heard."

I told him I had been in the hills, and he went on. "They took Granville just the other day. Bob Armstrong is killed, his body stripped and mutilated. The prisoners went to Kittanning."

I whistled soundlessly at the enormity of the thing. Bob Armstrong was a fine young fellow and mighty dear to his older brother. "Granville's less than twenty miles from here. Tell me, is John Coleman in this section?"

Coley answered my question in person, for he was just coming into the room. He looked better now that he was shaving more regularly, and someone had done something for his clothing. He was wearing what he considered a smile. "You tired or ready to travel?" he asked.

I excused myself to Croghan and followed the ranger outside, where he told me he had been waiting for me for several days, feeling sure I would come when the word about Granville reached me. We set off at once but lay overnight in the bushes. In the morning, the sun was kind to what was left of the small post bravely called Fort Granville.

The comer of the stockade reached the top of the undercut bank of the river. Here the savages had approached under cover of the same bank and mined away the stockade comer so they could rush in. Coleman told me somebody had opened the gate when Bob Armstrong refused to surrender. The fellow's name was Turner, and he had been taken to Kittanning. Armstrong had died in the rush of fighting when the enemy came in from both the gate and the breach. There had been several hundred Indians and French. Armstrong, as was usual, had only a skeleton garrison; most of his men were out guarding farms, for it was the season of harvest. Croghan had buried the remains of the dead. Shingas had led the war party, and the hatchet and knife work had been pretty horrible.

Looking down over this ghastly evidence of savage power, I had a feeling of impotence. It seemed nothing could make this frontier country safe. The fall of this fort would strike terror to every home west of the Susquehanna. True, I knew Colonel Armstrong was mustering men, but they would be so few in this vast thinly-peopled land.

Coleman was impressed and profane. "This damned business won't stop till every war party is chased home or to hell. Somebody ought to burn that Kittanning town."

I looked sharply at him. "Do you know Armstrong's plans?"

He gestured toward the ruins and replied, "Armstrong's dead."

He was grinning quizzically. I might have known that every frontiersman in these parts would be aware of the important move now shaping in the Cumberland country. Secrets do not grow old on the frontier.

As we moved down the valley, I knew I had been right. The settlers were leaving. Shingas had boasted he could take any place that would burn. The settlers believed him. Harvests were deserted in the fields; wagons and pack horses were carrying the settlers' movable possessions out of this rich frontier land. It was one of the saddest sights Coleman and I had ever seen.

John Armstrong, grim and quiet, had returned to McDowell's Mills. All he said to me of his loved younger brother was: "They buried him?"

"Yes," I answered, "Croghan did that and put up a marker."

"Well, you're here on time. Most of the men have gone to the Beaver Dams with Captain Potter. Our contingent will rendezvous at Aughwick."

Somehow it seemed to me that this thing should have begun with the sound of trumpets; that is if there were trumpets. But Armstrong was as casual as if this were merely a trip up to Harris Ferry instead of the launching of the most hazardous venture thus far undertaken in the English colonies. Our map drawing, our scouting, Armstrong's trips to Philadelphia, the governor's visit to the frontier—all pointed to this expedition.

We marched the next morning; better say we straggled, a hundred men. We passed through Cowan's Gap and stopped for a little at the place they call Fort Littleton, thence on to Aughwick. Potter had gone with the best men; Armstrong had held those who might need further discipline before they could fight as a unit.

Few of those who went to Aughwick realized what John Armstrong had in his stern Scotch-Irish mind. Terror walked the hills and valleys in those days like packs of ghostly wolves. But if he drove deep into Indian territory and spread terror there, he would raise a banner of courage where now only fear was. He proposed to go to the heart of Indian and French power, to do what Braddock had tried and failed to accomplish. And he proposed to do it with a minimum loss of men.

There were times, as I swung along those days when I thought of Braddock's army, which I had seen. He had batteries of cannon; here was nothing larger than an open-bored musket. Braddock had a wagon train; we had two carts, and those were left at Aughwick. There were not a half dozen uniforms in Armstrong's whole force and not a single drum. Our "band" was made up of a half dozen whistles carried by our officers on lanyards about their necks.

We had trouble in the first few miles. The men with the two carts lagged behind. Colonel Armstrong ordered me to take charge. "Watch yourself. Don't fool with those men; they're half drunk," he cautioned.

I found the cart and the three men. When I told them to hurry, they laughed. One spat a stream of tobacco juice at my feet.

"Huh," he grunted to the others, "he's one of Jack Armstrong's pups."

It was necessary to handle them in a way they would understand. When we came into the Aughwick camp, two of the men had to ride on a cart, and it was my luck that we drove straight into the section where Hugh Mercer's company was camped. The first man I recognized was Mercer and behind him was his lap dog, Parr. Mercer never hesitated. He pointed to me. "Arrest that man for brawling!"

Half a dozen men edged forward. Then Parr yelled. "Come on, men. That's Grove, the powder runner."

Parr's eagerness was his undoing. He came too close before his fellows could help. I had a glimpse of Mercer, who was smiling as his pack closed, and I was trying desperately to get through to him when they pulled me down. Of course, I had this advantage—everyone I struck or hurt was an enemy. Then someone kicked me. Consciousness exploded into a shower of stars.

The next thing I realized clearly was that two men were holding me. They were Coleman and Solly. The crowd of toughs was standing back, and facing them was Armstrong, livid with rage. I caught the last of his harangue.

"So you gang up on the man who walked the hills through the winter so you could sit on your lazy asses in the chimney corner! Parr, Miller, Leffler—get out of my camp! If you're here an hour from now. I'll take personal pleasure in running my sword through your guts!"

"Captain Mercer!"

The officer stepped forward and stood ramrod stiff before his raging commander, his thin face expressionless. Armstrong looked at him a long time. My senses were back. Much as I disliked this Mercer, I hoped Armstrong would not reprimand him before the men. But the Colonel had sense. "You will get these powder wagons up and be ready to start in the morning."

The soldiers cleared away; Mercer saluted and left. Armstrong, Coleman, Solly, and I remained. "Colonel," Coleman spoke, and his voice was deceptively gentle, "if that damned Mercer ever so much as looks crooked at any of us three here again—I'm going to let his pill-stuffed guts out with my war ax."

"Coley," Armstrong said sharply, "Mercer's a surgeon. I'm not losing men on this trip for want of a doctor."

Morning dawned a little gray. The men got fires going promptly, cooked their breakfasts, and were assembled afterward on the ball ground behind the post. There Armstrong talked to them.

"Men, as most have guessed, we're going to Kittanning. It's risky. If any of you talk too much or fail to obey orders, we all lose our hair. You volunteered. From this minute on, you'll obey every last whisper of an officer even if he tells you to put on skates. That's the way we'll have a chance—the only way we can be safe. You understand?"

He faced them like an old eagle, his blue coat buttoned to the chin. Most of those before him knew of the death of his brother. They would follow Jack Armstrong to Kittanning or Fort Duquesne or anywhere else if he gave the word.

"We march by way of the Standing Stone to the Beaver Dams where we meet Potter," he went on.

He struck his hands together. "Remember, there's a hornet nest of Frenchies and Indians less than twenty-six miles from Kittanning. If one Indian scout from here on in gets back with word we're coming, we're sunk. Officers, inspect the men."

Croghan came out as the long lines of militia began filing away. I heard Armstrong tell him softly: "George, see to it that your folks stay here this one week. I don't want one word loose that we're on our way to Kittanning."

Croghan nodded. "I'll hold them. After you pass Standing Stone, your men will stick. They'll have to if they expect to get back."

"So I figure," Armstrong answered dryly.

Coleman, Solly, and I were stuck in the pack train as I expected. We had thirty horses loaded with food and ammunition. There were scouts out all about us, and we would be safe from Braddock surprises.

Our little army didn't look too military if we were to judge by British army standards. Outside the officers, there wasn't a uniform in the body. But the men looked alike since nearly all wore buckskin breeches and linen or buckskin hunting shirts. Most wore hats of dark colored felt common on the frontier. I doubt if there were a half dozen pairs of shoes among the whole, for even the officers wore moccasins. The important thing was that somehow Armstrong had obtained a supply of good muskets, and these and the rifles carried by a good number were in excellent condition. There were even many pistols. Each man was well equipped to come hand-to-hand with his foe, for we had hatchets and knives and a few short swords. These last were sharpened to razor edges. Some of the farmers carried the heavy straight-bladed corn knives. Truly, it was a formidable force, fitted for the task ahead.

It was curious how little loud talking there was. Officers spoke in conversational tones; their commands were relayed back to the men at the rear. Each officer carried a whistle on a thong about his neck, but they used these rarely. We marched rapidly and rested a full ten minutes out of each hour. There were no stragglers. At noon we ate from our war bags, being allowed thirty minutes, and we stopped at four o'clock each day, building fires of dry wood to prepare the meat, tea, and corn cake. The cooking over, all fires were doused. Armstrong was taking no chances.

On Wednesday afternoon, we came over a ridge and went down toward the broad flat which hunters call the Beaver Dams. From the hillside, the place looked deserted, but Potter and his whole force were hidden in the thickets. Even with the excitement of the merging of our forces, there was little loud talk. Each man knew the seriousness of this business. We bivouacked together that night, having come thirty miles that day.

Captain John Potter was easily the most popular of the captains. He had a pleasant, easy way with the men and a knack of getting on with his fellow officers, even Hugh Mercer, whom most of them seemed to dislike. Captain Hamilton, an older man who had come with our group all the way from McDowell's Mills, was also liked well for his quiet, competent ways.

Potter, one evening, stopped with me and Coleman for a few minutes. "I wanted to see you, men," he said, then he pointed to Coleman's ax. "There's another."

We looked at him; he smiled. "I noticed the flat handles. You can get a grip."

I placed my ax in his hands, for I was proud of the weapon. Even VanCamp had approved it. He turned the weapon over and over, then passed it back. "Remember, boys, if ever you take another trip to the Sinnamahoning, I'd like to go along."

I did not have a word ready for the moment; then Coleman pronounced the accolade. "You'd do, captain."

Potter understood. He smiled, snapped his hand up in a salute we did not understand how to return and walked off.

About noon, the line stopped, the word drifting back from officers up ahead. Way out front, we could see men in buckskins talking with Armstrong, Potter, and Hamilton were up there. Bits of news came filtering back along the lines.

"Indian hunting party up ahead . . ."

"Killed a bear . . ."

"Went toward Kittanning."

When we moved again, I spoke softly to Coleman. "You think we'll make it, Coley?"

He craned his neck to look back over the long files. There were now three hundred seven of us. "Well," he said, "it's a good outfit, ain't it?"

I was inclined to agree with him, certain that I felt safer with this small frontier army than I would have with Braddock.

They told us the next day we were fifty miles from Kittanning. The going was getting worse by the mile. Here the hills were high, with slopes and crests covered with laurel thickets. Armstrong finally sent Captain Hamilton and some scouts forward to reconnoiter. Late the following afternoon, they rejoined us on the march with the news that all was clear. I was close and heard the interchange. Hamilton had fallen ill and did not go all the way. Colonel Armstrong was talking to the scout who sat on a rock, his clothing torn, and weariness in every line. "You went far enough to see the town?"

The man nodded.

Armstrong continued, "You didn't see many warriors?"

The man shook his head. Armstrong looked at him a moment and turned away.

"They hadn't time enough," Coleman whispered to me.

That evening the Colonel sent for us. He was seated on a log alone. "Colonel," Coleman said, "let me and Peter go ahead and scout."

Armstrong shook his head. "No, I'll ride my luck. We couldn't turn back now if there were a thousand warriors down there." He took out his map. "Here, Peter, show me."

Using the stub of a candle, I indicated what I remembered from a boyhood visit to the place. "The houses stand every here and there. No streets, Colonel. There's a high line of hills on our side, a narrow flat for the town, then the river, more flat land, then another line of hills. It's not a big river."

"How many houses?" he asked.

"There were about twenty. There's no cover, either."

Armstrong sat silent for a little, then: "Peter, you, Coleman, and Solly work to the left when the fighting starts. Watch the river, stop any going down. Try for Shingas."

I laughed. "What do you think I came out for?"

"God knows," he said shortly. "You Dutch are stubborn."

"Night-march," came the word down the line. There was a little soft grumbling, but the force moved forward silently. My eyes are good at night. It thrilled me to see this long ribbon of men flowing forward. After a couple of hours, word came for Coleman and me to get up front. The line was halting as we ran past.

Armstrong stood by a tree and pointed.

Ahead was a broad high flat. Out there, far off, was a faint glow.

"Campfire," I said, and Coleman seconded me. "We'll scout it, Colonel."

He stopped us, and, calling two others, sent them forward. "Listen," he said as we stood crestfallen, "I'm not risking men who can stand up and shoot when they're being shot at. We'll need you tomorrow."

Presently the scouts were back. "Four warriors asleep by a fire," they reported.

"You're sure that's all?" Armstrong's voice was doubtful.

They were sure, but I remembered the warrior at the edge of the brush on the Sinnamahoning, the one over whom we stumbled.

"Detour, camp ahead," the word went back. Once more, those three hundred men did the impossible. They circled that camp of sleeping warriors and went on without being discovered. But before we turned off, we corralled the horses. In the dark, rations were served out and powder. From here on we would not need transport.

Lieutenant Hogg, who was our youngest officer, was detailed with twelve men to watch the camp and to wipe it out when the sound of firing from Kittanning reached him.

There were times when we thought we were getting close to our destination, but we tramped on, hour after hour, over ridge after ridge. Finally, there was one higher than the others. When we came out on its broad, bare, rocky top, the sound of Indian drums and distant yelling drifted up to us. None of these men needed to be told what was going on down there where some poor devil might be dying at the black post.

Presently we saw the shine of their fires and the sheen of water beyond. A company which reached the river sent back a man.

Armstrong stood there in the gloom, fumbling with his watch: his officers were close to him. "We're south of the village. That's good; we can cut them off from downriver. Mercer, take a company up along the ridge. No firing, no noise until we engage!"

When the halt had come, the men had dropped where they were and sprawled out on the ground. Now the officers moved among them. "Get up, men. Get up."

Three hundred tired men came to their feet. Mercer's company filed off to the right; the rest of us moved south of the village into a big corn field. Orders came to lie down, and there was little noise, but a soft rustling as each man eased himself to the ground.

Coleman, Solly, and I were together and lying not far from where Armstrong had taken his post with Baker, the chief scout.

The sound of the dancing began dying down; the moon slipped behind a big cloud. Out on the bank of the stream, a bullfrog sounded one single deep note. The smell of wood smoke hung heavy here in the light mist rising from the river.

Suddenly, not fifty yards ahead, there was a sharp whistle. It speaks well for those men lying there in the corn that there was no ejaculation such as startled men might make. Only Armstrong started to rise, but Baker pulled him down. "Calling his squaw," he whispered.

We heard her coming through the corn, heard his grunt when she came up. For minutes there was the stirring of them close to us, then quiet.

"Colonel," Baker was very close to Armstrong, but I heard him. "Shall I slip up on the ornery son-of-a-bitch?"

Armstrong must have said no, for Baker lay down again. Coleman shook with laughter, his shoulder moving against mine.

The night dragged interminably. Part of the time, I slept like the other utterly weary men. Part of the time, I lay there thinking of many things. My mind flashed back to the quiet of that Ephrata village. Much of my thinking was of Faith, who this night seemed very far away and not more real than a fancied shape in the mist. Once a sickish sweet odor reached me, the Indian smell, and I realized how close we were to the Indian houses that loomed huge and black in the semi-darkness.

Three hundred men lying there as quiet as the mist that moistened their buckskins like light rain!

With the first gray of the morning, there was a rustling, and I understood what was happening. Each of us was looking to the priming of his musket or rifle. The soft snick of well-oiled gunlocks could be heard. We were ready to open fire.

Out front, the squaw protested sleepily. Armstrong was on one knee, poised. Baker looking at him. The Colonel turned to an officer and asked a question. "Mercer's on the bluff?"

The man nodded in assent. Baker was waiting. Armstrong had his big watch in his hand again, but he had trouble seeing the hands in the poor light. Then he closed the case, put the timepiece back in his fob pocket, and nodded.

Baker slipped away into the corn.

CHAPTER FIFTEEN

THE HARDEST part of any battle is the waiting that often comes before it opens, and that morning under the light mist rising from the corn field before Kittanning was no exception. The three hundred of us made little sound save slight rustlings among the cornstalks. We were disciplined by the danger that hung over us. The scout, Baker, seemed to have been gone an interminable time, and I believe only woodsmen trained in stalking shy game could have kept such an iron control over themselves. Then it came—the sound of a butcher's cleaver as he works on flesh and bone. The air ripped apart with a wild high scream.

Men part way to their feet stopped in the middle of their movement, arrested by that awful sound. It came again, to be stopped short in a strangling, half-human gurgle. There was no holding us now; we came up and forward in a long wavy line, moving toward the bulking shadows of the buildings.

Coleman, Solly, and I obeyed orders, working left toward the river until we were at the end of the line and I could smell the mud. A figure showed between the houses, but it was cut down instantly by rifle fire. We reached the edge of the dancing ground and found it littered with skin, bone, and charred wood in the usual filthy Indian way. Half way across this was a blackened post, the thing to which so many had been tied in their last hours of awful agony.

A shot answered our first volley, and smoke blossomed at one of the loopholes in a house. The bullet struck near me and whined away. Dogs began an infernal clamor, and one mangy cur darted across clear ground only to be hurled from its feet by a bullet. Figures appeared at several of the houses, figures that darted, crouching and drawing our fire.

There wasn't much surprise to this business. Volleys ripped from the houses, and all the buildings were wreathed with smoke that hung low in the dampness of the morning. A man dropped near me, then struggled to his knees, saying over and over: "Oh, oh!" Finally, he dropped with a long sigh and lay still. The first of the seventeen men who died here this morning had answered the roll.

"Take cover!" The order passed down the line from man to man, and we dropped behind anything that offered even a trace of shelter; logs, stones, clumps of brush. The sun was lifting higher, a good shooting light, and another man pitched his rifle into the air and dropped. Those French muskets used by the savages carried a huge slug and hit hard at this short range.

For two bitter hours, we had the worst of this firing interchange. The savages were sheltered; we were in the open. They kept up an almost continuous fire. Likely the squaws were reloading. Some of the men worked a log up from the river bank, shoving it along with their hands. Suddenly one swore; a bullet had clipped off the end of a finger. He rolled on his back, tore a strip of linen from his shirt tail, bandaged the finger, and went back to firing behind the log.

There were those who later said there were forty houses in Kittanning town, but I am sure there were not more than half that many. The place was no larger than when I saw it as a boy.

Now, anxious about the fire that swept our line, I noticed something. A thin line of brush ran from the comer of the largest house to our lines, and I saw that it marked a shallow gulley. At once, I went crawling to where Armstrong lay. "Colonel," I demanded. "Give me a horn of powder. I'll fire that big house."

He scowled at me a moment, then beckoned to one of the lieutenants who gave me a full horn. Into the open end of this, I thrust a string which I had first passed through my mouth and then rubbed with powder, making a rude fuse. Then I fastened this with the horn's stopper. Crawling again, I reached the gulley. George Feldbaum was smoking; I took his pipe. Armstrong had checked the firing. As I raised my hand, he signaled it to begin again, and I edged along the gulley to the house and reached a spot where they could not fire down at me from a loophole. All this was accomplished without drawing fire.

The house was carelessly built. I worked my horn into a big crack in the logs and bark chinking, then lighted my fuse from the pipe. It smoldered, then began burning furiously. I leaped to my feet and ran for it, with bullets kicking the ground about me. Ten feet from our line, I tripped on a root and fell to safe cover. I had time to duck my head, then the corner of that house was a sheet of flame. Not a minute later came the roar of a terrific explosion.

It is my notion that there was a great store of powder in that house since I do not believe one horn of powder could do so terrible a thing. The building went to fragments. Pieces of roof were hurled about us; a black cloud lifted high into the air, and something that looked much like a human leg dropped from it.

I was lying there staring when somebody nudged me in the ribs. It was George Feldbaum. "You bring back my pipe, Peter?"

I looked down at my hand; it still gripped the pipe. "Here," I said. "Guess it's not out yet."

The explosion hurled flaming timbers and shingles to the roofs of other buildings. All were burning in a matter of minutes. Savages appeared in the open, and we had good targets. But the firing from the houses had not stopped. Above the bang of guns, we could hear a high shrill keening that Coleman said was the death song.

Just as he finished telling me this, his eyes widened in surprise. Then he leaped across me. I turned; he was holding Solly's head in his arms. The boy's hand was pressed against his side, and blood flowed through his fingers. "Grandpap," he mumbled.

Solly was gone. Only a few yards away, his father and uncle may have died at the torture post, for they had been captured by Indians.

There was no holding the men when the Indians were in the open. They ran forward, hatchets loose, faces hot and flushed. Some captives appeared among the milling Indians. I saw Armstrong wave his arms; then, he dropped to his knees, and one of the lieutenants caught him.

Explosion followed explosion. Bursts of flame leaped from roofs and doors as the immense stores of powder either exploded or burned. A huge savage emerged from a building. I recognized the giant form of Captain Jacobs, but one of Potter's scouts appeared and flung his hatchet. The big chief dropped with the ax in the back of his neck.

It was a matter of straight murder now, the whites performing as the savages did on a settlement raid.

Knots of Indians were moving upstream; likely, there were fords that way. Then I remembered Armstrong's order. No person was to be allowed to escape downstream where only a little over a score of miles away were the French and Indian forces in and about Fort Duquesne. My rifle was empty, but I darted away down along the stream and burst through a screen of bushes where three canoes were drawn up. Two Indians had just appeared, one grasping at the bow of the first canoe. I dropped him with a pistol shot. The second warrior was small and very quick, and he did not seem to have a weapon. But he fooled me; his body had hidden his war ax. With a quick twist, he turned and hurled the weapon at me. The blade missed, but the handle took me a clip on the side of the head that dropped me to my knees. He had the canoe half in the water my head would clear enough to let me rise. The man was Shingas! There was no mistaking that seamed, evil face!

I had no thought of weapons. I would kill this man any way I could. His hair was loose from the usual braids. He wore what looked to be the same filthy shirt, and he knew me at once, for his lips twisted. Twenty feet from the bank, the current was fast. Shingas was trying to get his craft clear when I snatched up a stone and hurled it, so it crashed through the flimsy bottom of the canoe, which filled with water immediately.

The old warrior's foot must have caught in one of the thwarts as he sought to get clear. He snatched out his knife as I leaped for him, but I gripped his wrist while he struggled like a trapped cat, yowling, drooling from his open mouth. "Shingas, remember me? You killed my father!" I said between my teeth.

He tore from me and made a sweep with the knife that nicked my shoulder. This time I caught his hair and jerked him off his feet. We floundered about in the knee-deep water, he trying to use his knife, I trying to keep my footing against his struggling. Once more, the knife went high, and I caught that wiry wrist. This time I was too strong for him. I caught the bright-bladed weapon as it fell, jerked his head back by his hair, and drew the keen edge across the scrawny throat.

His evil eyes were wide open, his lips moved spasmodically, then I dropped him into the water, and a pool of red came up and widened as I watched.

Wading slowly to the bank, I knelt and washed my hands over and over to rid them of the feel of that unclean beast. When I fumbled in my pocket for a handkerchief to dry my hands, I felt the tiny wooden bead Faith had given me. Perhaps her wish had kept me safe while unarmed; I had killed the best knife fighter among the savages.

In later years it was often reported that Shingas led warriors in this place and that. When I heard, I smiled, for I had seen those dying eyes and watched the broad-bladed knife cross his throat.

Desperately weary though I was, I took time to ruin the other canoes to prevent escape on the part of savages to Fort Duquesne, where an alarm would mean pursuit and destruction of our small force. Then I moved toward the yelling and firing, but my legs dragged until I sat down for a moment on a stump and tried to clear my thinking. The bushes rustled, and I knew too late that neither my rifle nor pistol was charged. Hugh Mercer and another man stepped into view. Mercer looked at me sharply.

"So," he said. "So this is where you fight."

I said nothing, but what was in my mind must have shown on my face, for he half drew a pistol then turned away.

The fighting was over. What Indians were left alive were children, squaws, and old men who huddled in miserable groups. The concern of the soldiers was rounding up white prisoners—eleven of them—poor, half-starved, filthy creatures who stared at their rescuers with lack-luster eyes. All the houses were blazing, and of these, the men made funeral pyres for our own dead, seventeen in all. Armstrong sat with his back to a rock, his face white and drawn from pain.

"Shingas?" he asked as I approached him.

"Dead, sir, and no one went downriver."

He stared a moment, then nodded his head while he raised his hand and touched the bandage on his shoulder. He muttered. "Mercer'll company'll bring up the rear."

I said nothing, but I wondered. Mercer was supposed to have led his men to the bluff back of the village. I had heard the order. Yet I had seen the man down by the river. Now he was to guard the rear.

The long line of us began to draw out of the shambles of the town. Most of the wounded could walk, and whole men strode beside them. The helpless were carried on litters. All the men had an odd look about them. They had marched thirty miles, fought a bitter battle. They were young men, but now they looked old. Their clothes hung upon them as though their bodies had shrunk. Of our small army, one out of twelve either lay dead back there in the fires or moved out wounded.

A lieutenant ran up to Armstrong. "Sir, Captain Mercer's wounded. He and six men have started home."

Armstrong's pale face blazed with sudden fury. "Great God of the Mountains, was the man afraid of blood?" he roared.

I was glad now I was not an officer. All I had to do was shamble along in the line and give an occasional man a lift with his rifle or a boost over a fallen tree. But the officers who were unwounded had to round up utterly weary stragglers and haze them into line to check muster rolls against those marching. Certainly, any straggler left behind would die most horribly.

We climbed steadily, getting up the slopes we had descended in the morning. Men would stumble, fall, then drag themselves erect by holding on to bushes or trees. At rocky ledges or especially steep going, Coleman or I or others who were still strong would clamber ahead then yank men up.

It was my thought that when we reached the flat hilltop, the going would be better, but here was the low-growing laurel that tripped tired feet, that jerked gun-barrels when caught in the crooked branches until the soldier carrying the weapon would drop it. I saw men on their knees trying to pick up such a dropped weapon and weeping like small children because of the sheer weariness upon them.

Well out on the tableland, Coleman came up to me, and we walked together for a while. He was thinking. "That goddam Mercer's up to something," he muttered to me.

I shrugged my shoulders, for I did not care if Mercer lived or died. I knew we were soon coming to the place where we had left Lieutenant Hogg and his twelve men to watch that camp of Indian hunters. Almost immediately, a man stepped from the bushes. He was wild-eyed, his clothing torn. "Where's Armstrong?" he almost begged.

We took him to the commander.

"Sir," he reported, "the lieutenant is just ahead, dying."

Armstrong went with us, and we were led to a small open glade. I lighted a short length of candle, and the Colonel knelt by the man who lay there on a bed of leaves. The young officer was nearly gone, but he tried to raise his body when he recognized his commander.

"Easy, lieutenant," Armstrong said. "We'll have men to carry you."

Lieutenant Hogg shook his head in negation. Bit by bit, he told the story how they had struck the camp and found themselves outnumbered two to one. Three of his men were dead, the remainder scattered. He closed his eyes. The young wife who had ridden to Aughwick with him would wait in vain. Gently Armstrong touched the officer's forehead. In a strained voice, he whispered: "The Lord keep thee in perfect peace."

He rose to his feet, but he needed Coleman's help. "Pass the word back—Indians in front," he almost whispered his order from weakness.

I believe that challenge of danger was the thing that saved us all. Men became alert, moving in the moonlight like hunting dogs, spreading out, searching every possible lurking place. Finally, we were at the place where we had left the horses and our heavy baggage. Too tired to eat, we flung ourselves down and slept the sleep of utter exhaustion.

Armstrong sent Coleman and three soldiers away in the morning on some mysterious errand. They rejoined us the following day, and they had Mercer with them. He had his arm in a sling but showed no marks of suffering. The Colonel saw to it that he examined each of the wounded, but I noticed he did not permit the captain to examine his own bad shoulder.

Two days later, we filed into Fort Shirley, as they called George Croghan's fort. There, Mercer, as second in command, paid us off in hard money at the regular rate of six dollars a month for privates and about twelve for officers. It figured to one dollar and a half for each one. The march and destruction of Kittanning had cost the colony less than five hundred dollars or pieces of eight. I saw one man looking at the coins in his palm. "Hell," he muttered. "Just about the price of a middling good drunk."

Seventeen men were dead, but we had brought away every wounded man because of the iron will of John Armstrong. We had gone where Braddock could not go and had destroyed the savages' arsenal. From this time forth, no Indian village could ever feel entirely safe. There could be no security about their council fires. Both Delaware chiefs were dead— Shingas and Captain Jacobs. Both had died of the cold steel they had loosed so savagely and terribly on defenseless folk.

It was now I remembered Conrad Weiser and his prophecy that Americans must win the war because the King's regulars could not.

For myself, I went down to Carlisle, to which many of us repaired to be mustered out. I hired a room at the Belford Inn, where I shaved, bathed, and put my clothing in some sort of order. After a good meal, I wished to walk about the town a little, but I had not gone three rifle shots from the inn when I encountered a sergeant and four men uniformed as provincial militia. The sergeant stopped me.

I had no weapon, and I was surprised. They crowded round me, and the sergeant spoke. "You are Peter Grove?"

I nodded.

"You are under arrest."

I stared at him in utter surprise. "In God's name, why?"

He shook his head. "Captain Mercer's orders. It's on an old warrant, something about powder and Indians."

They led me away like a weary old sheep and locked me up securely in Carlisle's neat stone jail.

There was no fight left in me. Six months before, I would have fought the sergeant and his men. Now I sat on the edge of my small cot, as weary and spent as a man will be from long running.

CHAPTER SIXTEEN

IT WAS MID-SEPTEMBER of the year of our Lord seventeen hundred fifty-six when I was thrown into jail in the village of Carlisle, this being the only stone prison west of the Susquehanna in those days, though there have been plenty built there since. The months of fall weather, when color touches the hills and countryside, came and went. For the first time in my life, I was shut in, and I found it numbing business. It is heartbreaking for a man who has so often slept under the stars to walk to a door and find it closed fast and to find that it will not answer the frantic fumbling of his fingers.

At such times I raged and broke the things kept in my cell. Allison Craig, my jailor, was a kindly soul. "Do not rage so, Peter. It hurts both you and me," he would plead, and I did not like to see the dismay on his face.

He would greet me with a smile each morning, even when I glowered at him or seemed ready to hurl a dish through the bars. No formal charge had been entered against me, and I was not brought to trial. Daily, Craig would recite the news to me. I would sit and listen with hands clenched.

The Indians were raiding again but avoiding the Cumberland country. Perhaps the cold gray eyes of the Scotch-Irish looked too menacing over a rifle barrel, but even east of the great river, small bands of savages were taking their toll. Craig had much to say of more fort building, even that Conrad Weiser was now a Colonel.

One splendid fall day, Craig came to my cell wringing his hands. "This is the worst."

South of Aughwick is the lovely little valley of the path where some peaceful Dunkards had settled. Their faith would not allow them to take up arms even in self-defense, and the savages came. But one man defended himself. He was the miller and not a very good Dunkard. When he saw a skulking warrior, he killed him and promptly reloaded. The second warrior dropped at his shot and fell into the mill race, floating down toward the big wheel. It now seemed an excellent time to take to the hills, which he did. From there, he watched the progress of the raid by checking the burning houses.

The Indians surrounded the little village and clubbed or hacked the men to death with mauls and hatchets. They took no captives, apparently enjoying this new plaything, a white man who would not fight but muttered: "Gottes wil es getan," which meant simply, "God's will be done."

Years later, a Cumberland man met some Indians at Logstown, and one asked if there were any more "Gotteswilikins" in the mountain valleys. He finally realized the savage meant the Dunkards.

"Craig," I demanded. "Get me paper and a pen—quickly."

There in Carlisle jail, I made my decision, the one Governor Morris expected of me. I wrote my letter, and it was extremely short and directed to His Excellency, Governor of the Colony. "Do as you planned. The time of locusts is here."

For one of my gold pieces, Craig took the letter and found a reliable man to take it swiftly to Morris. One month later, a printed proclamation was posted all over "Improved Pennsylvania": "One hundred dollars or pieces of eight will be paid by the proper colonial officers under the direction of the governor for the scalp of a male Indian over twelve . . ."

It provided bounties also for women and children and placed the red men of the colony on the same basis as wolves and furbearers. Truly, "the only way to fight the devil is with fire." But, within limited time, Morris was ousted as governor, and the profligate Denny took his place.

In this month and the few weeks after, I had done a number of things, one of them breaking jail!

When I sat at my window and twisted my neck a little, I could look down one of the main streets of the town, a thing I seldom did. But, this day, I was looking. True, I had just a glimpse. At first, I thought it a boy riding a rangy chestnut, then I saw a hand come up. It was like a bugle call or like that explosion which happened at Kittanning.

That was not a boy but Faith Horn, and she had put up her hand to tuck a strand of brown hair under her leather cap!

Carlisle jail is a good one; there is no gainsaying that. Yet, an hour after I had seen Faith ride by, I dropped lightly from my window and hunted the remainder of the daylight hours through the town for another glimpse of her, but without success. She seemed to have vanished.

A short time after nightfall, a frantic and utterly chagrined Craig heard my knocking and re-admitted me to jail. That evening I walked the floor and cursed impartially, Mercer, the Assembly, and anyone else in power.

It is possible that I might have won my release from jail any time by calling on my friends. But the fight had gone out of me to the point where I was ashamed. I was here because of my violent temper and ways. For years things had turned against me. Let me figure in any locality, and presently there was trouble. No wonder the Indians called me Powder Horn. Even here, I had embarrassed the kind Craig by breaking from his jail at the mere glimpse of a girl who was going to marry a British officer—if she had not already done so.

So, for a matter of days, to please Craig, I faithfully read Roman History and found it passably interesting. Then, greatly excited, my good jailer appeared, looking very pleased. "You have a visitor, Peter."

"Tell him to go to hell," I growled ungraciously. "I don't want to see anybody."

Craig's spirits could not be dampened. "Mayhap, he will go there someday, but now he will see you."

He led me out into the big jail lobby. Two men were over at the window, one in a blue uniform coat, the other in brown civilian clothes, and both turned as we entered. John Armstrong strode across the room and gripped my hand; Hugh Mercer remained at the window. "Peter, I have just heard through Morris himself, who was informed by God knows whom, that you were locked up. My wound, my duties—Sir, I am ashamed, but why did you not get a lawyer or send word to me?"

I did not reply at once but kept my eyes on Hugh Mercer. The palms of my hands ached with the intensity of my desire to take him by the throat. Now he spoke. "I have withdrawn the charges against you. Grove. There was some confusion. The Indians call you Powder Horn; that and some other circumstances confused me. I offer my apologies."

Often since, I have wondered what Armstrong said to Mercer in private to make that stiff-backed doctor, lawyer, apothecary, soldier, apologize. I am certain that cold steel could not have done it, yet, Armstrong angry was a fearsome man.

Having done his duty and, I believe, a little eager to get out of the room, Mercer left. Armstrong lingered a little. "I go west with the British general, Forbes. This time we will take Duquesne. Presently this war will be over. Will you come with me as a lieutenant, Peter?"

For a long moment, we looked into each other's eyes. He was sincere, a man I could have followed anywhere. There was iron in the man. I remembered the long files of weary men and the driving will that took them clear of possible pursuit after Kittanning. Slowly I shook my head.

He stepped forward; his long, strong fingers closed round mine. "I'm sorry. It's no wonder you are a little bitter. It would have been a comfort to have had you in my force."

Craig helped me gather my belongings which were still in the inn room where I had left them months before. He declared that he did not know who had informed Morris of my imprisonment and was so vehement about the matter that I did not believe him. He further declared that he knew nothing of a young woman on a horse in the streets of Carlisle town. So, I gave him a gold piece for his kindness.

"If ever," he said in parting, "you want to be in jail again, come back here, my friend."

In another hour, I had shaken the gray dust of Carlisle from my feet and was bound north. Two miles out of town, where a farmhouse stood by a great free-flowing spring, I bought a horse and an old saddle for the flimsy reason that I might think my way through problems better if I rode.

I always liked to meet John Harris. He was voluble this day though harassed by many duties. In fact, he offered me a post with him within the first half-hour, and I refused as gracefully as I could. "War's on its last legs. Forbes'll clean out Duquesne. Scalp buying will dry up the raids.

When a dead redskin's worth a hundred fifty dollars, it ain't safe for him to take his hair to war. There's just one big danger."

He waited in order to impress me, then continued: "An Iroquois scalp looks just like a Shawnee or Delaware top-knot. A fellow hunting red meat's likely to get a Seneca scalp now and then."

From Harris, I traveled toward Lancaster. The Blue Goose looked very quiet. I stopped and learned that Mistress Wright had sold the place. Strangers attended to my needs. In Lancaster, I got my money together and fought the same old battle with myself. I wanted desperately to go to Horn's place for word of Faith. The impulse was doubly strong now since I had seen her in Carlisle. Once more, my Dutch stubbornness wrapped me round and kept me blind.

Philadelphia meant John Bartram. He had been on a long trip to the southland, and I helped him with specimens. He was interested in my plan to attempt to raise ginseng. I bought a small field and settled on my experiment. There I planted young maple trees to shade my plants. Bartram said I must, for he shaded those he had saved.

The Sinnamahoning country was too far; besides, I believed the Indians of some villages in the valley of the Standing Stone saved these seeds, so I needed to be away. The fact was that the city irked me; I wanted the taste of freedom in my mouth.

So, once again, I passed the Slide, which did not look such an evil place from the other side of the river. The little village of "Leatherton" had not changed much. After all, it was supposedly a neutral place without warriors other than old men and boys. But there was one man who recognized me. He took my hand in white man fashion. His wrinkled face broke into a smile. "Yes," he said. "Young Powder Horn, come back. But, our Mikwah is dead."

I was in the village two days while some seeds were brought to me from a valley in the hills where an old man gathered them. The chief told me about Mikwah. She had been found dead at the foot of a rocky ledge. She had the pistol I had given her, but it was broken. Also, the horn of powder was gone. Bruised and broken by her fall, it was still possible to tell that she had been brutally beaten.

The old headman or chief finished his story. "There was a man, Parr. He cheated a man called Charteris. We found this Parr tied to a pine tree. He was dead of many arrows. We hid him for fear we would be blamed. He was scalped. The young Powder Horn sees clearly as in a bright morning?"

Certainly, I "saw clearly" and thought about it on my long ride back, bearing my seeds. For once I owed Charteris something though I doubted the half-breed's part in the affair.

Bartram worked with me and my plantings during those days when the colony went mad at the news of peace. Armstrong was right, Forbes took Duquesne and in the north, Wolfe ended New France on the Plains of Abraham.

The great botanist heard me through one evening while I told him the tale of Mikwah, of Parr, of Charteris, and of Judson.

"Of Judson, I know something. He now runs a small and humble shop. Likely he was in the powder trade; also, he wanted to learn of the Indians' lead mine. But, it is said about this city that Charteris tricked these merchants. The outbreak of war came too soon; they lost a great deal of money. Now, with peace, trade with the savages will begin once more."

He tapped me on the leg. "I am glad, friend Peter, that you seem settled here."

I sat thinking, then turned to him. "Suppose I found that lead mine now; what would I do with it?"

He studied for some time, then answered. "As a loyal subject of the English king, you should turn it over to the military. But—hearken to me. If ever you find it, go to Morris; tell him."

It cannot be denied that I had some of my father's skill as a trader, for, in these days, I did well buying and selling small lots of peltry. Ginseng was brought to me, and I resold it. But I found little zest in this business. Now, in times of peace, the tiny wooden bead's message meant little, excepting that once Faith had thought kindly of me and wished me well.

Then suddenly, in the midst of the false peace, the war cry sounded again. Pontiac, of the Ottawas, united the Indians. All of them hated the English; even Sir William Johnson's hold on the Iroquois was feeble. One by one, this mighty Indian took the frontier posts, finally besieging Fort Pitt and the northern post on Lake Erie called Presque Isle. Bands of warriors were once more on forest trails spreading death and horror among frontier villages and homes.

I could stand the city no longer and told the Bartrams so. I was surprised to find them resigned to have me go.

"You have been restless. Perhaps, after all, you belong out there. Promise that you will come back to us. Ofttimes such a pledge will work to keep a man safe," John Bartram said.

I promised, and Ann Bartram tied a bright red scarf of China silk about my throat and kissed me on the forehead as she would have done to one of her sons. The smaller children filled my pockets with cookies, and once more, I was on my way to Lancaster dressed in buckskins and carrying my war gear.

My own home did not appeal to me, thronged as it was with reminders of my father and Mart Reed, so I found quarters in a Lancaster inn. Nobody seemed to recognize me there, so I ventured to make some inquiries about the firm of Horn and Teague.

"Oh, yes," the innkeeper said. "There was such a post here, but Horn is now in the land business. His daughter aids him."

"She is married," I said slowly, "to—"

He interrupted. "Oh, no. Her fiancé, Lieutenant Orme, poor fellow, was killed near Quebec."

I was trembling when my informant finished, and he noticed.

"Ah," he said, "perhaps the lieutenant was a friend of yours?"

"No," I said quickly. "I scarcely knew the man; I have been ill. A little fever returns from time to time."

Faith Horn was free! I gripped the small wood bead in my fingers. It seemed warm like the tones of her hair, like the friendliness that so easily came into her voice.

True, she had ordered me from her house, but she had left for me a tiny bit of wood and with it some hope; I must try to see Faith before I took to the frontier and the killing that so distressed her.

An obliging barber trimmed my black hair and lent me a decent shirt, for I had no clothes except my buckskins. Then he knotted at my throat the bright scarf Ann Bartram had given me. His mirror showed me tanned from sun, darker than an Indian. I shook my head at what I saw, but he said he thought I looked pretty fair. However, I set that down to the gold piece he received for his interest and help.

The Horn and Teague post was closed and empty but for an old caretaker who sold me a gill of priming powder that I might need. "Colonel Horn no longer trades. He and his daughter are upriver on their lands," he told me.

There was naught I could do but turn away.

CHAPTER SEVENTEEN

TREMENDOUSLY stirred by my news of Faith and forcing myself to be content with the small crumb of information as to her whereabouts, I went upcountry and walked right into the naked terror that showed its ugly face along the great river. It was the same thing as in the days of Shingas; people reluctant to leave their hard-won farms in the mountain valleys yet having no other place to go.

At Fort Hunter, I was introduced to a Captain Campbell of a British highland regiment. I liked the tall, lean, quiet man at once.

"I have heard of you," he told me. Then, with apologies, he asked me many questions. He wanted to know distances, grades, compass bearings, number of Indians, and other things. When he finished and put away his notebook, he spoke deliberately. "You have helped me greatly. Mister Grove. I fear our new commandant, General Amherst, does not know Indians."

A woodsman sitting near us broke in. "He's the one who wanted to send the blankets of the smallpox sick to the savages to spread the disease."

Captain Campbell looked at him oddly, then turned to me. "I am hoping that you will go to Carlisle. Bouquet could use you."

I told him I wanted to go upriver and that I would make my decision on what I would do from what I learned up there.

With a store of parched corn, meal, dried meat, and bacon in my haversack, I took to the hills. I was homesick for the smell of sweet fern, for the sight of long slopes and narrow valleys, for the feel of the forest floor on my speeding feet. Croghan was no longer at Aughwick, so I went up to Fort Augusta, the strongest post on the river. From there, I crossed the river and reached Fort Menninger, which stood close to the Widow Smith's mill. I was rewarded by finding Coleman and Pence. In the next hour, VanCamp came in.

The four of us had a real reunion, celebrating with a bottle of the Widow's blackberry wine which Pence said was "damned fine-tasting medicine, but lacking authority."

Coleman knew that Colonel Henry Bouquet, commandant in our colony, was moving west to relieve Fort Pitt. "He's a good man, hell on discipline, but he'll take a rifle and go out with his scouts."

Pence snorted derisively. "What chance would a British officer in a red coat have getting close to Indians? Me, I ain't got any time for soldiers anymore."

Finally, Pence and Coleman left us to step over to the mill. I turned promptly to VanCamp and asked about the Great Island country and Horn. "He's the big man up there—land, influence with the Senecas. Stays near a little place they call Fort Horn. He's not popular—too much property. Folks wonder where he gets his money. They wonder if he's in cahoots with the Connecticut people."

"What's become of Faith Horn?"

I tried to speak naturally, but he glanced sharply at me. "She was to marry a Britisher, but he got himself killed somewhere up in French country. She's with her pa most of the time. They ride good horses; she dresses in buckskins and rides a horse like one of them Virginians. They're nearly always together. Horn gets on with Senecas pretty fair."

That was a long speech for VanCamp. The others were returning, but I had one more question. "Where is their house?"

VanCamp shook his head. "I'm not sure where. They say there's a stone house being built, big as a trading post. The story is that he'll have slaves and that his outfit will make John Harris' place look like stables, but I never saw the place."

I sat a long time thinking and smoking. There was a small amount of gold in Lancaster. I had refused wages from Bartram. I owned several suits of buckskins, a worn rifle, a pistol, knife, and ax. Finally, this inventory of my possessions amused me, and I chuckled.

"Well," Coleman demanded, "what tickles you? What's funny?"

"I was thinking of Horn with his wide acres, living like a lord, when all I have is what I stand up in."

They looked at me quizzically. "You missed the harvest. Some fellow got word to Morris to offer a price for scalps. Well, we really went into the hair business."

"I'm willing to wager there were some Seneca wolf pelts in your fur take," I commented.

"No, no, friend Peter," Pence said ponderously. "The Senecas are children of the Great White Father, the King. No honest young men would think of harming these kindly red children who are only playing when they wind a man's guts out of him on a hot gun barrel. Tell me, Peter, does a dead Delaware stink worse than a Mohawk?"

"Depends. Come with me and find out. There'll be all breeds out in this war," I challenged.

Sitting there, looking west and north at the mountain barriers, I wondered what evil brooded behind them. For a moment, I thought of Penn's Creek that day and of Solly with his young lips set in a straight line lest his grief master him.

None of these men had any idea of enlisting, and they tried to laugh me out of the idea when I told them I was going to Carlisle. I said I knew the town well, having been in jail there for a few months. They were all too polite to ask me what the crime was. "I'll see this new commandant, Bouquet; I'll see if I want to follow him."

When they felt sure I was going, they overhauled my equipment. First, they stuffed my pouch with parched corn, the tassamane of this country. To this, they added maple sugar and some fine dried venison. VanCamp went over my ax and hatchet with his oilstone. Pence had provided the food. Coleman checked over my rifle. Then they stripped me of my buckskins and mended each rip and doubtful seam. Pence gave me two pairs of moccasins since we were about the same size. When I left, they were lined up grinning. We said no formal word of parting, only Coleman called after me. "Don't be a damned fool, Peter. Don't let good Dutch hair smoke in a horned Ottawa's lodge."

I swung away up the wide and deep creek they call the White Deer and was soon in a country of immense pine timber, dusky even at noonday.

Underneath, the ferns grew so luxuriantly that they carpeted the forest as they do in the south. Game signs were abundant, but I did not like this country as I did the Sinnamahoning, where all the little streams are bright and the timber lets in the sunshine. Here were rhododendron trees six inches in thickness that lifted ghostly white flowers up among the pines until the place seemed a vast cathedral with pine trunks for columns and the white flowers for dim candles.

It was in my mind to do one small piece of exploration while I was in this section—before I went to seek out Faith, to see her dear face once more, whether kindly toward me or no. After that, Bouquet and the relief of Fort Pitt in the Indian War. Knowledge of trails through here might be highly useful to a retreating army if worst came to worst.

I wanted particularly to find what is called the Buffalo Path, which crosses somewhere from the Shamokin to the Kittanning Path, but I did not find it the first day or later. It began to rain at evening. Next morning I found myself in a country of small hills clustered in a wide mountain gap. Finally, I climbed to a high tableland. The rain had stopped; a little sun broke through, and I looked down on fog that swirled among hills like steam in a giant's kettle being stirred by a mighty spoon.

What happened to me that evening I have never been able to explain. Perhaps I had a fever. When I tried to sleep, figures seemed to be all about me, and I tried to talk to them, but they would not answer.

Next morning I could scarcely rise, and so it was for two days. There would be times when I could walk, others when I lay in the bushes shaking like the leaves. Sometime in those strange days, I came to a valley with a high bold point beyond it. I reached this hill and clambered halfway up its side. Suddenly, in my weakness, there was something familiar. It was a wind harp such as Armstrong, Potter, and I had seen far to the south. Nearby was a small pit with the signs of old digging, and about were a few of those heavy gray stones like the pebble that had been in my father's handkerchief. Here then was the lead mine of the Indians!

Somehow I crawled down the hill; then, my head was mercifully clear once more. I remembered the terrible thing that lead meant, how my father had died because of this gray metal. Lead made war possible.

The fever was on me again. I worked rapidly with flint and steel. Presently the brush and small trees on that hill were burning. I was wiping out landmarks. No one would find the place without months of searching.

Next morning my head was clear. I was beside a large creek, and I was able to eat some parched corn. On its strength, I tied two dead logs together with grapevine and floated down the stream on this make-shift raft until I came to the great river. Twenty-four hours later, I was in Carlisle with no fever and a tremendous appetite.

The landlord of the big inn was an intelligent man. I asked him if Morris ever came this way now that he was back in his former legal business, which he had left to become governor. The man smiled. "Yes, he does. As a matter of fact, he is upstairs now."

Even in my impatience, I would not rush in upon the great man, but the maid who had gone upstairs returned immediately with the direction that I should go right up.

He looked little different from the time when he was bidding for Shingas's scalp in this same town.

"So," he cried, "here is our Peter Grove again, our Indian Powder Horn. Tell me, what new thing have you exploded?"

As best I could, I told him of the lead mine and Bartram's counsel that I should come to him. When I finished, he went to the window and stared out for a long time. Finally, he came back and drew his chair, so he faced me. "Peter, it was not lead that killed your father. It was powder. Shingas wanted him to tell how to make it. Your father played him along in the hope that he would be told where the savages obtained lead. So, he was killed. Traders like Judson and others were trying for the metal, humoring the Indians to learn of it. Now—I could be hanged for what I shall say, but here it is: Let the secret of the lead be between us. Bouquet will break the Indians. For a while, there will be peace. But there will be another war. You and I and many more do not like the British king. There will come a time, Peter, when this mine may make the difference between freedom and losing to the king. Tell no one till that time."

He did not dismiss me but after a little, I rose and took my departure, leaving him sitting there, his heavy eyes half-lidded. Next morning, early, his coach left the inn.

Carlisle was a town of dismay. It was crowded with refugees to the point where brush shelters had been built in the nearby fields. Food was scarce, the people from the surrounding area had fled their farms leaving everything behind. It had been so in the French wars, but now there was something different. The will to fight had left them. The only cheerful note was that Bouquet was coming.

My heart strained to be away in search of Faith. For what, I asked myself—for one look, mayhap one more rebuff, while the wild scream of Indian terror threatened the few last redoubts that kept her and these people safe? Not even the white-hot, foolish hope that I might yet have favor of her could bear the temper of this reason.

Colonel Henry Bouquet, commander of his Majesty's forces in the colony, arrived next day with five hundred soldiers from the Forty-Second Highlanders and the Seventy-Seventh Light Infantry. He had expected to find it possible to obtain supplies here in this rich farming area but instead, he had to share his military supplies with the half-fed civilians.

I saw the Colonel on his first day in town. Not a large man, he was immaculate from his polished buttons to the lace at his wrists. His light sword was carried at exactly the right angle; his face was austere, and it was easy to see that while his men might respect him, they would not love him.

Two days later, I called and was shown directly in to the commandant. I told him I wished to join his forces and understood he needed men.

He smiled. "God knows we need every good man. Amherst says no more soldiers can be spared. I know something of you from Armstrong, who spoke of your work at Kittanning."

I nodded, and he went on. "There is another woodsman here, a man named Coleman."

"Coley," I cried. "He and I are old friends."

Bouquet looked at me as though slightly displeased with my show of sentiment. Then he gravely administered the military oath and counted into my palm the advance pay of twenty shillings. I was assigned to transport duty until we reached Indian country.

I found a sheepish-looking Coleman, and we pummeled each other and traded jibes. "Coley, I knew you couldn't stand to be safe."

"Aw," he answered. "It wasn't that. I just got to hankering for this marching stuff. It keeps the bowels loose. Besides, I ain't had me an Indian for two years, and I'm getting tired of bear hunting."

Next morning a messenger brought word that Presque Isle had fallen, leaving Fort Pitt alone to hold out. Of course, we did not know about Ligonier, which was heavily invested. Now, even nearby farmers moved into town.

On the eighteenth day after Bouquet's coming, we marched out, bound west. Our lumbering wagons were drawn by slow horses. In four of them rode the sixty men not yet well enough to march. As the Highlanders and brightly uniformed infantry' strode along, people stood to the side, some of them weeping. Bouquet had explained that with his force moving west, savages would not dare come into the settlements.

The trim commander had a real problem. He must travel two hundred miles through the wilderness and relieve two forts unaided. He was moving against the most resourceful Indian yet to take the warpath against the whites.

From what I could see, war to Bouquet was a problem worked out along certain lines and taking into consideration certain factors. He had a corps of trained soldiers on whose discipline he could rely, a forged weapon to be handled in battle like a sword. Whatever his thoughts, he rode his small mare at the head of our column with the confidence of a man riding to a picnic or the races.

CHAPTER EIGHTEEN

EVEN A SMALL army on the march is an impressive thing. Our Highlanders marched with a free stride, their bare knees moving in unison, each man with his bonnet worn a bit to one side. Our foot soldiers wore the traditional white cross-belts making a fine appearance. The Rangers were in green, and there were too few of us in buckskins to spoil the show.

Bouquet was pleased when we reached Shippensburg in our first day, though the town was even more congested and frightened than Carlisle. From there, our force moved south-westward at the slow pace of the teams. I suppose the colonel wanted to reach the Forbes road where his transport could make good time in the hills. At our Fort Loudon halt, Bouquet summoned Coleman and me. He gestured to camp chairs.

We sat down gingerly, and Bouquet smiled. "Men, I need information. This Shawnee business concerns me; it is so often on the map."

Coleman looked at me, then answered Bouquet's question. "Sir, it was not a large nation. The name means wanderer. Old people say they came from the south, and they have been making trouble all over the colony ever since. The Senecas licked them a couple of times."

Coleman stopped but went on at the Colonel's signal. "This country was their hunting grounds where they used to be thick. West of here are some round hills they call Shawnee Cabins because they look like Indian huts. Peter, tell him about Charteris."

Bouquet was a good listener. He turned to me with a courteous smile.

"He is a half-breed, sir. His father had a post in Lancaster county at Piqua. The son travels with a small band of renegade Shawnees, and the traders do not trust the outfit, though the Quakers used to think well of them; too many pack trains looted in the hills. Charteris went over to the French in the late war. He is a keen man, sir, and a dangerous one."

Bouquet startled us with a question. "Do you know if any Iroquois are out with Pontiac?"

Both of us stared at him and likely answered his real question with our attitudes. I thought of the West Branch country where Faith would be, for that was Seneca country. Coleman spoke. "Do you mean Senecas, sir?"

Bouquet nodded. "Word is that some Shawnees were about Fort Augusta. Supposedly they wanted to stir the Senecas up for war."

Coleman shook his head vigorously. "No, them Shawnees is old enemies with Senecas. Likely the braves could be Delawares."

Bouquet smiled. It was plain Coleman had not convinced him. "There was a white man with them, a big fellow who wore a black hat with a feather in it."

"Charteris," I thought with anguish. "If that devil is loose on the Susquehanna—" But there was work to do.

Our army was now in the hills, the road itself climbing steadily. On the twenty-fifth of July, we marched into Bedford post with the Highlanders' pipes shrilling.

I would have preferred to stay with the main body, but that first night in Bedford, Coleman and I were again summoned. Bouquet did not waste words. "Lieutenant Burns and thirty Highlanders are to march rapidly to Ligonier. Can you men guide him?"

I nodded. "Yes, sir. I traded in this country. Coleman has hunted over it."

The matter was settled, but Bouquet leveled a long forefinger at us. "Remember, these Highlanders are good travelers and fighters, but they can get lost in a field of wheat. You men will watch in this matter. Also, keep them out of sight. We want the savages to think we all stayed here at Bedford."

It meant a good bit to have this officer take us thus far into his confidence, but Coleman wasn't pleased.

"Them damn Scotch," he muttered as we went to our quarters.

The following night Lieutenant Burns and his men followed Coleman and me out of the post. Whatever else these "damn Scotch" might be, they traveled well in the rough country, and they obeyed instructions to the letter. The morning of the second night's travel, we saw the lights of Ligonier, and about it, like fireflies, were the campfires of the besieging savages. Our problem now would be getting through to the fort.

Lieutenant Burns smiled when I told him my worry. "Leave it to me," he said. "We planned for this."

At daylight, we could see the post plainly with the main fort not over five hundred yards from us. It looked small, but there were long outer works; timber supported re-doubts, showing the muzzles of brass guns. We moved forward cautiously, stopped. Burns signaled to one of the soldiers.

I had noticed the package but did not know what it contained. The man unwrapped a set of bagpipes, and I heard Coleman groan.

The pipes screeched out; we moved forward at the double in two columns, muskets ready. For a while, I thought we would win through without drawing a shot; then Coleman fired, and an Indian rolled into the open from the bush where he had been hidden. It was the signal for a heavy fire from both sides. One Highlander tripped, went down, but scrambled up. Lieutenant Burns barked an order. The right file swung around, fired its volley into the trees, then ran. A moment later, the second file repeated the maneuver, and presently we were leaping over the earth-works into the arms of sentries posted only a dozen feet apart all along their lines. We had relieved the fort at the cost of one man wounded. Bouquet would be pleased, for this was his favorite outpost.

The little post had not suffered for either food or munitions, but being cut off for weeks from all communication had its effect. The soldiers and settlers crowded about, pumped our hands, made heroes of us, though all we had done was march and hurry a little. When they learned that the main force was near, their joy was the greater. We were given the best quarters the place could afford.

August second, we heard the pipes again. This time every man and woman rushed into the parade ground to see our main force come in.

The savages seemed to have melted away; no one fired on the array of soldiery or the slow-moving baggage wagons.

Late that night, Coleman came to our small hut when I was half asleep. "Peter," he said softly. "I've been spying."

I flung back my blanket and sat up.

"Yessir, I spied on the Colonel. He's got a man to help him with that mustache and likely to get them tight pants on. Me, I always hated to take my clothes off because in a couple of hours, I'd have to put 'em on again. Now, if I had a feller to kinda help—"

I threw a chip at Coleman. He rolled himself into his blanket and slept.

We were moving by full daylight. Bouquet had picked up thirty woodsmen at Bedford and had scouting fringes all round us. He knew Indians and their love of butchering stragglers. We had a scant fifty miles to reach Fort Pitt, and he would not take chances in this country of ambuscades.

This day, August fourth, we did not travel far. It was our twentieth day out of Carlisle. Here was lovely rolling country, wooded hills, and gentle valleys that would make good farmland some day. The plan was to spend the night at an abandoned post on Bushy Run, and by one o'clock, we had traveled seventeen miles. Byerly, chief scout, said the creek was less than a half mile ahead. It had been hot; the soldiers in heavy uniforms suffered, but the prospect of a rest and good water made them step out briskly. Then it happened!

Far up front, a single rifle cracked, followed by a long moment of profound silence.

It was as though a clamp had suddenly gripped those five hundred men, stopping them dead in their tracks. Then a volley crashed out. I had been riding pretty well back in the pack train. By rising in the stirrups, I could see our scouts running back to the main force, turning at times to fire at an invisible enemy. The fire became general; a man dropped, and an Indian leaped into view to scalp the fallen man, but a dozen rifle shots dropped him.

The firing shifted to the right flank. Up front in the train, a horse screamed and reared. Other animals began to drop. A small brown horse flashed past the train, and I saw Bouquet rise in the stirrups, point with his sword to a low open hill. The line of men turned. Highlanders with fixed bayonets went forward at the double. Campbell, their commander, was running ahead, his claymore out, his bonnet gone. Into the circle formed by the soldiers about the top of the hill went our pack train. Horses were plunging, dropping. Some clever brain among the savages knew the importance of wrecking our transport. It was a sad thing to see horses suffer so. Mart Reed would have hated it.

Lieutenant Randall of the Rangers took charge of the train. "Pile off the bags, men, make a barricade."

We worked like beavers, unloading and piling the heavy sacks into a small circle. They tied up what was left of the horses just south of this barricade.

All the while, the Highlanders and Light Infantry were taking terrible punishment, for the fire of the attackers did not drop off one iota. The Rangers were sprawled on the ground at the point of our farthest advance and were firing slowly and coolly. For the first time, I observed British volley firing. They did it by platoons, one firing, one reloading, one in reserve. It meant a steady sleet of lead fired into the brush, and there was no lack of targets. Our wounded were coming back to the circle of bags.

The dweller in safe lands and towns can have but little idea of the way Indians can fight. Man for man, they can beat white regular soldiers. Only the backwoodsmen fight with the same fury of these men of the woods. This day at Bushy Run, the savages fought like reckless devils, crowding close whenever the chance came. Also, they fought with the assurance that they could wipe us out as they once had Braddock. The only reason they did not overwhelm us that day was because we had this slim, erect man with the pointed mustaches to lead us.

Under the heavy sun, men were panting from the terrible labor of fighting. They were licking cracked lips before the battle had raged an hour. By three o'clock, there were some who were reeling from heat and exertion. The only water available was in a few canteens, and this went back to the wounded.

Those Indians knew our predicament. Several, out of range, poured water on the ground in mockery. Over everything hung the thin smoke of powder fog. Through that long afternoon, "them Scotch" held their posts, meeting every rush with bayonets and standing firm.

Tige, the Colonel's big dog, was everywhere. I saw him among the Highlanders. An Indian came pretty close, and the big animal leaped out for him. The savage turned, his war ax high. In that moment, the nearest Highlander, a giant of a man, threw his musket like a spear. The bayonet went through the Indian's chest. The Highlander was upon him as he dropped and wrenched his weapon clear, plunged it again through his foe, and leaped back to his line. I heard the burr of the sergeant reproving the man under the din of the firing.

To most of us, it was like the battle in which the sun stood still for Joshua, but if it did that day, Joshua was on the side of the savages. The hours dragged. I do not know all that I did that afternoon, but my clothes were cut by bullets, and I carried a pebble under my tongue because of thirst. The heavy firing continued steadily until dusk. Even after dark, for an hour or so, a sporadic firing continued. Outside our circle of steel, the savages howled like wolves. Some taunted us from the darkness in English. In the ring of bags, the wounded just lay and suffered.

Sometime in the night, Coleman and Byerly each brought a hatful of water from the run. Two rangers loaded with canteens tried it later. One returned laden with his canteens, but they caught the other out there in the dark. We heard them howling over their victim like wolves will over a deer they have draped down. Then came one long scream of utter agony. The word was that the man who had died out there, in some unholy way, was Lieutenant Randall, who had been in charge of the wounded all afternoon.

I saw Bouquet sitting at a field table, writing by the light of a carefully shaded candle. Since, I have learned that he was setting down an account of what had happened. He was sure we would be destroyed in the morning and wanted to leave a record. Yet, in the morning, he was alert, immaculate, cheerful, setting his lines with the care and exactitude of an army on maneuvers.

They were at us before the sun was up, and it was plain they thought this early attack would wipe us out. They came forward recklessly, exposing themselves, howling, posturing, waving bloody scalps. I happened to walk past Bouquet, who stopped me. "You've had experience with wounded men, haven't you? Get up and help the surgeon; Ivry needs a man."

Half an hour after I had crawled over the barricade, two Light Infantrymen brought in Coleman. He was shot twice through the chest. Bubbles of bloody froth were on his lips. I picked him up and laid him in the shade cast by the barricade. He was conscious and wanted to speak.

"Senecas," he whispered and gestured feebly. "Senecas. West Branch."

I nodded. Perhaps I knew better than he what that news meant. Death and destruction had so far passed that country by, but, with Senecas out, that region would suffer. Gently I slid down and cradled the shaggy head in my lap. We had been together on many long marches. Outside was the crash of firearms, the screeching of savages. Likely we would finish our course almost together for we had little chance. Coley smiled a little.

"You'll go?" he whispered.

"Yes, Coley."

Minutes slipped away; his eyes were glazing but he managed one last smile. A moment later, I drew a blanket over his still face and went to the other wounded.

Now came the magnificent final gamble of our Colonel Bouquet in this battle at Bushy Run. The line of Highlanders, which had held firm all yesterday and this morning, gave slowly back. I could not see the Light Infantrymen. Triumphantly the Indians followed the retreating Scotchmen brandishing knives and hatchets. It looked like a rout, the beginning of the end. I checked the charging of both my rifle and pistol, loosed my weapons in my belt.

The backs of the Highlanders were not fifty feet from the barricade that protected the wounded when that whistle shrilled. Through the brush to the right came the bright red coats of the Light Infantry. A second whistle sounded, and from the left came the Rangers and scouts. Trapped, boxed in by the tricky maneuver, the savages fought desperately, but they could not face the bayonets. They broke, and volley after volley poured into them at close range.

It was all over in another half hour. We moved the wounded down to the water between long lines of uniformed men whose bayonets still showed red. The battle of Bushy Run was over.

One short attack struck us before we reached the fort. We did not lose a man, but, back at the main battle, one out of every four had been struck down by a bullet. On the second day, we came over the hills and saw, flashing in the sun, the tremendous "V" of the rivers and the British flag snapping on its halyards over Fort Pitt.

CHAPTER NINETEEN

A FEW MILES outside Fort Pitt, Bouquet halted his column, and word came down the line to order our uniforms as best we could. Even the scouts shaved hurriedly and most fastened a bright scarf at their throats. The soldiers, of course, had their bright uniforms. So, later we swung into the fort with a swagger. We were the iron men, what was left of our five hundred. We had broken the best the tribes could fling at us.

After two days' rest, I sought out Colonel Bouquet and told him of Coleman's dying message. "Sir, I have friends on the West Branch. I want to get to them. That's Seneca country."

He nodded, having known all along that the Senecas of the Long House had gone out with Pontiac. He turned, and his quill scratched busily. He handed me my release from the service. "So," he said. "Powder Horn is on his own again. Guard yourself well."

He looked at me sharply, studied me from head to moccasins. "I believe you can do it," he said shortly and did not explain further as I took my leave. Ahead of me lay close to two hundred miles of wilderness.

Ensign Forbes was to take a squad of troopers to Kittanning. I rode with them that far and left them on the grim hills from which we had looked down on that bloody place so long ago.

Before me was a vast, high, wooded tableland, the wildest and most unsettled area either by white man or Indian in all the colony. There were fast streams to cross and miles of tangled laurel thickets which even the deer avoided. There were forests and swamps, high rocky ridges, and heavy forests.

The Senecas were out, and this country belonged to them. True, I would not find them excepting at streams and trails. But, I had to cross these north and south routes used by the savages. My trail would take me past Canoe Place and other old camping grounds. Near any of these might be hunters keen of senses and hungry for scalps.

The West Branch of the Susquehanna, which joins the other river at Shamokin, flings itself about this tableland in a great loop. Its farthest north is where the Young Woman's Creek enters at the place where we found the Indian war party camped when we followed them to the Sinnamahoning. I would cut across this loop, then follow the river to Great Island. Truly, ahead of me was good country in which to lose either myself or my hair.

Yet, knowing the dangers ahead, on the very first day out, I did a most foolish thing. It was near evening, and I had just crossed a low, wooded hill. Below me, near a stream, was a cabin. That a building should be there surprised me out of my regular caution. I dropped down to take a look at it.

It was old and set in a small natural meadow. The stick chimney had collapsed, weeds choked the doorway, and there, a rattlesnake disputed my passage. I killed him with a limber stick and entered. There was an old table, its legs fastened in auger holes. The snake might have warned me had I taken it as an omen, for certainly no Indian would come this way without investigating the cabin. But I seated myself on a block of wood and ate my frugal meal from the table. The rattle of the nearby stream was soothing; in the corner was a deep drift of leaves. There I made my bed after making sure there were no more snakes about.

I must have been wearier than I thought, for I overslept; bright morning was in that small room when I wakened, and there was something else! I raised my head slowly and saw in the doorway the faces of two Indian warriors, each with white circles painted about his eyes, their bodies striped with vermilion that looked like knife cuts. Both had hatchets ready as I came slowly to my feet and crossed to the table. I noticed that one of the savages had an eagle feather in his braided scalp lock.

Any man who says he has never been frightened has had little contact with danger, or he is a liar. Cold fear gripped me now; my stomach felt empty, and my wrists ached at the memory of the Mohawk thongs I had felt on the Wyalusing Flats. I did not believe my life was worth a pinch of powder from the horn which hung over my rifle a good six feet away.

Wearily I allowed my body to slump until I was seated where I had eaten my evening meal. The savages stared steadily, but when I drew my knife and laid it on the table, one raised his ax. I placed the palms of my hands on the rough planks and looked back at them, keeping my eyes steady.

Very slowly, the warrior with the feather in his hair edged forward until only the table separated us. His fingertips rested, as did my hands, on the planks. Despite the paint, his face wore a look of incredulity as if he saw something he could not believe. When he spoke, it was softly, and he used good English. "My father is dead. I saw Shingas strike!"

Sometimes my mind works quickly, sometimes it is slow, but in this moment, when my life hung on a thousand-to-one chance, I understood as though a warning bell had sounded somewhere deep in my consciousness. Perhaps something watched over me that morning, the something about which Mrs. Harris loved to talk. The Indian before me thought he was looking at a man already dead. To him, I was the ghost of my father.

I twisted my body, touched my back between my shoulders with my fingers. "The knife went here, my brother."

He stood straight and backed up a little; then, he bowed. It was his first experience with people who have been dead a long time. His beady eyes saw the knife. It had been my father's, and the end of the handle was carved in the shape of a man's head. He pointed a long, incredibly dirty finger. "The knife, it was in your sheath."

Suddenly I scowled, snatched the weapon, and pounded the table with its haft. "Shingas is dead. I killed the Delaware chief with his own knife. I came back from the Spirit Land."

He touched his breast humbly. "I am Aurtah. I was in the canoe with Shingas that day, but I did not strike, my father."

I nodded slowly.

"You are the son of the Half King who died of a fever at Harris Ferry. Guyasuta claimed he was poisoned."

This odd name, Aurtah, had been familiar once. That I knew something of him confused the savage even more. I pointed a finger. "Your father is happy in the Spirit Land, for peace is there, but Aurtah and his friends go to Great Island to take white men's scalps."

Aurtah was thoroughly frightened. It was plain he wanted to bolt out of the cabin and get away from this place. Yet, he felt compelled to answer me. "It is as my father says. We go to Sinnamahoning and meet there other warriors of the Seneca clan. We have come from the Forks of the Ohio."

I drew the point of my knife across the table and allowed my voice to trail away as if I was very weary. "Aurtah, I am very weary. Bring me meat. It is a long way to the Land of the Spirits."

The pair backed out the doorway. I heard them gabbling with the others of the party; then, Aurtah entered and put a piece of battered-looking venison on the table. I nodded slowly and let my head sink forward into my cupped hands. Presently I knew that I was alone.

Believe me; I did not rise until I saw the last of the band disappear in the brush far down the stream. Then I traveled most thankfully at the best speed I could get out of legs that persisted in trembling a little.

Later, when I told this story to VanCamp and Pence, VanCamp merely grunted. Pence preserved what looked like an impolite silence. There are smart Indians like Shingas, but it had been my incredible fortune to fall into the grasp of one who was stupid and too credulous. In all my lifetime, I was not entitled to another chance like this. That my face was so like my father's might not again turn aside death as grim-faced as it was that morning.

Wild things do not worry about danger after it is past, but it does make them more alert. It was like that with me. I put Aurtah and his evil band out of my mind as I jogged on eastward. My mission might be futile; surely, the West Branch people had been warned by this time. But there could be danger to Faith which I might avert. Again, it was possible she was safe in Lancaster; yet, as I traveled over that immense washboard of hills and valleys, she seemed close, as though her light steps followed me through the laurel thickets.

Just at evening of the second day, I found a high rock with a drift of leaves before it. There I built my fire of dry sticks and cooked Aurtah's venison, his gift to the wanderer from the Spirit Land. I grinned at the thought of him as the meat cooked. Next, I mixed cornmeal and huckleberries together to make a cake. I had snatched the berries from the bushes as I walked. A man needs something sweet to keep up his strength when he has no fat meat, and I had forgotten to bring a cake of maple sugar from the storehouse at Pitt.

After I had eaten, I wanted to sleep in that inviting bed, but when I had smoked my pipe through, I was uneasy and had no mind to argue with that feeling. With only a glance at the leaves, I set out and traveled until it was dark. Then I slept most uncomfortably under the bushes.

I was awake with the first faint purple light of the sun in the east, and I did not stop for breakfast but nibbled at meat and my cake as I traveled. At first, my leggings were soaked by the dew, but they dried as the sun mounted and as I climbed the long slope of a great ridge. From its top, I could see below me the long ribbon of river, and clustered beside it were three or four sun lodges. A spiral of smoke lifted from the fire down there, and its acrid taint reached my nostrils. I had done very well, for this must be Canoe Place, and I was a full fifty miles from Kittanning. It was certain I must now make a wide detour and create no suspicion of my passing.

When I was finally down by the river, I crouched in the brush for a long time, and it was good I had done so, for around a bend came a canoe. There were three Indians in it. A man sat in the prow with every muscle relaxed; a child slept on a bundle of skins; and the squaw wielded the paddle. I raised my short rifle. It would be an interesting thing to surprise this warrior, but I dropped the muzzle again, a little ashamed of the foolish idea.

I crossed the stream and waited another quarter of an hour to be sure I had not been observed. Then I struck away in the direction of the Black Moshannon country. From there, if I found it, a short march would take me to the river. Then I could find a log for a raft, perhaps even a canoe, though that meant Indians.

It was hot. I removed my hunting shirt and slung my rifle over my shoulder, and drove myself hard. When night came, I felt I had missed the Black Moshannon, likely passing north of it, although I could not be certain.

It was a second miserable night. As soon as the sun dropped, I was chilled in my sweated buckskins, and I had been setting myself too hard a pace for such long marches. Besides, I was hungry most of the time and needed fat meat. The lean venison was gone; I gagged at raw cornmeal. So I woke in a vicious humor and took stock of myself.

I had slept near a natural meadow with its small stream under-cutting the banks. In ten minutes of careful fumbling, I had three big trout, which I rolled in cornmeal and roasted over my fire of dry sticks. The world looked better after this fine meal. In the middle of that afternoon, I came out on the broad reaches of the main river.

I followed the stream for the remainder of the day. It was flowing south, so I knew I was somewhere below the great north bend. My "sun traveling" had not played me false all the long way from Kittanning. The problem now was to find a log big enough to carry me yet small enough so that I could launch it. Just before dusk, I had my warning that I was not alone on the reaches of the river. A canoe appeared, and I took cover to watch. Three warriors were in it, each with a feather in his hair. At this time of day, it was likely they would camp soon.

Here the mountains came down sharply to the water, leaving a narrow beach covered with round stones and pebbles which make treacherous walking. As I watched the canoe, my main concern was that the savages would camp on my side of the stream, for I had resolved as suddenly as I had seen it to have that craft. If they crossed to the far side, I would have to swim for it, and I had no mind to attacking three warriors with a wet rifle and pistol.

Luck was with me. My Indians swung in at the mouth of a small creek and started a fire with a celerity unusual to savages. Likely they had come a long distance and were as hungry as I knew I was when the smell of roasting meat came to me. A half hour after they finished their meal, the three were rolled in their blankets. No watch had been set. I waited a long time. It was pretty dark, but I could see well enough, even though I do not have cat's eyes, as some say. The mosquitoes were a bother, and when I rose from my hiding place, a sleepy bird sounded a feeble chirp. At first, I thought it a signal, but the Indians were asleep, their equipment strewn about carelessly. I slipped their rifles into the creek, found the canoe was a good one, and eased it down to the edge of the river, having made sure of the paddles.

It was my Dutch stubbornness that turned my bloodless victory into a shambles. I remembered the smell of roasting meat and was determined that savages should not sleep well-fed while I was hungry. Good sense told me to get away; appetite sent me searching for the food, and I found it in a bag. But as I tossed the bag into the canoe, a sleeper sat up, saw me, and yelled. He died under my hatchet, but too late. He had roused the others. The second brave took the charge of my pistol at less than six feet; the third rolled from his blanket and scuttled into the brush on all fours.

I recharged the pistol and fired another shot in the direction he had gone, but there was no sound from the darkness.

I felt sure these warriors were Senecas, though I am never certain about tribal markings. I searched the camp more thoroughly, finding more meat and some corn cake. Their best blanket, folded, went into the canoe to furnish me a soft pad on which to kneel as I paddled.

About an hour's paddling brought me around a bend of the river and face to face with the winking fires of a big encampment on the right bank of the stream. I paddled quickly to the far side but could hear the muffled barking of a dog and the faint single beat of a drum.

Here, in the heavy shadows, I beached my canoe and climbed the steep bank to reconnoiter. It was at once plain that I was farther down than I had thought. There were no fires on my side but on the other, widely spaced, there seemed to be three Indian camps. Likely, hundreds of warriors slept between me and the people I wished to reach.

This canoe was a good one, well braced, and answered to the lightest paddle stroke. I sat far back, so the prow was high, and put all the power of my shoulders into swinging that ash wood paddle.

The first camp was on a small island, and I passed it in the shadow of the left bank; the others were on the main shore and offered no threat to my passing, though fires smoldered at the water's edge.

The Great Island is really a peninsula lying in a loop of the river and facing the mouth of the creek we call Bald Eagle. This favored spot contains nearly a square mile of land as flat as one's palm. Almost in its center is a huge bubbling spring, and about that is always an Indian encampment. Fires were smoldering there this night. Perversity led me to take a risk here. I found the landing beach and ruined ten good canoes, four of which I set adrift. The braves on the island would wade or swim to join in any murders tomorrow.

The river would be dangerous for me in daylight with Indian rifles on the shore. So, at dawn, I hid my canoe in the willows, found a thick mass of brush a half mile or so away from it, and there slept like a tired bear.

The sun was well along in the afternoon when I woke. I ate what food I had left, then climbed a nearby hill and studied the country. A mile or so below, I could see a small stockade on the bluff. With my destination that close, I was willing to take a chance, so I launched the canoe. Some zealous person sent a shot my way when I tried to land, so I stood up and yelled until they allowed me to come in.

This was not Fort Horn. I had missed it and come past it to Antes Fort. People thronged about for a little, then paid no further attention to me. A general exodus was under way, with settlers from upriver gathered here, preparing to go all the way down to Fort Augusta. It was the old story of leaving behind the labors of years and escaping with their lives and the little they could take with them. The concern now, of most, was to get some sort of craft to bear them on downstream. Finally, I found one man idle. He was a big fellow seated on a stump placidly chewing on a wad of tobacco. "These folks is in a hurry," he commented, gesturing toward the throng at the river edge. "I brought the warning," he continued. "Where did you pop from?"

I squatted on the ground. "Fort Pitt,'" I answered.

His eyes widened, and for a moment, he stopped mauling his tobacco. "Great God," he cried, "that's a long stretch. How did you come?"

"Kittanning, Black Moshannon, the river."

He came to his feet at my answer in one smooth motion. "You come along, stranger. Colonel Antes'll want to talk to you."

Antes proved to be a small man with a short brown beard and a kindly, if worried, manner. He extended his hand. "I think I know you. Your name ought to be Grove."

He asked many questions. I told him of Bushy Run and the defeat of the tribes, of conditions in the Cumberland region, and of what I had seen on the river. His final question was: "If Bouquet believes all the Iroquois are on the warpath, does he think we have a chance?"

"Sir," I answered, "only the Senecas are out. Bouquet will force a peace this summer. If we had a company of regulars here, we could stop the Senecas in this valley."

He shook his head sadly. "I asked for one. They sent a single man, and he tells us there is no course but flight."

"Colonel Antes, is there a man here named Horn?"

He looked at me sharply; there was reserve in his voice when he answered with a question. "You mean Horn, the trader, and his daughter?"

I nodded, and he continued in a cold voice. "I have not seen him, but the Fort Horn people are above us along the bank."

I was turning away, irked at his answer, when he stopped me with a further remark. "You know, Horn comes and goes, owns vast tracts of land above here, and is, unfortunately, not popular with the settlers who claim he is too friendly with the Senecas. Some claim he deals with the Connecticut people. Of course, I know he is merely a shrewd man of business intent on land deals."

I said no further word to Antes, and on the upper beach, people either shook their heads or grunted uncivilly when I inquired. Some Indians had been sighted across the river, and they had no interest in anything else. Finally, some little distance upstream, I saw a single man working on a flat boat. He scowled when I approached him. "No room on this boat," he growled.

I felt now I had a key to some of the boorishness of these people. They were afraid I would ask for space in crowded crafts. "I don't want any," I answered civilly. "I want to know if you have seen Horn?"

He turned to his work. "You go to Hell, trapper!"

Two hundred miles of wilderness—now this. I looked at the man's heavy shoulders, his hairy arms, the shock of hair falling forward over his narrow forehead. "Brother," I said softly, "better talk."

His answer was to throw his hammer straight at my head. Too many Indians had tried that with keen-edged hatchets, and this man was clumsy. I stepped in close and took out on him with my fists, all the tension of these last few days. He dropped twice, and the second time I kneeled on his chest. "Where's Horn?"

He tried to shelter his battered face with his hands. "Back—at the fort—in the magazine."

I heard them coming and was on my feet with my pistol ready before they could rush me. It was a crowd of the settlers. Rifles showed.

"Listen," I snapped at them, "the pack of you. I came from Pitt to help you and to find Horn. This lousy sheep tells me you left him behind."

One man sneered. "I don't give a damn for Horn or his friends, but I ain't seen him."

Two strides brought me to him. "You damned boor, the Senecas can have the likes of you and welcome. Neither do I care for Horn; but is his daughter with him?"

The man's face twisted. "If you mean that hard-riding little wench . . ."

I think I struck him harder than I have ever struck a man before. I saw his shoe soles as he went over. "You lousy, cowardly scum," I muttered. Turning my back on them, I started upriver. Not a man followed as I began my trip back to Fort Horn.

CHAPTER TWENTY

A HALF HOUR'S good stiff walking cleared away some of my temper, but it did not help the fact that I had very little information. The fellow I had beaten had said "Fort—magazine." The forest up there would be overrun with Indians, and scant opportunity would be afforded me to do much searching.

It was dusk when I topped a small hill and looked down at a stockade which must be Fort Horn. It was built well back from the river, which accounted for my having missed it. Nothing down there was moving except the main gate, which stood wide open and swung a little in the breeze. No smoke lifted from the chimneys. The place looked like a child's toy, abandoned while its owner slept.

To the south, a narrow gap cleft the high, dark ridge that pitched sharply up from the level stretch of river-bottom land on which the small fort stood. To my right and the north, I could catch glimpses of the river. Whoever had built this place had done it well; trees were cleared away to make a field of fire. A tiny stream entered under the wall, solving the water problem.

As I studied the place, I thought of that fort of meal sacks at Bushy Run and remembered how thirsty we had all been. But down there somewhere might be Faith Horn with her chestnut hair and her laughter like the sound of bright water over stones.

Suddenly the same feeling of weariness and dismay that had possessed me at Carlisle seized me. For many nights I had slept like a beast in the forest, and now I would see Faith if indeed she were here and still lived. If she had been hurt—if they had laid their hands on her!

As suddenly as I had become weary, the hatred of Indians flooded up in me—the smell of them, the hellish cruelty of the best of them. In a little while, I would be down there in the shadows where they might be lurking. I was strong once more.

After it became fully dark, I closed my eyes for a long time, then I could see pretty well. As I have often said, I could not see in the dark as a cat can, but I could do it better than many others. It would be too dark to see rifle sights, even the silver barleycorn fitted to the brown barrel of my piece, so I slung the weapon across my shoulders. My pistol was thrust loosely in my belt, but I carried the small flat-helved ax in my hand, ready. Long ago, VanCamp had convinced me that I must depend on that keen weapon in night fighting.

Nothing happened as I went cautiously down until I reached the brush that fringed the cleared land. Then I crouched, for I had caught a strange odor. In another minute, a heifer walked past me unconcernedly and approached the small stream, and drank thirstily. I had smelled her, and this looked like a good omen, for Indians always kill cows.

Yet I did not walk across the open space but crawled from patch to patch of shadow and so reached the swinging gate. Inside the fort, I moved close to the log palisades. The moon had risen early; the center of the place was light, and then the cow I had seen wandered in, likely searching for someone to milk her. It came suddenly—the thrum of a bowstring, and the animal went down into a struggling heap. A second thrum and I could see the arrow protruding from her side.

That Seneca or Delaware—I cared not which—was too intent on his murder of the animal to be alert. I struck him twice after he was down. Then I stepped into the cabin from which he had shot, the pent-up viciousness in me craving a further victim. But there was no one else there.

The stockade was empty; no sight or smell of an Indian and nothing that looked like a magazine. Then I remembered instructions that went out when the chain of forts was built. Magazines were to be outside and connected with the main works by a covered or underground passage.

A small, strong gate like a door let me out behind the fort. Here the shadow was deeper because the timber was closer and higher.

I found what I expected in a matter of minutes, not twenty yards from the palisades, a stout door of timber set into the side of the hill. It was closed with a log set against it.

Once more, I stopped and listened. The Indian back there might have been some sort of outpost, for they are seldom alone at night. Then I worked at the log, lifting with all my strength until it fell clear and the door came open as though set on a spring. Something bright flashed in the moonlight.

"Put it up," I whispered hoarsely. "I'm a white man."

"Who is it?" My heart leaped, for it was Horn's voice, quiet, restrained as I would have expected it to be. He would know how far a human voice carries at night and be cautious.

Then there was a stir behind Horn. My throat closed as though I had swallowed a thing too much for me and my hands trembled as I peered into that small black opening of the door. Was she there in the shadow?

"Peter Grove, sir," I answered finally. "I'm alone."

"Peter, Peter!" It was Faith's voice, glad beyond any measure of caution.

Thunder pounded in my temples. Her arms were about me like a glad child's. "Peter, Peter, I prayed and prayed, for I was not ready to die."

I patted her shoulder and could find nothing in the world to say. It was like hunger too well satisfied or cold, cold water after a long march. Then I spoke to Horn. "Sir, get your things. The woods are full of them."

They had a candle shaded by a wooden bucket. After he had drawn the heavy door shut, Horn took this out so we could see better. He had not changed, nor had Faith. She was dressed like a boy in buckskins, with a white linen shirt open at her rounded throat.

Horn handed me a small flat parcel wrapped in oil skin. "That is valuable. If anything goes wrong. Faith will open it."

I tucked the thing carelessly inside my shirt, caring little for its importance. It was better that he had a good pistol thrust into his belt and that he carried his slim sword. Faith picked up a bundle of clothing, and I could see both had good moccasins.

"Any food?" I queried.

Horn shook his head. "Only a little corn meal. They left us very little when they abandoned us. You know they expected the savages to get us."

I led them to the corner of the stockade. "Wait, there's meat down there."

With only the moon for light and with the pressing need for hurry, I made bloody business of butchering the dead cow. My butchering work would give me away, but the Indians would be after us in the morning anyway, and I could not risk hunting after these wolves were in full cry. With the meat in my war bag, I went to the main gate and listened. A whip-poor-will was calling from the direction of Antes Fort. Presently it had an answer, then another. All the calls were right with the little tap that follows each call, but there were too many night birds. The woods through which I had come were full of the enemy. There would be no escape that way. When I turned back, I saw another thing even more startling—the body of the dead Indian I had killed was gone!

I wasted no more time but found my people and bade them follow. "We'll try for the gap first, then for Augusta."

It was Faith who saved us, for I had been watching behind us. She saw the glint of the campfire first. It was small as a man's hat, but about it were a dozen dark bulks—blanket-shrouded Indians!

When we had crept away, and it was safe again to whisper, I took Horn's sleeve. "They are all about us. By now, they know there is an enemy lurking about. They'll watch hard downstream. The only way out is upstream, for they won't expect us to go that way."

He studied a moment. "You're sure they saw us?"

"Yes," I answered, "I killed one brave. They rescued his body."

"Then let's go and fast." His voice was decisive.

The mountain rampart on our left guided us. Sometimes we caught a glimpse of the river, and, once in a while, a campfire looking as small as a firefly's light glanced down there. The Indians were in the river valley in great numbers. We walked smartly for long hours, stopping now and then to rest but not long enough to stiffen our muscles. Before morning I found a dense hemlock thicket where an icy stream escaped from a bowl-like spring.

We spent the day there, and I risked a bright fire to broil some of the beef and told them about the cow and how she had been killed.

"Poor Becky," Faith said. "She was always straying—now we eat her."

Her appetite was excellent. After they had finished their meat, I showed each how to mix a portion of tassamane with water, roll it into a ball, and eat it in the form of small pellets.

"Blue corn is best," I claimed, and Horn agreed. I had forgotten that he had probably sold tons of this sort of food to traders. Having plenty of time, we washed our feet several times during the day in the icy water to toughen them. I explained it would be better if we had hot water; then, we could make an infusion of the hemlock needles which would really harden our feet for long, fast going. Faith was too sleepy to be interested.

When one slept, two watched. It was too dangerous to trust one weary watcher, and I slept my share because I knew how much depended on my strength and judgment. Next night was the same, with us marching and resting throughout the time of darkness. Horn showed signs of strain but said nothing about discomfort. Faith was doing as well as I. Close to morning we came to a tremendous gap through which came a wide stream. When I had my charges safely hidden in another hemlock thicket, I slipped down to the stream intent on trying for trout to eke out our slender supply of provisions. I found my fish all right under the undercut banks in a sort of natural meadow, but as I turned to leave, I saw another man. He was moving not a hundred yards away. The next instant, I recognized Pence and signaled to him with my raised hand.

His rifle went up like a striking snake at the sound of my low whistle, but he saw me and ran forward. He pounded me on the back. "Well, well, here's my damned Dutch lion. Don't you know the Senecas is as thick here as fleas on a cheap dog?" I told him briefly some of the things that had happened—Coleman's death, my rescue of the Horns.

"Well," he said, "I don't wonder them folks left Horn for the savages. With Faith, of course, it's different."

"Why do you all hate him?" I demanded.

He scratched his head a moment. "It's hard to say, Peter. One thing, he's getting rich on land deals, and folks is jealous. Then he keeps to himself; he's mysterious. Why, he owns Great Island or will have it when we get rid of these Senecas."

Horn recognized Pence, and the Ranger was obviously pleased with Faith. His eyes followed her as she moved about in her neat buckskins; his face reddened at her ready friendliness. The trout made us a good meal. Pence told us as we ate that he was returning to Fort Augusta and insisted on leaving with us his entire supply of corn meal. When I asked for advice, he studied quite a bit.

"Well," he said slowly, "one man going fast can get through, but not a party. Best hole up somewhere. The talk is a Seneca chief was killed upriver couple of nights ago. They're wild about it, and they've seen Peter. Every stinking brave would like to have that black scalp. They know it's Powder Horn, and they want that hair."

"How would the Black Moshannon country do?" I asked.

"Fine, Peter, fine. They don't like that country for some reason. Get your folks there, stay a week or so, and VanCamp and I'll be in to help you out. But be careful till you get there. There's a small band some-wheres above you, and I don't think they're Senecas."

Horn looked at me sharply when Pence was ready to leave. "Peter, would you mind letting Pence take that packet to Fort Augusta to the commandant?"

I took the thing out carelessly and handed it to the ranger, who thrust it into his war bag. Either Horn did not trust me, or he had little faith in our escape. I am afraid I cared little for his opinion.

We had come so far without molestation that we were inclined to be a little less cautious. It was hard to lie quiet all day. Late that afternoon, I announced that I wanted to get some berries. Our little camp was in a place of huge rocks halfway up a steep ridge.

The wild blue huckleberries were plentiful. I filled my war bag and, before starting back, had a good look at the country, for the march that night would put us in the wild Black Moshannon area, and I wanted to know the lay of the land. As far as I could see, there was nothing below us but tumbled hills and small valleys. No smoke showed; certainly, there was no sign of habitation. Then came the sound of a single shot.

I went down the mountainside on a dead run, unslinging my rifle as I went. A second shot, muffled a bit among the rocks, sounded. Then I saw.

One Indian lay on his side, dead. Horn stood with his back to a huge rock, his slim sword gleaming. Faith crouched nearby. Three warriors were edging in toward the swordsman. Even as I looked, one came too close; he screamed as the thin blade stabbed through his chest. My rifle shot dropped the second Indian as he swung his hatchet to hurl it at Horn. My pistol shot missed the third warrior, who bounded away.

I loaded rapidly both pistol and rifle. Blood was dripping from Horn's arm, but his hard face twisted into a smile of triumph.

"Wait," I said as I started after the running Indian.

Instantly Faith was at my side, her hands gripping my sleeve. "What are you going to do, Peter?" she demanded.

I frowned at her. "Get the other, of course. He'll carry the word."

"No," she said, "let him go."

"Listen, Faith," I remonstrated, "he'll bring others like wolves after a crippled deer. If he escapes, our danger is greater."

She tossed her bright head. "Then we'll face it. Stay for my sake."

For a moment, I wanted to shake her, but I looked into her eyes and saw the smile that thanked my forbearance.

The wound in Horn's left arm was a bullet-cut through the muscle. We cleansed it thoroughly, using brandy from a small silver flask the trader carried. We bandaged it with a strip torn from the sleeve of his shirt. Later he carefully cleaned his sword.

"You're a real swordsman, sir," I said a little grudgingly.

He smiled. "Yes, but that red devil would have finished me with his ax. Why didn't they shoot again?"

"Captives," I answered. "They wanted to burn you."

We had to leave that place of rocks quickly, but first, I wanted to get a good look at the dead Indians. Horn joined me.

"Those men are not Senecas," I said.

He bent and turned over the one he had killed with his sword. "Shawnees," he announced grimly.

I looked down at the dead man. Despite the paint, I knew I had seen him before. This one had been with Charteris back near Old Town when Reed and I captured the renegade. I whistled softly. "You're right; Shawnees, Charteris' band!"

The full implication of the thing struck me as we went along. If these really were Charteris' men, he would be on our trail like a hungry hound, and he would not give up until he had found this woman. There was no telling how many white captive women had gone through his bestial hands in the years he ranged the frontiers with his renegade Shawnees.

But this was no time for argument or too much speculation. We traveled. Horn's arm would be giving him trouble in twenty-four hours, and I wanted the safety of the Black Moshannon country. We turned wide away from the valley we had followed, and dawn found us on the crest of the mountain that hunters call Rattlesnake. There we rested, looking down into the country that was to be our refuge.

To me, there are few wilder or more beautiful bits of country than this was if we except Aughwick and Great Island. It is a high tableland through which wanders the stream the Indians call Black Moshannon—the black moose stream. To the north, the land dips down, and the stream escapes through beetling walls of sandstone to come into the river at the end of a long narrow gorge. On the plateau is the quiet of a land shaded by tall trees. Here a small lake glimmers like silver in the sun and pushes back the shadows of timber along its edges. Trout break the mirror surface, deer come down to drink, sometimes a lumbering bear comes as well.

Within an hour after we reached this lake, I had a young spike buck hanging up. Another hour after that chore was done, we dined on cornbread and the liver of the animal. Horn and Faith ate with real hunger.

For the first time in my life, I had the challenge of providing in the wilderness for a woman. From high up on Rattlesnake, I gathered the goldenrod that grows there and which makes a tea full of spiciness. There were berries, too, picked into a bark container.

Horn helped as much as he could in setting up our shelters close to the lake. It was evident he was in pain, but he stuck to his work doggedly. The lean-to we made for Faith was in the center, and we were careful to do a good job of it, making thick sides of branches. I fashioned her a bough bed which I knew would be as soft as any she had ever used and more fragrant. Inside a day and a half, we had food, shelter, and a good measure of comfort. I whittled a laurel wood pipe and divided my small store of tobacco with Horn.

Faith called me at noon when she bandaged his wound. I noticed that his face was flushed, and the bullet hole was a little inflamed. She looked at me with questions in her eyes. I suggested that she make compresses of pieces of his shirt and keep them cool with water. "I'll get some balsam," I promised.

It took a longer trip than I had planned, and I did not get back until dark. The campfire glowed cheerily. Faith had meat and corn cake ready and some tea steeping in a bark bucket. She had boiled the water by dropping in hot stones, as I had shown her.

"See," I showed what I had found, "this will take away the fever." I had some of the gum that exudes from young balsam trees and a quantity of buds. Seated before the fire, we worked the gum with our fingers until it was like putty. This paste we laid on the bullet wound and bandaged it well. Before he slept, Horn said he was feeling better.

Next morning he was much improved as far as the wound was concerned, but there was something else wrong with him. He was not surly, but he would sit quietly, paying little attention to what was going on. Faith, however, entered with real zest into each thing we did.

Hidden away in my war bag was a tiny parcel I had almost forgotten. In it were two of the trout flies tied for me by old man Kreiner back in Lancaster town, and coiled with them was a ten-foot length of braided horse hairline.

Faith turned these things over in her slim fingers. "What are they, Peter? What are they for?"

"Do you like fish?" I smiled as I asked.

"Yes, I'm afraid I have a most unladylike appetite, but these are not fish," she answered.

She followed me while I found a young sapling of black birch, which I trimmed carefully and to which I attached my line. Then I bent on one of the flies, which Kreiner had called a "Coachman."

At my second cast, a great trout rose and snapped the fly. To save my tackle, I had to race along the bank until he tired and came to us flapping. His sides were dark because this was dark water, but his spots were bright red and gold. Truly, he was a magnificent fish.

Faith was as excited as a little child. "Oh! If I could do that," she exclaimed.

For answer, I placed the rod in her hand and was most thankful when at her first cast, a trout took the fly, and she managed to land him.

That same afternoon I killed two grouse with a club. Faith did not like the way I set about preparing them by first drawing the birds, then rolling them, feathers and all, in blue clay mud, and putting the whole in the coals. But when I had drawn out the hard lumps and cracked them with my hatchet, she was delighted with the clean meat; the feathers had stuck to the clay. Horn enjoyed his portion, and he ate more heartily at that meal than he had thus far.

We had been in the Black Moshannon a week, and I had never been happier. The world of war was far away. There was no need of killing but for food. High overhead, the sky was an inverted bowl of blue and fair weather greeted us each day. Faith and I tramped the hills from far Rattlesnake mountain to the gorge through which our stream turned down toward the distant river.

So it happened that we came down the mountain like two children, her hand in mine lest she slip on the steep going. And so she did, and I caught her, so for a moment, her slight weight was in my arms. I think I waited for her to release herself, and perhaps she was tardy, but my hunger drove all sense from me. My arms closed tightly about her. Presently she lifted her face.

I know there was little gentleness in me as I crushed her lips with mine. But, it was the hunger and the long waiting. Her hands stroked my hair; she locked her arms about my neck. "Oh, Peter," she cried softly. "I have waited so long."

I released her suddenly. "You did not wait," I blurted. "There was Orme."

"Poor, poor fellow." She turned up her small nose suddenly and stuck the tip of her tongue out at me in most unladylike fashion. "Men are so thick-headed, you most of all, Peter Grove. You are a big man, smart about fighting and woods lore, but you know nothing of women."

I only stared at her until she laughed and went on. "So very little despite Indian women and the wide-hipped landlady of the Blue Goose."

My face must have been as scarlet as an Indian brave painted with vermilion. What I wanted to say stuck in my throat. She came close again. "There never was anyone else, Peter. Never from the time you came to the post with your father. Some day you'll understand.

"Oh," she breathed a little later when I released her, "you say little in words, but—you do love me?"

She stopped me with her flattened hand pressed against my chest. "No, not again. My ribs must be guarded. I am sure you said 'yes.'"

Horn must have seen that something had happened to us, but he did not say anything. Surely we were so happy that any man must know there was some reason for it.

"Your father's wound—tonight, we will put the pounded buds on it and not the salve," I said.

She looked at me. "Peter, it's time you knew. Samuel Horn is my uncle, not my father."

I stared at them, and Horn smiled. "Yes, she is my dead brother's child. It seemed best that she should be my daughter, living on the frontier."

He looked at her fondly. Whatever Horn was or did, he loved Faith. "What was always plain. He retired early that night—the last night of our safety. Faith and I sat listening to the whip-poor-wills and the crickets. Occasionally we would hear the splash of a trout breaking water. Far upstream, a bullfrog sounded one full note, and we laughed. "Just turned over in bed," Faith said.

Finally, our small campfire was down to a single brave coal that lasted long after the others were embers. We watched it, and when it was gone, we rose, and she stood on tip toes so that I could kiss her goodnight. She went into her bough shelter, but I had to walk about a long time before I could compose myself enough to sleep.

CHAPTER TWENTY-ONE

ABOUT A RIFLE shot from our camp I had found a thing which pleased me a great deal. It was a sand spring only a short distance from the main stream. Its clear, icy water spilled into a small rock basin, then escaped to the main creek. These springs are lovely, with their sand-filled rising bubbles looking like those in a boiling pot. I have often tried, in drinking from them, to get grains of sand into my mouth but never succeeded. About this rock basin, I had erected a screen of branches so that Faith could have privacy in her bathing. Both spring and bower looked down toward the long defile where the creek broke from our mountain valley.

I was busy with the morning fire, but I had time to look up when Faith appeared from her sleeping lean-to, where she had been humming for the last ten minutes or so. Her hair was loose about her shoulders, and her white feet flashed as she ran toward her booth. Horn had not stirred or had been very quiet in his shelter. Far out on the lake, a big trout broke the water, and I watched the widening rings a moment or so before I went on with my preparations for breakfast. One of my concerns was that our corn meal was getting low, and we had no means of replenishing it. For myself, I could have lived well on meat and berries, but I wanted better fare for Faith and Horn. Then a piercing scream brought me to my feet. A moment, and it came again.

Surely I, who had lived so long amid frontier alarms, should have known better when danger sounded an alarm as imperative as this. My weapons—knife, rifle, pistol, ax—were in my shelter and should have been sought first. But it was Faith's voice telling her desperate extremity. I ran without a thought of any weapon.

Recklessly, I reached the screen of evergreens and brushed past Faith's white naked body; yet in passing, I saw her eyes wide with terror. Then I stopped and looked at him standing there gloating. Nose broad and flat, high Indian cheekbones, eyes feeding lewdly on the beauty before him, the hat with the feather pushed back on his head, stood Charteris. I had time to note his one affectation—the white linen shirt open at his brown throat. In his hands was a double fowling piece, both wicked hammers at full cock!

An Indian would have killed me on sight, but instead of firing, the half-breed gestured with the gun. "Get your hands up!"

Slowly my hands obeyed, the fingers tingling to close on that brown throat so marked above the white linen. If I moved, he would fire and, with the scattering charge, would kill both Faith and me. Had he carried a rifle, I would have chanced the one bullet at so critical a time.

His face twisted into a gloating grin. "So," he mocked. "I find Powder Horn's white flower who is fairer than the dead Mikwah or the tavern woman with yellow hair."

My mind was a racing, selecting thing. A bit of morning breeze touched something to my face, and I knew. Before I stepped from my lean-to that morning, I had flung on my hunting shirt with its tasseled fringes, and one of these strands had touched my face, reminding me. There was a cape across my shoulders, and under the cape—

The knowledge that it was there came with such a shock it seemed the man with the gun must know it, too. Between my shoulders under the cape was the flat sheath that carried my heavy throwing knife, the one I had used that day in the village before Shingas. My father had taught me how to throw it with all the power of arm and shoulder.

Charteris looked and gloated. He would have this woman and think more of it because he had taken her from an enemy who cherished her. He was moistening his thick lips with his tongue and a little intoxicated by what he saw. My fingers dropped back over my shoulders.

"Get over," he snarled, gesturing with the gun. His signal to shoot would be when I had stepped far enough that his charge of shot would not kill the girl also. The buckhorn haft of the knife was in my fingers; the weapon came up smoothly into my hungry palm. Then I dropped my head a little and threw; putting all my abhorrence and hatred of this man into the cast. The heavy knife was like a flick of light.

At this distance, I could have split a copper penny or driven that double-edged blade through an inch of oak. It caught Charteris by the side of his misshapen nose and went home to his twisted half-white brain through the right eye socket.

I leaped before Faith. The man's body lurched, his arm jerked up, hurling the fowling piece into the brush. Miraculously it did not discharge. His body pitched forward; the blunt fingers of his outstretched hand touched the small heap of her garments.

"Oh," she sobbed. "Peter, Peter!" My hand rested a moment on her satin shoulder, and I drew her close until she ceased trembling. Then I snatched up her garments and gave them to her. A moment or two later, she came out of her bower dressed, and we walked slowly back to camp where my freshly built fire was crackling cheerily; Horn had come out. We told him the story while his face became grayer and grayer. Then he spoke. "We must get away from here. Charteris would not have been alone. I am glad this beast is, at last, dead."

Leaving Faith, we walked to where the dead man lay and then scouted the defile a mile or more without finding any of that Shawnee crew. It was my idea that knowing we were up here, he came along so he would not need to share his captive as he had done with other women. Horn stood looking down at the renegade, and his lips were grim. "I should have killed him long ago."

I remembered the hat on the chair in Horn's room so long ago and wondered. Charteris must have been about the trading post when my father and I stopped that night. Not many men wore a broad black hat with a goose feather in the band. Now, as I looked, something about this same hat band caught my eye, a hint of brightness as the sun touched it. When I picked the hat up and saw the thing, it stunned even me, who had seen so many savage and devilish things on the high frontier.

The band was woven cunningly of strands of the fine hair of women. There were golden hairs, auburn and black, all plaited together. This was a trophy, a thing of awful evil. My heart sank to think that Faith's brown hair might have been added to it. With infinite care, I removed the band and buried it deep under the shadow of a white sandstone boulder. Then I dragged Charteris' body down the defile and flung it among the rocks as one would do with an unclean animal.

We remained in the Black Moshannon country two more days despite the danger from Shawnees. I wished to look over this valley carefully once again and slipped away up Rattlesnake for a while. I was about to return when a sharp whistle startled me. It was Pence, and he came at a run when he saw I recognized him. "War's over," he called as he came. "Pontiac's dead down on the Mississippi. Bouquet licked Guyasuta and forced the old devil to make peace."

We hurried to the camp, and Horn was much brighter as he heard the news and asked questions about the outside. "Your paper's with Hunter," Pence told him, and he nodded.

"We came here in war; we leave in peace," Horn said when we had climbed Rattlesnake and looked back to where the bright water meandered through the meadow and under the shadow of the tall pines. Only Faith's glance swept down toward the defile where the stream broke white among the rocks.

It took us a good four days to reach Augusta, but we took our time. Horn wanted to get out on the West Branch to see how much damage the savages had done. Fort Reed, above the Great Island, had been little more than a large cabin. The walls were still standing, though fire had gutted the interior. Pence busied himself scouting and found a big canoe hidden in the mouth of a creek. There were no paddles, but we solved that easily enough with our axes and plenty of good wood about.

We saw no Indians; no smoke rose from the site of the village on the Island itself. Likely the Senecas had gone back to the council fires of the tribe for the discussions that would come after the forced peace. Horn seemed to rouse from the mild dejection that was upon him as we passed nearly around this expanse of level land almost clear of trees.

"It's rich land, Peter, hungry for the plow and waving grain," he commented.

I thought of a stone house said to be building, but neither he nor Faith mentioned it. I agreed about the land and its richness. There the valley along the river, which is so long and narrow as it comes down from the mountains, widens until it is a fair land indeed, with the hills close enough to be friendly but not so close as to crowd the fields which would come in due time.

We stopped at Fort Horn, which was almost intact, then Antes Fort. None of the settlers had returned, but we felt sure the next spring would find the valley settled once more. Evenings, we would sit by the campfire and talk. That is. Pence, Faith, and I talked while Horn smoked quietly and listened.

"What will you do now, Peter, since peace has come?" Pence asked me.

"Ginseng," I answered. "Those roots are brown gold. I'll be up the Sinnamahoning, and I'll load a war canoe with the stuff, take it down to Wright's Ferry, then by pack horse to Philadelphia. With the money, I shall buy land. I want a huge farm and a stone house and—"

Faith's laughter was like the chime of tiny bells. "Listen to our Indian fighter turned Dutch farmer. He will follow a plow instead of the long trail. He will grow pleased with himself and sit in the shade and smoke a clay pipe," she mocked.

I tried to scowl at her and waved my hands. "I'll have John Bartram up to show us how a stone house should be built. He will lay out gardens like those he has by the Schuylkill. There will be tall corn and fine cattle." Faith's eyes twinkled. "And you will no longer get into Carlisle jail nor—"

"What?" I demanded.

Horn answered. "It was a headstrong girl that learned you lay in that place, and she nearly killed two horses getting to Governor Morris for you."

So that was how it happened! Faith turned to Pence with a question. "And you, what will you do?"

"Travel," he answered. "I aim to see a lot of country now. I won't be bothered looking after my hair. I'll see the big rivers. I'll travel fast and far and maybe get back in time to help Peter with his tall corn."

"The old ones watch, the young ones do," Horn repeated from an old German proverb. He seemed to consider himself an old man. That had been apparent for days.

We had good canoeing all the way to the meeting of the rivers, where we crossed to the brown stockade of Fort Augusta. The fort itself was built of huge white oak logs and had small brass cannon commanding the broad reaches of the rivers. But, for all its strength, it was not in good repair. The moat banks were crumbling, and there was no water in it. One gate was off its hinges. It seemed to me the Indian village was much smaller and farther back toward the hills.

Colonel Hunter, the commandant, was an austere and worried man. He was glad to see Horn and Faith, paying the deference as befits a beautiful woman and a wealthy man. For Pence and me, there was courtesy but no excess of it. In our worn border dress, we were just two more forest runners, of whom there were many in this country. He told us some of the upriver settlers were still here but getting ready to go up the river again. The greater number, however, had gone farther south.

Since most of the soldiers were away, there was plenty of room. Pence and I were assigned to a cabin and were able to buy enough clothing to make ourselves presentable. Then I went to the commandant's quarters, found Faith, and we walked about the enclosure, coming finally to the bastion that overlooked the river.

We stood for a time, then I tried to thank her for getting me out of Carlisle jail.

"I saw you that day," I said. "And I was so hungry to see more that I slipped out through a window but could not find you."

She laughed. "I was on my way up the valley," she explained. "It was not so much. I was always taught to help the needy and sometimes the stubborn."

She stopped my grasp at her by putting up her hand. "Listen," she said. "I must go in. But, uncle wants to talk with you this evening."

"I had rather talk with you," I said stubbornly.

"It is really important," was her answer.

Horn was seated at a long table on which candles already burned. Before him was a packet of papers which I recognized. We sat down, Faith and I, as he indicated, on either side of the table, so we formed a triangle. Faith and I facing each other, he at the apex.

His strong white fingers loosened the tape. "Faith and I think it high time to settle some things that have bothered you and have been a problem to us," he announced.

The papers were open. I looked down and read in utter astonishment a patent to the Great Island drawn in my name. Horn smiled at Faith when he noted my surprise. "Yes, Peter, you own your broad lands already—the Great Island and many acres more. Besides, there is money in the counting houses of Philadelphia and Lancaster. You are in the way of being a very well-to-do young man. Faith has her own lands, her own money, too. I flatter myself that I have been a good steward of both."

He leaned forward, took our hands, and joined them over the papers. Nothing loth, we held to each other's hands while he finished.

Peter, you have hated me at times, and I did not like your carelessness or the reckless devil that looked out of your eyes. When your father died, his affairs were much involved. He had lost some money years before, then turned everything over to me. I was land speculating. When you asked about his money, I told you part of the truth. It took time to get my deals through; they could not be interrupted without endangering the capital invested. It has only been lately that things have come about as I wished. Faith shared with me the idea that you should not know lest, in Dutch stubbornness, you stop what we were doing."

For a long moment, we looked steadily at each other. I noted the strength and weariness on his face. It was good to sit there feeling my antipathy for this man fade, to feel that I must apologize, to feel myself cleansed of doubts and old angers. "Sir," I said, "if you will forgive my doubts—"

The grip of his strong fingers met mine. "I, too," he said softly, "am Dutch and wondrous fond of my own way."

I had placed the papers in my pocket and was standing a little dazed at the fortune that had come to me when there was a sharp rap. The door opened almost immediately to admit Colonel Hunter. "Mr. Horn, I have just remembered something and hasten to tell you. Some weeks gone, an English officer and a half-dozen troopers came here asking for you. My word to him was that you were somewhere upriver, that the tribes were on the warpath."

Horn nodded gravely. Hunter hurried on. "I told him you were usually in Lancaster around the first of each month, that he might find you there."

Horn waited a moment, then asked. "He was a tall man, a little younger than I am, a little stooped—?"

"Yes," Hunter interrupted, "he was extremely abrupt. Gave his name as Creston, said he would find you."

"Thank you. Colonel Hunter. It is extremely likely that Creston will find me sometime—"

Hunter retreated from the room. Horn added quietly, "about the first of the month."

CHAPTER TWENTY-TWO

WE REMAINTED two more days in Fort Augusta, though Pence left on some errand of his own about which he chose to be mysterious. It was on the second of these days that Horn asked me to come to his room.

"Peter," he said thoughtfully. "I do not like to be mysterious, but I want you to do something."

I nodded slightly; there seemed nothing to say and after a bit, he continued. "Draw a rough map of the place where you found the savages' lead mine."

I stared at him incredulous, for I had spoken of the place only to Morris. Horn was smiling—one of his rare smiles. "Presently, you will understand, but I urge you. It may not be important now, but—it will be."

Even so, I gave no promise. While I had been confused in the latter part of that journey, I knew the general directions and could set down enough information that would lead to the mine.

Colonel Hunter offered us horses to go down the river, but we liked our big canoe better. We took our time, drifting for the most part, coming at evening of our second day to the beach at Harris Ferry, above which loomed the new stone house that took the place of the broad cabin that had been so homelike.

Late in the day though it was, Mrs. Harris and her women prepared a regular feast for us and served it on her new china, which seemed very fragile. Silver spoons appeared and some of the new forks. When the eating was over, Harris brought a bottle of dark wine, and the company stood while they toasted Faith and me and wished us happiness. Harris added this pertinent bit of news. "The Reverend Paul Brandon comes through here soon. Best not miss him."

I liked to see color flame on Faith's cheeks, but I did not enjoy Harris's boisterous way, so I was glad when the women left us to smoke before the big fireplace. Suddenly Harris smote his fist into his palm. "I forgot, Horn. A Britisher was here a couple days ago asking for you. His name was Creston, a kind of surly cuss. Said he was going to Carlisle, but he'd see you in Lancaster."

Horn looked at our host a moment, then said; "Thank you, John. I'll see him in good time."

In the small hours of this same night, I was roused from deep sleep by a hand on my shoulder. It was Horn, fully dressed and carrying a candle. "I must get to Lancaster," he said. "Could you get horses? I don't want Faith or Harris to know until we are gone."

My answer was to swing out on the floor and to dress rapidly. "Get your things. I'll have horses in a hurry."

Twenty minutes later, I had kept my word, and, walking the horses, we rode out of the village. I was fully armed according to custom and I saw Horn wore his sword.

We rode out the darkness and the forenoon of the day before stopping. Then we left the road and entered a pine grove where we cooked and ate some of the provisions Horn had brought in a sack.

"I left a note for Harris about the horses," Horn explained. "I don't want him raising the colony hunting horse thieves." He chuckled and was almost immediately grave. "I have so many things to tell you. It's a complicated story."

He put his pipe away and settled himself on the pine needles. "To you and others, I have been Samuel Horn, trader. I am Dutch. But, Samuel Horp was my brother and Faith's father. Your father and I came to this country because we did not like the insolence of the English in the Low Countries. Here we joined the French in one of the old wars, and I was captured. Because they found I was Dutch and fighting with the French, I was placed in a prison. Michal Grove rescued me. I was out of my cell, had recovered my sword, and was slipping along the corridor that led to freedom when a young British officer met me. In a fair fight, I killed him and then reached your father and the boat."

Now Horn spoke hesitatingly, as if reluctant to bring the story into light. "The officer I had killed was the illegitimate son of some duke. The English set a price on my head for murder, and I have been hunted ever since. In the Netherlands, they locked my father in a prison where he died since he could not tell them where I was. They did brutal things to my sister. Luckily my brother escaped to America. He fell ill after telling me what happened in the old country. When he died, we buried Hendrik Horn. I took my brother's name and his child, who is Faith, and came to this province. The English are stupid and never suspected me nor your father. But this Creston, whose name you heard, is a bloodhound. He has found me at long last."

Deeply moved at what this man had endured, I stared at him, then questioned. "But how did they learn; what set them after you?"

He cleared his throat. "Outside your father, two others knew my story. One is former Governor Morris, who is coming to Lancaster to-night; Pence went to get him. The other was—Charteris. He was with the French in those days and knew me."

At last, I understood the hat on the chair and the quiet statement on Black Moshannon—"I should have killed him long ago." For years Horn had been at the mercy of that renegade. Even I could not guess to the full what that must have meant.

Horn stood up and smiled. "I am afraid I am old before my time, Peter. We Dutch are stubborn. If the English take me, they will confiscate my property. Most of it is in Faith's name and beyond even their greedy reach. We are going to Lancaster where Morris will arrange that not a penny of Horn money goes to enrich the English crown."

He smiled. "I am no longer young, but I have kept my sword arm and hand supple."

We arrived in Lancaster a little after nightfall and stabled the horses in my barn, after which we walked over to Horn's post. The place was empty, of course. We had entered the house part. Here was Faith's spinet, and I touched the wood gently as if something of her lingered. Over there was her sewing basket, but I knew the wooden beads would be about her slender throat.

In the trading room, I lighted the candles set in brackets on the wall while Horn busied himself with his strong-box from which he took some papers. He had just finished when there was a knocking which Horn answered. Even in the poor light, I could not mistake Morris with his heavy brows. The other man was VanCamp, dressed soberly in black coat and breeches but fully armed.

We shook hands all around.

"This is a great honor, Judge Morris," Horn began, but the jurist held up his hand. "I shall not forget the services you rendered when I had the doubtful honor of being governor. Nor do I forget Peter or Pence or VanCamp—nor Michal Grove, dead in our service. We have been waiting here in town. Friend Horn, until this hard-riding son of Holland, VanCamp, saw your light. Let's to our work."

We found a table, and with the many candles, the room was cheerful. Morris sat, reading carefully the papers Horn gave him. "Quite simple," he said finally. "We'll assign your remaining property."

He scribbled rapidly on each deed, and VanCamp and I signed as witnesses. After the final signature, Morris tied the bundle of papers together and fastened it with a seal. "I'll put these on record in the city. Now," the big man demanded, "Friend Horn, when do you expect Creston?"

Horn shrugged his shoulders. "I do not know, perhaps the close of the month, maybe tomorrow. It could be within this hour."

Morris shook his heavy head. "It will be difficult to get you off. A lot of influence is still alive—"

Horn interrupted with a touch on his arm. "That does not worry me; it was this property. I—"

There was no time for him to finish. The door slammed open, and in stepped a tall officer in the uniform of a captain of foot. Behind him were three soldiers, each armed with musket, hanger, and pistol. For a little, the officer stood blinking in the bright lights. I saw that he was a bit stooped. He had the usual arrogance I associated with these people, but his thin face carried the look of a tired hound that has, at last, brought his quarry to bay.

Almost unconsciously, the four of us who had been in the room set our backs against the long counter. But as he passed me, Horn thrust a piece of paper into my hand. "For Faith," he whispered, and I nodded.

There could be no doubt that Creston was enjoying himself, standing with booted feet apart, his right hand thrust into his tunic. "Ah," he said, "so here we are—at last."

That nasal, arrogant accent reminded me of another officer who had come to my house. I understood how Horn had allowed the semblance of that engagement to Faith for a purpose. I believed she knew her uncle's story and had tried to protect him.

Morris was most distant from the intruders. He looked out under his heavy brows as one will at a critical moment in a stage drama. VanCamp scowled, the candle behind him turning his hair golden in its light.

The officer bowed. "Gentlemen, I am Captain Creston of His Majesty's Thirty-First Foot, on detached service."

His hand was still in the tunic. He was having a fine time and was in no hurry. I doubt if he recognized that Morris was a former governor of the colony. "In the King's name, Hendrik Horn, I arrest you for murder." His voice reminded me of crackling parchment.

The hand whipped out, holding a small scroll of paper—his warrant. Now he thrust it back, drew his sword, and stepped toward the man he had come to take. I saw one of the soldiers take a pair of hand irons from his pocket.

"A long chase, Creston; but it was no murder. It was fair fight." Horn's voice roused the Captain to sudden fury. His voice answering was high pitched.

"You would have me believe that? He was the best swordsman in the regiment. You could not have fought him, you Dutch swine; you murdered him."

Horn's slim blade hissed from its scabbard. He pointed to Creston's weapon. "Get it up, you British lout. I'll answer your charge."

I know little of sword play, and I would not like to depend on this weapon. Yet, there in the candlelight, I was to see two men who seemed to know every use of the slim blades. Creston pushed the fighting with every evidence of his desire to kill his older, slighter adversary. Their blades met with a sharp clanging as when one pounds metal with a hammer. A soldier moved his hand toward his pistol. VanCamp gestured with his rifle barrel aimed at the man's stomach. I drew my pistol and moved to his side, ready to help.

Those two men out there on the floor had hated each other for long. Creston lunged and cut, grunting with the force he put into his blows. Horn's face was set, his slender blade flickering in the candlelight like a moonbeam on bright water. Suddenly he shifted his feet wide apart.

"For my father, dead in your foul prison," he said between his teeth.

I could not follow the blade's movement, but I did see the blood leap from Creston's split ear. "For my sister."

Creston could do nothing about it. His other ear was slit; blood was running down both sides of his face. The blades clanged, locked; then, the officer's sword was twisted from his hand and thrown into the air. It dropped with the point in the floor, the hilt quivering.

"You, Creston—you said I am no swordsman. Now I have marked you to remember."

Creston cursed softly. Instantly Horn was at him, beating him with the flat of his blade. "Pick up your sword. Remember, they tortured me. Pick it up before I spill your foulness on the floor."

Creston brushed away some of the blood and seized his weapon but could not protect himself. Again his sword went spinning. Horn stepped close to him, tore the lace from his throat, and calmly wiped his blade with it. Then he turned his back on his adversary and walked slowly toward the opening in the counter.

None of us could have prevented it, for our eyes were on Horn walking so calmly across the floor. Creston snatched out his pistol and fired. Horn slipped slowly to the floor, his face half-turned toward his murderer.

VanCamp knocked Creston senseless with his rifle, and turned to Morris. "Will it help if I kill him, sir?"

Morris shook his head, spoke to the soldiers. "Carry him out; he has murdered a man before witnesses. If he is here in the morning, officer or no, he will be tried for murder."

We carried Horn to his bed, but he was far gone. He looked at Morris. "Peter will make the map—lead."

Morris nodded. Horn half-rose, insistent. "Tell him—powder . . ."

His eyes closed, then flashed open, but they were glazed.

As he dropped back, I caught one final whisper. "Michal."

Morris talked with me a long time later when VanCamp had gone to tell Faith. "He would not tell you, Peter, but Horn was another of my men working with your father, VanCamp, and others. Charteris had a hold on him, as you probably know. Horn pretended to be with the powder ring moving powder to the savages, but west of the river, it was always destroyed—until the business became so bad the ring lost interest in the traffic. He was a man like your father who took you away from the frontier because he did not want his son mixed in such dangerous business. Besides, he may have felt his young Powder Horn was too impulsive."

He smiled at this last, then was thoughtful.

"So another of my men is gone, though he labored under a cloud; but, I forget, I no longer need men like these in the prosaic business of the law."

When I went over to my home to care for the horses, I sat for a while in my father's chair. All my questions were now answered through no wit of mine. It seemed odd that one who had done so little toward righting things should have the privilege of seeing them come right. I felt very humble. So much more than I deserved had come to me.

During the remainder of the night, I worked on a rough map of the lead mine country, which I gave to Morris next morning. We buried Hendrik Horn beside my father on Watch Island, for his last word had been the name of his friend. Under the pines, they would take their last, long, quiet rest together.

Faith was her brave self while Morris read the sacred words of comfort. We then returned to Lancaster with him, where he helped us set things in order. We were solemnly pleased when VanCamp bought the trading post. One day, when business was completed, a messenger came from Harris telling me that the Reverend Paul Brandon would be at the Ferry the following two days.

There we were married under the great tree Harris' father had left standing so that children born later might see what trees were like in the early days. We could look across the river to sunlight touching the line of blue hills now empty of menace. For just a moment, my mind strayed to the country out there but came back as Faith's fingers tightened on mine.

The quiet voice of the preacher went on: ". . . and forsaking all others, cleave unto each other so long as you both shall live."

Faith stood there, the light breeze having its way with the rich brightness of her hair. In her eyes, there was peace. Suddenly she held out her slim hands toward the river, the hills, the rich flat land in a gesture of promise.

THE END

Made in the USA
Middletown, DE
27 February 2023

25450006R00132